31143011594802
M Maxwell, E
Maxwell, Edith,
Mulch ado about murder /

Bookvan

Bookvan

D0389360

Mulch Ado About Murder

Books by Edith Maxwell

A TINE TO LIVE, A TINE TO DIE

'TIL DIRT DO US PART

FARMED AND DANGEROUS

MURDER MOST FOWL

MULCH ADO ABOUT MURDER

Published by Kensington Publishing Corporation

Mulch Ado
About Murder

EDITH
MAXWELL

KENSINGTON BOOKS
www.kensingtonbooks.com

To the extent that the image or images on the cover of this book depict a person or persons, such person or persons are merely models, and are not intended to portray any character or characters featured in the book.

KENSINGTON BOOKS are published by

Kensington Publishing Corp.
119 West 40th Street
New York, NY 10018

Copyright © 2017 by Edith Maxwell

All rights reserved. No part of this book may be reproduced in any form or by any means without the prior written consent of the Publisher, excepting brief quotes used in reviews.

All Kensington titles, imprints and distributed lines are available at special quantity discounts for bulk purchases for sales promotion, premiums, fund-raising, educational or institutional use. Special book excerpts or customized printings can also be created to fit specific needs. For details, write or phone the office of the Kensington Special Sales Manager: Kensington Publishing Corp., 119 West 40th Street, New York, NY 10018. Attn. Special Sales Department. Phone: 1-800-221-2647.

Kensington and the K logo Reg. U.S. Pat. & TM Off.

Library of Congress Card Catalogue Number: 2017933098

ISBN-13: 978-1-4967-0029-2
ISBN-10: 1-4967-0029-5
First Kensington Hardcover Edition: June 2017

eISBN-13: 978-1-4967-0030-8
eISBN-10: 1-4967-0030-9
First Kensington Electronic Edition: June 2017

10 9 8 7 6 5 4 3 2 1

Printed in the United States of America

For my Wicked Cozy partners in crime: Jessie Crockett/Jessica Estevao, Sherry Harris, Julie Hennrikus/Julianne Holmes, Liz Mugavero/Kate Conte, and Barbara Ross. You're the best. Really.

Acknowledgments

Once again I am grateful to so many for helping me get this book into the hands of readers. I'm always stunned by the beautiful covers the gifted Robin Moline creates. Thanks to my agent John Talbot, who found me this contract in the first place. Many blessings to my always responsive Kensington editor, John Scognamiglio, and the entire Kensington team, who bring the Local Foods Mysteries to the reading public. Sherry Harris once again expertly edited the manuscript before I turned it in, finding the unwritten emotions and gaping plot canyons. My gratitude, always, to Sisters in Crime, both locally and nationally. I read a number of scenes from the book to my critique group, the Monday Night Writers, and benefited as ever from their keen eyes. And of course the Wicked Cozy Authors (see the Dedication)—my friends, my lifeboat, my inspiration—I couldn't do it without you.

Thank you to Matt Iden for inspiring the title, my farmer son John David for the idea of organoponics, and my son Allan for remembering details about his long-ago high school track meets. I was delighted to include a scene set at Throwback Brewery in Hampton, New Hampshire, as well as a recipe from their fabulous pub restaurant, used with permission, of course. No one is killed at the brewery or dies from eating their food! I think every book in this series has a scene set at the real Newburyport watering hole, the Grog (again, no deaths result from the experience). The Market restaurant is fictional, though—and I wish it wasn't.

Thanks once again to Amesbury Police Detective Kevin Donovan, who is always willing to answer my questions, often at the last minute, about police procedure. Any errors remaining in this book are because I (foolishly) thought I could swing it on my own.

I am one of the Flick Chicks, a group of women friends who've been meeting monthly for more than two decades for wine, high-fat appetizers, conversation ... and sometimes even a movie. I hope Deb Hamilton (equestrian), Judy Smith (re-enactor), Janice Valverde (Girl Scout leader), and Kim Wegrzyn (volleyballer) are pleased getting a tiny walk-on role in the Memorial Day parade, which is modeled directly on the West Newbury parade we all were part of for many years when our children were younger. I also used Deb's beach house as a model for the final climax scenes and hope she doesn't mind.

The character Sue Biellik was born because Daphine Neville was the very generous high bidder on my 2015 donation to the Merrimac River Feline Rescue Society. I love to offer the right to name a character in one of my books to support the cause of rescue cats, and in recent years the MRFRS Fur Ball even brings me up on stage during the live auction. Susan Biellik is Daphine's good friend and an animal lover. I hope you enjoy your time on the farm, Sue!

It's been a real pleasure to stage a mystery series on a small working organic farm. It's what I did for a living long ago, and where I set my very first crime fiction. I hope, readers, that you'll support your local farmer. Go buy your produce, cheese, eggs, and meat from a farmers' market, CSA, or farm stand every chance you get—the farmers appreciate and need your business.

To my family and dear friends—I love you and am grateful beyond words for your continuing support and delight in my successes.

Dear Readers, Librarians, Cozy Fans: I'd be nowhere without you! I thank you deeply for your kind and enthusiastic words about my stories. You have my continued gratitude for helping me spread the word about these books.

Mulch Ado About Murder

Chapter 1

Cam Flaherty sank her head onto the steering wheel in the parking lot outside the Seacoast Fresh greenhouse. The repeated refrain of the protesters on the sidewalk behind her swirled like angry wasps. She straightened and whacked the wheel with her fist. "I do NOT have time for this."

"Hydroponics has to go. Soil-free plants, no, no, no." The small clutch of demonstrators formed an infinite loop with their signs.

Cam climbed out of her old Ford truck and retrieved her delivery from the back. A dark-haired man hurried toward her in the parking lot, but he stared at the ground and was on a collision course with her. She cleared her throat.

He glanced up with a pale, sweaty face and haunted eyes. "I'm sorry." He swerved around her.

She whipped her head to gaze after him. She'd never seen him before. Had he been in the greenhouse? He looked terrible, no matter where he'd been. Like he'd seen a ghost.

Nicole Kingsbury, the owner of the new hydroponic greenhouse in town, had contracted with Cam to start basil and lettuce seedlings for her at Cam's Attic Hill Organic Farm. Cam stared at the two flats of baby basil plants in her arms. She hadn't expected to encounter her own mother in the small group of locals marching in a circle on the sidewalk in opposition to Nicole's venture.

Deb Flaherty had arrived last week with Cam's father, William, for their first visit since Cam took over the farm from her great-uncle, Albert St. Pierre, a year and a half ago. And somehow Deb had jumped into the fray of the debate about what "organic" should mean. Nicole said she planned to feed her water-grown crops organically. Purists like this group of protesters maintained that organic should mean food grown in soil, not in solution, that organic growing included the whole naturally balanced system of soil, water, micro-organisms, beneficial insects, and healthy crops and animals. Cam held an opinion somewhere in the middle.

It hadn't occurred to her parents to ask their daughter if she had time for them to visit, time to show them the sights of northeastern Massachusetts.

"No," Cam muttered to herself, "I certainly do not have time." The end of May was crazy busy on a small organic farm. She had a zillion seedlings to plant out in the fields now that the frost-free date was past. She needed to harvest asparagus, rhubarb, and scallions. And she definitely didn't need her quirky, peripatetic academic parents to be hanging around her farm and the small town of Westbury, where it was located. One town in from the coast, two towns south of New Hampshire, as she liked to tell prospective customers.

Nicole had let out a nervous, jerky laugh when Cam had asked her about the name of her business.

"Isn't Seacoast Fresh a little odd, since Westbury is a good ten miles inland?" Cam asked, when Nicole showed up at her farm a couple of months earlier.

"Sure, but I like the name," Nicole said. "And I'll be using marine products in the feeding solution." That day Nicole wore black jeans with a red jacket. She'd worn red and black every time Cam had seen her since, which went with her high-energy personality. It was like being in the presence of a hummingbird when she was around Nicole: always moving, and always moving fast.

"How did you find me, anyway?" Cam asked.

"Bobby said to call you."

"Bobby Burr?" The handsome carpenter had rebuilt Cam's barn last summer.

"He's my cousin," Nicole had said. "He's helping me put up the greenhouse."

Now one of the protesters shouted, staring at Cam as she reached for the greenhouse door, "Why are you dealing with her? You should join us instead."

At least the shouter wasn't her mother. Cam shook her head without speaking and let herself in. The greenhouse door clicked shut behind her.

"Nicole," she called out, "I'm here with your seedlings." The air pressed in warm and humid, with a familiar scent of moist potting soil and plastic. She sniffed, detecting an acrid note of chemicals, too. That was odd for a supposedly organic business.

The only sounds were the whir of the big ventilation fan in the end wall and the now-faint repeated calls from the demonstrators. Parallel rows of white pipes at waist level stretched out in front of her. Two-inch holes pierced the tops, some with green leaves spilling out of the holes, others awaiting the potential crop she was delivering. Cam needed to get back to her own farm this afternoon. Days stretched long a month before the summer solstice, and she usually worked outside right up until dusk.

"Nicole? You here?" Cam's voice didn't quite echo, but it rang out like she was the only human in the structure.

Strange. Nicole had said she'd be on-site all day. Like Cam, she was going nuts getting her business under way in time to take advantage of the plentiful light of a New England summer. She had a well-equipped new greenhouse, though, and a visible spot right on Main Street near the center of town. Nicole had moved to Westbury from Florida in a postdivorce scenario, according to Bobby. Cam didn't know much about her except how she dressed and that she was a devout Catholic. Bobby had told Cam that Nicole's divorce proceedings were caused in part by her affair with someone she'd met at a religious retreat and that she was anguished at being out of favor with her church because of the divorce.

Nicole still didn't answer. Cam shrugged and headed for the opposite end of the long structure. She approached the worktables where she'd seen Nicole direct-seed crops and assemble the nutritional slurry that was sucked into the feeding pipes running under the plants' roots. The open slurry vat, three feet in diameter and about the same in height, stood in the far corner behind white plastic shelving.

Cam set her flats on the trestle table next to a travel coffee mug. She dug a scrap of paper and a pen out of her messenger bag. The pen poised, she shook her head before stashing them again. Instead she sent Nicole a quick text.

Left you the seedlings. Let me know about more. Sorry about the protest—not my doing.

Cam turned to go. A *ding* sounded a few yards away. Cam twisted her head to look. Had Nicole gone out and left her phone behind? The sound came from beyond the open shelves holding various planting supplies and tools. Cam looked harder and gasped. She took a step, but her foot felt anchored in thick mud and her gaze would not leave the far corner. She took another step, and another, until she was dashing, barely breathing, nearly tripping to the vat.

"No," Cam wailed.

Nicole sprawled jackknifed over the vat, her red shirt hiked partway up her back. Her head hung just above the slurry. Her left hand dangled outside the vat clutching a string of tiny, bright red beads with black dots at their ends. The gold cross on the rosary glinted in the filtered light. Nicole's eyes didn't glint. Nicole was dead.

Chapter 2

O r was she? Cam reached out a shaking hand to feel Nicole's neck. She couldn't detect a trace of a pulse under the cool skin, which had a bluish tinge. A shudder rippled through Cam. Goose bumps popped up on her arms and legs. Nicole was beyond help. *Poor Nicole.* Cam shook her head fast and pressed nine-one-one on her phone, which she still gripped.

She'd found a body in her own greenhouse a year ago, but he'd been a victim of murder. She narrowed her eyes, blinking away her reaction. Surely this wasn't murder, too. Had Nicole tripped? But how had she died? Did she have a heart attack? She was young, around forty, Cam thought. Or maybe she'd killed herself. But Cam couldn't see blood or a wound.

"Hydroponics has to go. Soil-free plants, no, no, no," drifted in through the plastic like a taunt to death.

When the dispatcher answered, Cam told her what she'd found and agreed to stay on the premises, not touching anything.

"Is the person you found in need of medical help, Ms. Flaherty?" the dispatcher asked.

"No. She's dead." Cam's voice trembled. She swallowed

hard. Her stomach jounced like she rode in a boat on rough seas. She sucked in a breath. That man with the haunted eyes she'd seen before she came in. He might have done this to Nicole.

A minute later, sirens roared up to the property. The Westbury Public Safety Complex was only a quarter mile down the road. Cam's childhood friend Sergeant Ruth Dodge hurried into the greenhouse, followed at a slower pace by George Frost, the town's chief of police.

Cam stuck her hand in the air and waved frantically. "I'm back here," she called, her voice scraping. At nearly six feet tall, Cam knew they could see her over the top of the shelving unit.

"What do we have?" Ruth asked when she reached Cam's side. Hefty to Cam's slim, she was nearly as tall, one thing of many that had united the two when they'd played together during Cam's summers on Great-Uncle Albert and Great-Aunt Marie's Westbury farm. Ruth was in the official black uniform of the force, her waist covered by a wide, heavy duty belt. She moved between Cam and Nicole's still form.

"I came over to deliver some seedlings I'd started for Nicole," Cam began. She waited to go on until Chief Frost ambled up. "She didn't answer me when I called out. I'd just sent her a text when I heard her phone ping. I saw red in this corner and I came over to check. She's dead, isn't she?"

"I assume you didn't touch anything." Ruth circled the vat and bent over to peer at the rosary.

Cam hadn't noticed at first that the string of beads seemed to have a few gaps. "I felt her neck for a pulse." Cam's throat thickened until it threatened to choke off her own pulse. "I didn't touch anything else over here. My seedling flats are on that table." Cam pointed as she swallowed and took in a deep breath.

"What's in this thing?" George asked, frowning at the vat.

"I don't know exactly what goes into it," Cam said. "But it's the nutritional slurry that feeds the plants she's growing. She says it's organic." She brought her hand to her mouth. "I mean, said." Her voice quavered.

"And maybe it isn't? That what those ladies out there complaining about?" he asked. He folded his arms across his chest and frowned.

Those ladies being her farm's most avid volunteers and customers: Felicity Slavin, plus Cam's mother and a couple of other locals. Cam blew out a breath. "It's kind of complicated. You probably don't want me to explain it right here and now."

"No, I guess I don't," Frost answered.

Two more people rushed in, this time carrying bright red bags. When they arrived where Cam stood with the officers, Frost shook his head. "No need for medical attention, I'm afraid. We'll need a pronouncement instead."

"You got it, Chief," one said. He carefully approached Nicole's body. Cam watched as he listened for breath, checked the pulse in her neck for what seemed like a long time, and shined a little flashlight in her eyes.

"I can use the paddles to make sure she can't be shocked back, but we'd have to get her out of there and onto her back," the paramedic said to Chief Frost.

"No." Frost shook his head. "We haven't even started with the crime scene. Just pronounce."

The paramedic checked his watch and somberly said, "Time of death, fifteen twenty-six."

The other paramedic stared at Nicole. "Reminds me of another death I attended," he said.

"How do you think she died?" Cam asked. She cocked her head. It had gone quiet outside. Seeing emergency vehicles must have stunned the demonstrators into silence.

8

The paramedic glanced at Chief Frost.

Ruth cleared her throat. "Not really your business, Cam." Her brown eyes were kind but firm.

"Did you have any grievances with the victim, Ms. Flaherty?" Frost asked.

"No! Not at all." Did he think she had hurt Nicole? What a ridiculous idea. "We were working together. I was growing seedlings for her. She could count on good organic stock, and I received a little extra cash at a time in the year when I need it. Like now. But I didn't know her, really."

"She pay you promptly?" Frost asked.

"Yes."

"Did you see anyone in here? Anybody leaving before you came in?"

"I didn't see anyone in here. Except Nicole. But as I arrived, a man passed me in the parking lot. He looked upset about something. I didn't recognize him at all."

"Describe him," Ruth said.

"Slight, dark haired. Green shirt. Haunted eyes."

Chief Frost raised his eyebrows. "Haunted?"

"I don't know. It was an expression on his face, in his eyes. Like he'd seen something bad."

"Or done something bad, more likely." The chief, who towered over Cam and Ruth by a good six inches, nodded. "We'll need a more thorough statement from you later, but you can go ahead and leave now."

"But sir," Ruth began. She glanced at Cam and back at her superior. "She found the body. Doesn't that mean . . ."

Cam knew Ruth well enough to know that she was questioning the chief. When it came to regulations versus friendship, for Ruth regulations won every time, and Cam respected her for that.

"Heck, we know Cam. She's been through this drill before,

9

and it's not like we don't know where to find her. She can go," he said gruffly. He narrowed his eyes at Cam. "By the way, you know any of those ladies walking around with signs out there?"

Rats. Cam cleared her throat. "The short one with the long gray braid is Felicity Slavin. The one with her hair pulled back is Deb Flaherty. I don't know the names of the other two."

"This Deb any relation?" Frost asked, his eyebrows raised.

Cam nodded slowly. "She's my mom."

Chapter 3

Cam followed the EMTs out of the greenhouse. The pair headed for the ambulance and drove away, sirens quiet, lights unlit. Cam hurried toward the clump of women on the sidewalk in front of the greenhouse. A fresh breeze ruffling Cam's short red hair was a relief after the warm humidity of the greenhouse, but the afternoon sun was still high and she had to shield her eyes with her hand.

"Cam, what's going on?" Felicity folded her hands in front of her chest, worry etched on her face. She wore an Indian print tunic in her signature colors of purple and turquoise.

"Police cars? Ambulance? At first we thought they were coming for us," Cam's mom said, her light blue shirt bringing out the blue in her eyes, eyes exactly like Cam's. She hurried to Cam's side but stopped short of actually touching her. Deb was shorter than Cam by a few inches and, despite being a lifelong academic, moved with the athleticism of her earlier days as a college soccer star.

"I think you'd better end your protest, ladies." Cam gazed at the group, her eyes moving from one to the next. She skipped over her mom and ended on Felicity. "Go home and put your signs away."

"We have every right to demonstrate, Cameron," Deb said, lifting her chin. "We've stayed on the sidewalk." She held a neatly lettered cardboard sign high. It read DON'T DILUTE ORGANIC. SAY NO TO SOIL-FREE HYDROPONICS.

A passing car tooted its horn, whether in solidarity or disagreement Cam couldn't tell.

"It doesn't matter anymore," Cam said.

"What do you mean?" her mother asked.

"Nicole's dead," Cam nearly whispered.

The collective intake of breath was sharp and fast.

Felicity reached out and touched Cam's arm. "Did you, is she . . ." Her voice trailed off.

"Yes, I found her. She's in the greenhouse. She's dead." The words were harsh, final, almost cruel. But that was the reality this afternoon.

"The poor thing," Felicity said, bringing her other hand to her mouth. "And poor you, finding another body."

The other two women looked at each other. One shook her head, her mouth pulled down and her eyes dark. "We didn't agree with Ms. Kingsbury. But we didn't wish her dead."

"Of course not," Cam said.

Deb blinked. "How did she die?"

"I don't know." It figured that her mom would go straight to the cause and bypass feelings altogether.

"But it wasn't murder, was it?" Felicity asked, eyes wide. She'd been involved with Cam's farm since the beginning and knew of Cam's connection with more than one murder in the past year.

"I don't know." Cam turned her head to take in the greenhouse. Its new pointed-arch supports were unbent and strong, the plastic still clean and stretched taut, the wood end walls secure. Unlike the owner's life. She looked back at the women. "But just in case, I sure hope none of you was in there alone with Nicole today."

Deb blinked again. Felicity opened her mouth, but when Ruth emerged from the greenhouse door, Felicity shut it again. Ruth glanced around. She made her way with deliberate steps to the group.

"Hey, Felicity." Ruth nodded at the diminutive woman, whom she'd met at Cam's farm. "Ladies, I'm going to need to speak with each of you." She pulled out a pad of paper and a pen. "Names and addresses, please?" She surveyed the group, focusing on Deb. "Ma'am?"

Ruth must not realize she was Cam's mom, and her mom probably had never met Ruth. When Cam's parents dropped her at Albert and Marie's farm every summer from when she was six right through high school, they never stayed long. They were always headed out on anthropological research junkets to various far-flung parts of the world. Cam had talked about Ruth to her parents in the past, though. Not that they'd listened.

"Mom, this is Officer Ruth Dodge. My *friend* Ruth. Ruthie, Professor Debra Flaherty. My mother."

"Nice to meet you, Professor." Ruth smiled and extended her hand.

Deb shook it. She'd taught Cam a few things, and among them was that women should always have a good, strong handshake. "Pleased to meet you at last, Officer. Sorry it had to be under these circumstances."

Cam groaned inwardly. A dig at her, she was sure. But when was she supposed to have introduced them? And it was just like her mother to not ask Ruth to call her Deb instead of Professor.

"Are your vehicles parked in this lot?" Ruth gestured to the lot behind the greenhouse, which it shared with the office building to their left.

"No," Felicity said. "We all parked across the street."

"I need to speak with each of you privately before you leave." Ruth tilted her head at the Westbury Police SUV parked in the greenhouse lot. "Professor Flaherty, let's begin with you. If you don't mind?" She gestured with her arm toward the vehicle in a way that left no room for argumentation.

Deb pursed her lips but followed Ruth to the passenger door.

Felicity stared after them.

"What?" Cam murmured to her, turning Felicity away from the other women.

"Your mom was in the greenhouse for a while this morning," she murmured. "She said she thought she could reason with Nicole. Get her to close the operation."

"Really?" Cam asked. This was very bad news. Mom, perhaps the last person who saw Nicole alive, and for a contentious reason? Not good.

"Yeah. I told her that was absurd. Nicole put a lot of money, time, and energy into this place. Why would she give it up?"

It was Cam's turn to stare at Felicity. "Then why in the world are you out here protesting? Isn't that exactly what you hoped would happen, that Nicole would give up the business?"

Felicity wrinkled her nose. "I was hoping she'd convert to a regular organic greenhouse, with plants grown in soil. She could have, you know. She already has the structure."

"Maybe," Cam said. "It's too late now, though. Too late for anything."

Cam's truck clattered along Bachelor Street. She rolled down the windows and luxuriated in a few moments of solitude with spring wind in her hair, the aroma of cut grass in her nostrils, and nobody to talk to. She was getting better at hanging out with people, but a classic introvert like her needed solo periods in which to recharge. She'd had almost zero time to herself since her mother and father had arrived last week. And they weren't due to leave until after Memorial Day, which was still four days from now. Moments alone also freed up her brain to think.

She breathed in the calm and energy of the fresh air and tried to breathe out how it had felt to find Nicole dead, letting go of the negative. She inhaled the good, exhaled the bad, over and over. It all sounded reasonable when her yoga teacher said things like that. Right now? Those feelings and that negativity weren't going anywhere. Her underlying sadness at seeing Nicole dead and her worries about her own mother refused to be vanquished.

Cam thought more about the dark-haired guy she'd seen in the parking lot. Who was he? Maybe he was Nicole's ex. She tried to remember anything else about him. Pale. Maybe about five eight. He'd worn a green shirt. But what was the other thing about him she couldn't quite remember? Had he killed Nicole? She shuddered involuntarily. He'd seen her. She'd seen him.

Cam's mom had been alone in the greenhouse with Nicole. If the police determined the death wasn't due to natural causes, Mom could be in deep trouble. That was a pretty big "if," though. Nicole could have had an underlying health problem. Cam had heard of a woman in her forties dying in her sleep of a brain aneurysm. Heart attacks happened at any age, didn't they? Or maybe Nicole had experienced an allergic reaction triggered by one of the chemicals in the slurry. And why was she holding a set of rosary beads? Cam wasn't a bit religious.

Had Nicole been praying for success in her business? Or a better love life? Unhappily her prayers hadn't worked out for her.

Bobby. He'd just lost a cousin, one he seemed close to. It might take a while for word to get to him, especially as he lived across the river in the town of Merrimac. Cam pulled to the side of the road and sent him a text.

Got a minute to talk?

She waited a few moments but he didn't reply, so she resumed driving. He would know if Nicole had children who would mourn for her, siblings, parents. Cam couldn't remember if he'd ever told her exactly how he and Nicole were related, if they were true first cousins or some other permutation of family connection and had just simplified the relationship to the word "cousin," as many did. Of course, if Nicole's death was murder, then she had at least one enemy out here somewhere, too.

Turning onto Attic Hill Road, Cam coaxed the Ford up the steep hill toward her farm. She was sure her mother hadn't killed Nicole. Debra Greaney Flaherty was governed by logic. If in some alternate universe she turned out to be a murderer, her crimes would be planned and plotted to the tiniest detail. No unpremeditated passion killing for her. Cam had always thought her mom was the least emotional person she knew, and Cam's upbringing had reflected that.

She'd always known she had a safe, stable home and two parents committed to each other and to her. But in their house there'd been no sitting on laps, no good night hugs, no tears at parting, even when they were about to be separated for two months and Cam's permanent front teeth hadn't come in yet. That is, her parents hadn't shed tears. Cam herself had cried plenty of her own. Thank goodness for Albert and Marie. Warm, low-key, and fun, they'd offered unconditional love, an unstructured summer, and an education in nature and living creatures without a single lesson. Thinking of Albert reminded Cam that she and her parents were due to have dinner with him tonight over at Moran Manor, his assisted living residence.

She took another deep breath in and let it out. She couldn't solve her mom's problems. Cam had enough of her own. And now she was headed home to her father, to whom she had reluctantly assigned a couple of farm tasks just because he'd insisted he could help. Who knew what this least handy of men had wrought in her absence?

A Baltimore oriole warbled its rich song as Cam slowed to turn into the long farm driveway at 8 Attic Hill Road. The sound brought a smile to her lips, despite what she'd just been through. Every year at this time the brilliant orange and black birds returned and began wooing their mates. Petty human grievances, up to and including murder, didn't faze them. "It's spring," the flash of color seemed to say as it flew in front of her, "and you can't stop me." If only her own spring were so uncomplicated.

Chapter 4

Not again. Cam stared at the fence in back of the hoop-house. Marie had always planted sweet peas in that spot. Last year Cam had planted a crop of early pole beans along the fence, but they had been mistakenly—or maliciously— pulled up by a volunteer. She'd decided to revert to sweet peas. People need food for the soul as well as for the body, and Cam's love for those sweet-scented, delicate flowers came from her great-aunt. Marie had been dead four years now. Cam still missed her, and smelling sweet peas would be both a comfort and a reminder of her competent, nurturing relative. The tender vines had been a foot tall when she left this afternoon, their tendrils already licking around the pickets. Now she saw nothing but rich, dark soil at the base of the fence.

Cam closed her eyes and pressed her hands to her forehead. *Daddy.* She should have told him to stay in the house.

"Hey, sweetie, how'd I do?" His voice called from over her shoulder.

She opened her eyes and turned to face her tall father hurrying in her direction. He was gawkier even than Cam, if that was possible. Neither of them possessed her mother's fluid grace.

"Um, Daddy?"

"See, I pulled up all those weeds for you." William Flaherty beamed. His buckwheat-colored hair, which he'd pushed straight back from his high brow, lay in sweaty strands on the back of his neck.

"Those weren't weeds." She shut her eyes for a moment. Her father was a brilliant scholar without a speck of common sense. She opened her eyes again and tried on a smile to cushion her words. "Those were flowers I'd planted. Did I ask you to weed that fence?"

"Well, no. But I finished the stuff you asked me to do. I was just trying to help." The pleasure disappeared from his face.

Now she felt bad for being harsh. Cam had asked her father to weed the potato field and had clearly pointed out the dark green rounded leaves, which looked very different from the grassy weeds sprouting around them. What she'd neglected to say was, "Don't do anything else!" Well, it was still early enough to plant new sweet peas, although they were much fonder of cool weather than of warm. And this spring was proving to be extra warm and dry so far.

She took another look at her father. He wore his usual khaki trousers, except these had had a pair of scissors taken to them, and not very evenly, either. His skinny legs emerged pale from a midthigh cut and ended in black socks pulled halfway up his calves. At least he owned a pair of sneakers and wasn't wearing black dress shoes.

"Daddy, did you just make those shorts?"

"Why, yes. It's awfully hot here." He looked down at his handiwork, which slanted from right to left on one leg and the opposite on the other. "And I figured if I was going to be working on the farm, I'd better get comfortable."

Cam couldn't help laughing. "Sounds like a plan."

"Where's your mother?" he asked. "She still out with those new friends of hers?"

Oh. How much should she tell him? "I expect she'll be home soon. She, um, well . . ."

"Did she go and get herself in trouble again?" he asked.

"Again?" What was he talking about?

"She's been quite the activist these last few years."

"Really? She was never like that before." Prior to Cam leaving for college, that is. While Cam was growing up, her mother had been completely absorbed in her teaching and her research. When Cam had needed cookies for a school event, her mom bought sweets at the store. She'd told Cam to make her own Halloween costumes. She'd sometimes attended Cam's track meets, and had always supported her academic endeavors. But she'd been more of a devoted professor than a devoted mother, and definitely hadn't become involved in anything political.

"She loves to join demonstrations for causes she believes in." Rather than sounding peeved, her father's voice held a note of pride. "She's gotten quite passionate." His cheeks colored.

Uh-oh. Let's not go there, Daddy. She cleared her throat. "When I was in the hydroponics greenhouse today, I found the owner dead."

"Dead?" William looked suitably shocked.

"Yes. Nicole Kingsbury, the owner whose business Mom and the others were demonstrating against."

"That's just terrible. I don't believe I've ever seen a dead person in this country."

"You've seen them elsewhere?" Preston, her cat and farm companion, ambled up. Cam leaned down to pet his luxuriant Norwegian Forest Cat fur.

"Well, of course, Cameron. Your mother and I are quite well known in certain circles for our research into cultural customs of death and dying."

"Really?" She saw her parents rarely in recent years and didn't remember a single conversation about that research.

"Yes, indeed." Her father's stomach growled audibly. "We're having dinner with Albert and his lady friend Marilyn tonight, I think you said." William raised his eyebrows.

So much for talking about research. Or death. "That's right. Anyway, the reason Mom's not here is because the police wanted to question her. But I'm sure she'll be home soon."

William made a *tsk*-ing sound. "She's not going to be happy about having to talk to the authorities, I daresay. She's more accustomed to being the authority."

"There's no arguing with the police when someone has died."

"I suppose. Now, what about your fellow, Pete Pappas?" he asked. "I hope he's invited for dinner tonight, too. I like him, Cam."

Cam had asked her boyfriend, Pete, to dinner the night before so he could meet her parents. She'd made pasta primavera with grilled lemon chicken, and Pete had brought his homemade spanakopita for an appetizer. By all appearances her parents had liked her man, and vice versa.

"Of course he's invited," Cam said. "But now I'm not sure he'll be able to make it." Pete was the lead Massachusetts State Police homicide detective for this region of the state. "If Nicole's death is murder, he'll likely be assigned the case."

"Murder? Surely that's not possible, my dear. I'll bet the poor woman merely suffered an irreversible health crisis. Or perhaps she ended her own life."

Maybe, maybe not. Cam frowned. If Pete was assigned the case, and if her mother was a person of interest, once again Pete wouldn't be able to spend time with her. He'd already had to suspend their relationship in the winter when Cam herself was briefly a suspect. That was reason enough to hope Nicole had died of natural causes. Spring was plenty manic on a small vegetable and chicken farm. She definitely didn't need murder in the mix, with the temporary loss of a boyfriend on top of it. Cam grimaced. It was heartless of her to even think that when a really nice woman had just lost her life.

"This is quite a delight." Albert beamed at his four tablemates in the Moran Manor dining room. Cam sat at his left at the round table. On Albert's right was Marilyn Muller, his new lady friend, then Cam's parents. "I'm just sorry Peter couldn't join us, Cam," Albert went on.

Cam gazed at the empty seat to her left. "He's sorry, too, but he had to work." That was all he'd said, but he'd promised to call Cam later if he could. His absence had to mean that either Nicole was murdered or they had reason to suspect a homicide. Small towns in Massachusetts called in the state police in cases of unexplained death.

An older woman appeared with two open bottles of wine—one red, one white—and set them in front of Albert. "Here you are, Mr. Saint Pierre." A teenage waiter followed her.

The facility allowed residents to bring their own wine to dinner, which Cam thought was a sensible and civilized approach to institutional living. All the men in the room wore blazers, as was required in the formal dining room, and Cam had changed into a springlike skirt and top before leaving. Her mom wore white Capris and a dark blue blouse, while Marilyn was attired in her usual comfortable slacks but with a string of pearls to dress up her flowered top. Cam was glad Albert had found Marilyn. The fact that he and Cam still missed Marie didn't mean Albert shouldn't be happy.

Cam's mom had showed up at the farm at the very last moment in the rental car and had quickly washed up and changed. Cam hadn't had a chance to ask her how the interview with the police had gone.

"Thank you, dear," Albert said to the woman, whose name tag read MANAGER above her name. "Now, who wants which?"

After the manager poured the wine and left, the teen asked, "Do you know what you want to order?" His voice cracked.

Cam perused the menu. At the bottom was a line she hadn't seen before: "All herbs from Fresh Page Farm." She pointed to it. "Do you know where this farm is?" she asked the waiter.

"It's in Salisbury, ma'am. One of those water farms."

"Do you mean hydroponics?" Albert asked.

"I guess so," the kid answered. "The owner just made a delivery. Do you want to talk to him?"

"We'd appreciate that," Albert said. "Right, Cam?"

She nodded. They each gave their dinner order to the teen and he left.

William raised his glass of Chardonnay. "Here's to your health, Albert, yours and Marilyn's."

They raised their glasses and clinked them in all directions. "Thank you, William," Marilyn said. "And safe travels to you both. Albert tells me you lead very exciting lives in the summers. Where are you headed this time?" She took a tiny sip of wine and set her glass down, aiming a cheerful smile at Cam's parents.

Deb glanced at her husband. "We're going to a village in the Amazon in Brazil. The Yanomami have some curious customs regarding death. Right, Bill?" Cam's mother was the only person her father let call him by a nickname.

"Yes, it's a fascinating culture," William added. "They cremate their dead and then the family members eat the ashes to protect the soul of the deceased. We've seen more unusual customs elsewhere, but the Yanomamis' is one of the more interesting."

"I hear we had a bit of drama in town this afternoon," Albert said, "that Deb and Cam were involved with. What can you tell us?" His eyes were serious under his snowy ski-jump eyebrows.

"What drama, Al?" Marilyn asked.

Cam looked at Deb, who pointed back at her. "I wouldn't call it drama, exactly. You know the new hydroponics greenhouse downtown?" Cam asked. Using the word "downtown" was a bit of an exaggeration, since all Westbury had for a center was a strip of Main Street with a post office, the Food Mart, a gas station, a pizza parlor, a barber shop, and a few other small businesses.

"Certainly. That's a fine new structure Mrs. Kingsbury built for herself," Albert said.

"It is," Cam said. "Bobby Burr helped Nicole put up the greenhouse."

"Must be a competitor to this Fresh Page outfit," Albert said.

"Did I hear the name of my business?" A tall man with blond hair turning to gray approached them. He flashed a toothy grin. "Evening, folks. I'm Orson Page. Kid in the kitchen said you wanted to ask me a question?" He stood with his arms hanging straight at his sides, his bony wrists extending beyond denim workshirt sleeves a bit too short for him.

"I saw the note on the menu about your business, and our server was nice enough to say you were in the building." Cam stood. "I'm Cam Flaherty, and I'm a fellow farmer here in Westbury." She shook his hand and introduced the others at the table.

The man's eyebrows went up. "Glad to meet you, Ms. Flaherty. What do you farm?"

Cam wondered if he'd heard of her before. "Organic produce, primarily. And I keep chickens, too. I didn't realize you were growing there in Salisbury."

"I've been kind of flying under the radar for years, growing and selling herbs," Orson said. "But when I saw that new lady set up shop right here in town, I figured I'd better get my name on the menus of all the restaurants I supply. Never had no competition before."

"Did you meet the proprietor of Seacoast Fresh?" Albert asked. "She was doing hydroponics, too."

"No, not yet. Well, nice to meet you folks. I've got to get back to the missus. She's an invalid and depends on me for just about everything."

"It was good to meet you, Orson." Cam pulled out her farm business card from her bag and handed it to him. "I'd love to show you my farm sometime." When a frowning Deb opened her mouth, Cam shook her head at her. They didn't need to get into the ethics of hydroponic growing here at the dinner table.

"Thanks. And you stop on by the greenhouse when you can, Cam. I'm on Ferry Road in Salisbury." He glanced around the table. "Any of you are welcome. I'd be happy to show you around." He ambled back toward the kitchen, shoulders forward in a self-effacing gait.

Albert watched him go. "He doesn't appear to know about today."

When Marilyn looked confused, Cam said, "I took a couple of flats of seedlings over to Nicole in her greenhouse today. But I found her dead. Right there in the greenhouse."

Marilyn gasped and brought both hands to her mouth.

Albert nodded. "That's what I heard."

"Al, you could have told me," Marilyn said to him in a gentle tone. She looked at Cam. "How terribly upsetting for you, dear."

"Before you ask, I don't know how she died," Cam said. "And yes, it was no fun to discover her body." She brought her own hand to her mouth, seeing again Nicole's hand clutching the rosary, her body splayed over the vat. Nobody should have to go like that.

"The police seem to think she might have died from foul play," Deb said. She sat erect in her chair, as always.

Cam wondered why they thought that so soon. Didn't they have to wait for an autopsy? Sure, if Nicole had shown evidence of suffering a gunshot wound or having been stabbed, but Cam hadn't seen any signs of either. If she hadn't died from natural causes, might it have been suicide?

"They questioned me for quite a long time," Deb continued.

"Why you?" Marilyn asked.

Deb sipped her Pinot Noir instead of answering.

"Because she had been picketing Nicole's business." Cam watched her mother. "And apparently had been inside alone with Nicole earlier. Isn't that right, Mom?"

"That is correct."

"How did it go, your conversation with Nicole?" Cam asked. "I assume she was still alive at the time?"

"You can't have a conversation with someone who isn't alive." Deb clipped off her words. "We're here to have a nice dinner, not rehash some idiot officer's questions. If you don't mind, I'd rather not repeat the grilling I received."

"And you shan't," William said, patting her hand. "Marilyn, we hear you're quite the wordsmith. Winning Scrabble every time and all?" He smiled at her. "I'd like to take you on after we eat."

"I don't always win." Marilyn blushed. "Albert here gets a little carried away in his estimation of my skills."

"Let's play," Albert said. "A family game. That'll be splendid."

Maybe, or maybe it'll be tense, Cam thought, just like things are right now. Her mom wouldn't meet her gaze. What was she hiding?

Chapter 5

The sun had set twenty minutes ago, but light still softened the night sky as Cam shut the chickens into their coop at eight-thirty. She and her mother had played a rousing game of Scrabble with Marilyn and Albert, with William looking on and offering whispered tips to anyone who asked. Cam had insisted on a timer, though. She hadn't expected to arrive home so late, and she needed to make sure her flock of several dozen hens was safely inside for the night.

Marilyn had won the game, as predicted. Her sweet demeanor didn't dilute a keen mind and a cutthroat approach to game playing. Deb had continued to refuse to talk about her interview, even in the car on the way home. Cam couldn't imagine her mother was hiding something, but she sure acted like she was.

Now mild air brushed Cam's cheeks. She leaned against the chicken tractor, which was really just a coop on wheels she could transport around the farm to let the hens fertilize different sections of ground. She and her father had moved it only this morning, so the fragrance of chicken manure was barely detectable. Tomorrow was volunteer day. William seemed to like the hens, so maybe Cam could get one of her regular volunteers to supervise him cleaning out the inside of the coop. She definitely wasn't letting him near any more plants, even weeds.

Cam's phone buzzed in her messenger bag, which she'd slung crosswise over her chest. The display confirmed Pete as the caller. She greeted him and sank onto the bench near the back wall of the barn. Preston sidled over and reared up to rub against her knee.

"Cam, I'm so sorry to have missed dinner."

"We missed you, too. Uncle Albert asked about you."

"I've been put on the Kingsbury death, as you might imagine."

"I was wondering. That means a suspected homicide, right?"

"There's just too much that's odd. That doesn't fit."

"For example?" Cam asked in a soft voice.

"I'll let you know a few details in person next time I see you. You know I can't talk about it on the phone, hon. How was it for you, finding the body?"

"It wasn't any fun. I keep seeing her in my mind and thinking what a terrible way it was for her to die."

"I'm sorry you had to go through that."

"Thanks." She couldn't see the farmhouse from where she sat, but Cam pictured her mom and dad sitting quietly side by side reading on the couch. The home movie of her childhood—all three of them reading every night instead of watching television. "Pete, is my mom in trouble? They kept her at the station for quite a while today."

"Trouble. Hmm. As far as I know she gave a straightforward account of her dealings with the victim. But the fact that she was engaging in public and vocal opposition to the greenhouse business isn't a point in her favor. Nor that she spent time alone with Ms. Kingsbury this morning." He cleared his throat. "I'm sorry, Cam, but that's the way it goes."

Her mom. A person of interest in a murder. Cam felt a rush of protective feelings. "Mom wouldn't have hurt Nicole. No way."

"Let's hope not. I've been in this business long enough to know that people aren't always as they seem."

"But—" Cam protested.

"Cam, hang on." Pete's voice was gentle. "Nobody's been accused of anything. We haven't made any arrests. We'll be investigating this death as thoroughly as any other suspected homicide."

"All right." Cam stared into the evening, which was getting darker by the minute. "I know you will." *But my mother did not kill Nicole.*

"And actually, Chief Frost and Officer Dodge shouldn't have let you go as soon as they did. You found the body. They should have obtained a full statement from you." His voice was low and ended in a sigh.

"But I didn't have any problems with Nicole," Cam protested.

"Doesn't matter. You'll need to come in and give a statement tomorrow."

"To you?"

"No, to Officer Hobbs. I have to be in court tomorrow morning."

Ivan Hobbs, Pete's assistant. Cam had seen how rigid he could be earlier in the spring.

He cleared his throat. "And anyway, I'd have to recuse myself from taking your statement."

"Of course." *What a mess.* "I miss you. When can I see you again?"

Pete remained silent for a moment.

"Uh-oh," Cam said. "Does this mean—"

He blew out a breath. "It's not quite the same as when you were a person of interest in January, Cam. But the fact that you found the body and that your mother is staying with you, well, I really can't be socializing with any of you."

It was Cam's turn not to speak. Dating a homicide detective was so much fun.

"I'm sorry," he went on. "You know that."

"I know." Her voice was heavy. "Call me when you can." She disconnected without saying good-bye. "Come on, Preston. Time to go inside."

A bat startled her by zigzagging almost silently through the air from the barn to a nearby tree, likely dining on mosquitoes or black flies. Too bad catching a murderer wasn't as easy.

Cam was almost to the house when a truck crunched toward her on the gravel of the driveway. She held up her hand to block the headlights as her heart thudded. According to Pete, a killer was at large. Preston dashed for his cat door, jumping through into the basement. The flap *fwapped* behind him. She hurried toward the steps, too.

"I couldn't reach you, Cam," Bobby Burr's voice said through the open window. "Hope it isn't too late to stop by." He turned off the engine and hopped out.

Whew. "Bobby, I'm glad you came. I was out to dinner and must have missed your text." She gazed at the curly-haired carpenter illuminated by the porch light, her pulse returning to normal. Had he heard the news? Had the police notified him, questioned him, even?

"I'm on a big job in Amesbury, didn't get off until an hour ago. What's up?"

No, he clearly didn't know. Cam gestured to the chairs on

the small bricked patio behind the house. She would have invited him inside, but she wanted to speak privately with him and it was a nice evening.

"Have a seat." She flashed back to the murder at the poultry farm in March, and how Pete hadn't wanted her to tell the widow and her daughter about the killing, how he'd insisted that he do it, that their reactions could be important. Should she even be telling Bobby about Nicole now that Pete thought her death might be murder? How could she not, though, now that Bobby was here? He was her friend. And anyway, lots of other people already knew about the death.

He sat, but looked puzzled. "What's going on? I mean, I'm happy to chat with you, but—"

She held up her hand. She took a deep breath and let it out. "Something awful happened today. I'm really sorry to tell you that your cousin Nicole has died."

Bobby jerked back in his chair as if someone had hit him with a two-by-four. "Nickie? You're not serious. She's only forty-one." His hands clenched the arms of the wrought iron chair until his knuckles were the color of a freshly cut piece of ash.

Cam leaned forward and touched his hand. "It's true. I was the one who found her. In her greenhouse."

His eyes filled. He sank his head into his hands and leaned forward. It took a few moments before he spoke. He addressed the ground. "We were like sister and brother. Neither of us had siblings. We always took care of each other, ever since we were little." He raised his head to look at Cam, anguish painted on his face. "I was so glad she left that jerk of a husband and moved back up here." He shook his head slowly. "My uncle, her dad, died of a heart attack in his forties. She must have had an underlying heart condition and we never knew it."

"I'm so sorry." What else could she say? Bobby's own mother had been murdered last fall. If it turned out Nicole had been killed, too, her death was going to hit him even harder.

"And you found her. That must have been tough." Bobby's characteristic caring side took over from his grief.

"Yes."

He folded his hands and stared at them. "God, now I'm going to have to deal with Rudin."

"Who's Rudin?" Cam asked.

"The just recently ex-husband, or maybe it's about-to-be-ex. I'm not sure if the divorce is final." He set his mouth in a grim line. "I never liked him. He's one of those men who wants to control everything, especially his wife. At least he paid her what he owed her. I mean, I think he was finished paying."

"The divorce settlement?"

Bobby nodded. "She didn't want to keep their house in Miami, so he bought her out. That's how she could afford to buy the property on Main Street, that little house and the land."

"That's right. A small house sits behind the greenhouse. Almost a cottage. Nicole was living there?"

"Yes. She owned the cottage, but she had to take out a loan to build the greenhouse. She'd come up with a good business model. She was going to make it work."

"Nicole seemed very devoted to the enterprise. Organized, hardworking."

"She was starting over," Bobby said. "Getting a fresh beginning in her life."

"Did she have any children?" Cam asked.

"No, and she was sad about that. But it's just as well she didn't have any with *him*." Bobby pronounced the pronoun like it was an obscenity. He stood. "I'd better go. Thanks for telling me, Cam. You're a good friend. I'd rather hear news like that from you than from the TV, or from whoever would have told me."

"That's what I thought, too."

He brought a fist to his mouth and blinked away a tear. "I need to call my aunt. The police probably already told her, right? She's next of kin, at least if the divorce is final."

"Yes, they probably have, if they could reach her."

"She must be devastated. They were so close, her and Nickie."

Cam stood, too, and held out her arms for a wordless hug. After they said good-bye, Bobby walked toward his truck as if he were dragging a twenty-pound sledgehammer in each hand.

Chapter 6

Death or no death, Cam still had a farm to run. She stood in the barn at eight the next morning. It was another warm day with not a rain cloud in sight, and her volunteers would be showing up shortly. She'd been holding weekly volunteer days for almost a year now. It was a big help to have dedicated customers arrive ready and willing to weed, turn compost, harvest, and generally lend hands and muscles. All of them were members of her community-supported agriculture program, her CSA. They prepaid to pick up a share of fresh organic produce every week all summer and into the fall. Cam really needed to hire at least a part-time worker for the busy months this year—but she'd been too busy to advertise and interview for one. So far the volunteers filled the labor gap. Even though she usually held the volunteer day on Wednesday, none of them had minded her switching it to Friday this week because of her parents' visit.

Cam had had trouble falling asleep last night. She'd chatted with her parents for a half hour after Bobby had left, sipping a little glass of Scotch, avoiding talk of death. But once she slid into bed upstairs, it was Nicole's death that filled her mind. Bobby's reaction. Pete's suspicions. The sight of Nicole's dead body splayed over the slurry vat. Even the rosary in her hand. Cam hadn't fallen asleep until after midnight. Now she yawned wide, then drained the last drop from her mug of French roast coffee.

Bobby had spent last summer rebuilding Cam's barn after the fire. Last fall, when things were getting rocky with her former beau, the volatile chef Jake, the very attractive Bobby had flirted with her. But her relationship with Pete had picked up once she'd told Jake she couldn't handle his jealousy or his tempers, and now Cam and Bobby had settled into a firm friendship. She was glad of it. She was happy with Pete—or would be again once this current mess was solved—and who couldn't use a friendship with a handsome carpenter?

Felicity Slavin popped in through the open barn door wearing a purple T-shirt and green work pants tucked into turquoise rubber boots. She hurried to Cam. "How are you holding up? It must have been just awful to find poor Nicole dead."

"Not much fun, for sure. How did your statement go?"

She lifted her shoulders and dropped them. "I told them I didn't know Nicole, hadn't met her. I just didn't want chemicals going into food. Any food, anywhere. And organic should mean food grown in soil, not in solution."

"Do you know for sure what she was feeding the plants?"

"It doesn't really matter. NOSB recommended hydroponics not be certified. It dilutes the standards, Cam!"

This was funny. Cam was the certified organic farmer, but her customer was throwing around acronyms like a pro. The National Organic Standards Board was trying to uphold the philosophy of organic, but the National Organic Program had allowed hydroponics to be certified organic. An unfortunate tension existed between the standards board—which wanted to uphold the entire relationship of water, soil, microorganisms, the works—and the certifying program, which dealt with working farms big and small as well as lobbyists from deep-pocketed farmers.

"NOP shouldn't have certified hydroponics. They should have listened to the board." Felicity frowned and crossed her arms.

"Since when did you become an expert on NOP? I thought you were more concerned about eating local food, being part of the Locavore Club and all."

"It's all tied in together, Cam. You know that."

Cam mentally rolled her eyes. She was committed to growing organically—it just made sense. But she didn't always eat local and organic herself and didn't go overboard about it.

"Did you tell the police about all the standards stuff? I mean, how it related to Nicole's business?" Cam asked.

"I certainly did."

Cam glanced up to see a sparrow fly into the barn and light on a rafter. She returned her gaze to Felicity. "I saw a dark-haired man in the greenhouse parking lot yesterday afternoon. Did you see him? He looked kind of pale. I don't know who he is."

Felicity cocked her head. "I can't say that I did. But you know the lot is shared with the Huntington Insurance Agency next door."

"That's right. He probably had business with them." Instead of business killing Nicole. Cam had never had a particularly vivid imagination, but it seemed to be going haywire lately, putting ideas like that into her brain.

A bicycle bell trilled outside, and Alexandra Magnusson strode in a moment later. "Am I late for a meeting?" she asked, lifting her helmet off her flaxen hair, worn as usual in two long braids.

Cam laughed. "No, but thanks for coming. How's your new job?"

"It's great. The environmental group loves my web design work. They want to bring me on full time, but I told them not unless I can have my farm mornings off. I would miss volunteering here too much."

Smiling, Cam thanked her lucky stars. These two women, along with Lucinda DaSilva, had become much more than customers over the last year. They were good friends, and her lifeboat. She knew they had her back as well as one another's.

"Are you distributing summer shares this Saturday?" Alexandra asked. "I've lost track of the start date."

"No, not until June fourth." Cam had fifty subscribers signed up for her CSA this year, and the beginning of the season was always iffy. She hoped she'd have enough produce to satisfy everyone. At least she had plenty of greens in the field. "You both can go out and cut greens for yourselves, if you want. Take some asparagus, too." The delectable shoots were popping up like crazy. One could almost watch them grow.

"Thanks," Felicity said.

Alexandra's expression grew somber. "You found that greenhouse lady yesterday."

"I did," Cam said. "We were just talking about that."

"She was actually growing vegetables? Or planning to?" Alexandra tilted her head. "When I hear hydroponics, I always think of pot farms." She shot a quick glance to Felicity. "No offense or anything."

"No offense taken." Felicity twisted her mouth. "That was Wes's doing, not mine." She brightened her expression with visible effort. Felicity's husband Wes was currently serving time for a serious error in judgment.

The petite woman was unfailingly cheerful and optimistic, Cam thought. It had to be hard for her to have her ex-hippie pot-smoking husband in prison.

Cam glanced at the door of the barn when she heard a knock. A smiling woman about Felicity's size stood in the doorway.

"Come on in," Cam called.

The rosy-cheeked woman, her gray hair held back by a bright green knitted headband, walked in and said hello. "I'm Sue Biellik. I just signed up for the CSA last week, and I saw your Facebook post about volunteering. I hope it's all right for me to join in."

"Of course it is, Sue. I'm Cam Flaherty, farmer in chief." Cam shook her hand. "Happy to have you." She introduced Felicity and Alexandra. "Do you have any experience with gardening?"

"Oh, yes. I've always had a garden. But now I live in a condo, and I miss it so. This seemed like a good solution."

"So you know your weeds from your seedlings," Alexandra said approvingly.

"Indeed I do," Sue said.

"Glad to hear it," Cam said.

Preston trotted into the barn. He stopped cold when he saw the group.

"Hey, kitty," Sue said, squatting. She held out her hand. Preston examined her. He strolled straight to her hand, letting her stroke his thick coat. She looked up at Cam.

"Who's this handsome fellow?"

Cam laughed. "Preston. You look like a cat person."

"I have three of these sweethearts at home." She gave Preston one more stroke before standing. "And an English springer spaniel puppy, too, who's driving me crazy right now."

"Sue Biellik," Felicity said. "You taught a knitting class at Newburyport Adult Ed, right?"

Sue laughed. "Last year, yes. Knitting is pretty much my life these days."

"I'm hopeless at it," Felicity said with a wry smile. "I guess I'd better sign up for another class with you." She glanced at Cam. "I wanted to say hello to your mom. Will she be helping us this morning?"

Cam's father peeked around the corner of the door. "No, Deb said she has some work to do. But I'm willing to lend a hand." He chuckled and made his way in.

"Daddy, please meet some of my friends and customers." Cam introduced him to the three women. "And this is Professor William Flaherty."

"No formalities, now. Just call me William." He shook each of their hands. "That is, I'll help if Cammie will let me. I made a big mistake yesterday, apparently."

This time Cam actually rolled her eyes. What was it about her father that made her revert to teenage behavior? "We won't be offering sweet peas in the shares for a while. So no, Daddy, you don't get to weed."

He spread his hands. "I admit my crime, your honor."

Alexandra glanced at Cam and covered her mouth, suppressing a giggle.

"But is there an alternative service you can assign me?" William went on.

"I'd love your help with the chickens," Cam said. "Think you can manage that?"

"Yes, indeed," he said. "You know, my grandparents had a chicken farm back in Paoli."

"I never knew that." Cam pulled a mock frown. "Really?"

"Indiana is a great place to raise birds. And of course your

40

mother and I see chickens, or a similar species, in most of the indigenous cultures we visit. I'm good with those silly birds."

"You got it, then. Alexandra, can you find him a mucking shovel and grab a wheelbarrow for him? Show him the ropes?"

Alexandra made a thumbs-up gesture and headed for the tool wall.

After the two tall figures went out, Felicity's face grew serious again. "Do you think your mother would mind if I pop into the house? I just wanted to say hello and . . ." Her voice trailed off.

"Sure, go ahead. I don't know what she's working on. I'm not surprised she doesn't want to help out here. She's not really the farming type." Cam hadn't thought she herself was, either, until Albert had to have his foot amputated at the same time Cam was laid off her job as a software engineer in Cambridge. He'd offered her the farm and here she was, making a go of it. And not just surviving, but loving it. The hard work and fresh air turned out to be so much more appealing than sitting in a cubicle with her face glued to the screen and her body bent over a keyboard writing and debugging software every day.

She watched Felicity walk briskly out of the barn. What did she want to talk to Deb about? Cam shook her head. Her mom and Felicity had had all day yesterday on the picket line to get to know each other. It could be anything. Cam headed out into the sunshine, determined to let good, honest hard work in the soil and fresh air take her mind off death.

When Felicity came back from greeting Deb a few minutes later, Cam asked, "You found Mom?"

Felicity frowned but nodded.

"Is everything okay?" Cam asked.

"I guess. I thought she'd want to talk about Nicole, but she doesn't."

"She's like that. I wouldn't take it personally." Cam felt bad for Felicity, with her genuinely sunny, open attitude toward life, as unlike Deb Flaherty as could be.

"All right." Felicity mustered a little smile. "Where do you want me this morning?"

Cam asked her to grab a hoe and join the volunteer in the potato field. After Alexandra helped William get started on the chickens, Cam set her to work planting out pepper seedlings. She directed several other customers who arrived to weed rows of lettuce and Asian greens and to hill up the potatoes. Cam rolled up the sides of the hoophouse. She began to water the lettuce starts and the new seedlings for the fall broccoli and cabbage.

Last spring hadn't been anywhere near as warm and dry as this one. She worried about her crops. She wasn't set up to do serious irrigation, and she was afraid her well wouldn't be able to handle being drained of massive amounts of water. The town water lines didn't stretch out here, but even if they had, the cost would be prohibitive. She didn't have a pond from which to pump water, and would have to acquire more hoses to reach sprinklers to the far field. But if she didn't water or if rain didn't come along soon, she'd lose her investment of seed and seedlings. Worse, she wouldn't have enough product to dole out to her CSA customers.

After she'd worked alongside her volunteers for a couple of hours, her phone buzzed in her back pocket. She pulled it out to read a text from Pete:

Statement? Ivan's waiting.

Cam groaned. She had to do it, but the last thing she wanted to do was leave the work party, get cleaned up, and spend an hour with a humorless by-the-book detective. She let Felicity and Alexandra know she had to leave before heading to the coop to check on her dad. He sat on the ground inside the fenced-off area with a full wheelbarrow of sawdust mixed with droppings next to him. He was singing, and hens were all over him. Mama Dot, Cam's Silver Laced Wyandotte, even sat on his head, her black-edged white feathers gleaming in the sun.

"You do like chickens," Cam said, smiling at him and his companions.

"Indeed I do." He beamed. He gently plucked Mama Dot off his head and set her on the ground. He boosted himself up to standing. "I noticed they've done a good job of laying. How do you want me to collect the eggs?"

"Follow me." She showed him the bucket in the barn. "The eggs need to be soaked and gently scrubbed before putting them in these flats." She pointed to the sink next to the egg refrigerator. "Then they go in the fridge here. Thanks, Daddy. I appreciate the help."

"My pleasure. I've been either in my office or a classroom all year. I like to get out and do something physical once the semester is over."

"I have to go downtown and give my statement to the police." Cam frowned. "I hope I won't be long."

"You run along, then. Don't worry about us."

"Okay." Cam turned to go, but stopped. "Um, Daddy?"

"I know. No weeding." He stood there grinning, his hair sticking up all which way from his head. Sawdust decorated the shoulder of his T-shirt, which read MY CAREER IS IN RUINS.

Cam surprised herself by throwing her arms around him and hugging. He flapped his arms, finally bringing them to rest on her back. Not hugging, exactly, but touching. She pulled back.

"I'm so glad you're here." And she was. She didn't think

she'd ever felt this kind of rush of love for her father. Something about her new life of farming, of developing close friends, even of solving mysteries, had changed her. And especially to have him here now, when she was getting involved in another murder, was a comfort.

"I'm glad, too." He ruffled her hair before reaching for the bucket. "Got to get to those eggs, now." He ambled off, bucket in hand.

Chapter 7

Ruth ushered Cam into an interview room thirty minutes later, her thick brown hair today in a tidy French braid. "Detective Hobbs will be here in a minute," she said. She lowered her voice and added, "He's kind of upset you took this long to come in."

Cam sighed. "I didn't do anything wrong. And I have a farm to run." She sat the table in the room. Westbury must have spent some money on paint recently. The walls were a warm cream color with butter green trim, and she detected a clean lemony smell. "It looks really nice in here. Like not institutional at all."

Ruth laughed. "The new thinking is to make people feel relaxed when they are interviewed. When you put people in an ugly cold room, people think jail and are less forthcoming. Or so the researchers say." She lifted a shoulder and let it drop. "I think the interview method is a lot more important than what the room looks like."

The door swung open. A thin Ivan Hobbs bustled in. "Ms. Flaherty. Officer, thank you." He shook hands with Cam before sitting at the end of the table. His dark blond hair looked freshly trimmed in a military-length cut, and his Oxford shirt was crisply pressed under a light blazer. He examined Cam out of dark eyes over a narrow nose. "I expected to see you much earlier this morning. Detective Pappas said he conveyed the necessity of this interview to you."

"Pete asked me to come in. He didn't say when." Cam folded her hands on the table in front of her. She was glad she'd changed into good slacks and a turquoise blouse. It couldn't hurt to look a little professional. It gave her a sense of confidence, as illogical as that seemed.

"Be that as it may. Let's get going then, shall we? Officer Dodge, if you don't mind."

Ruth did something with a panel on the wall. "Recording," she said. She remained standing with her hands clasped behind her back.

The detective identified himself and the date and asked Cam to state her name and address.

She obliged. "Just to be clear, I understand this is a homicide investigation."

Ivan stared at her for a moment. "I'm afraid it is. Or at least an investigation of a suspicious death." He pulled out a ballpoint pen and laid a legal pad covered with illegible writing on the table. "Please describe the events of yesterday afternoon."

"I brought two flats of basil seedlings to the greenhouse yesterday at about two o'clock."

"That would be the Seacoast Fresh greenhouse at"—he checked the pad—"71 Main Street."

"Yes. After I climbed out of my truck, a dark-haired man pushed past me. His face was pale, and he looked worried. Or nervous, or something."

Ivan sat up straight. "Can you identify him?"

"No. I'd never seen him before."

"Height? Build? Other identifying features?"

"Maybe five eight. He was wearing a green shirt. I told Ruth and Chief Frost that."

Ruth nodded. "You did. And you said he had haunted eyes."

Cam squeezed her eyes shut, trying to bring up the thing that had been dancing outside her memory. She opened them. "I think he was wearing a chain around his neck. I only got a glimpse, but maybe a cross hung from it? I can see a flash when I try to picture him, like a flash of bright metal on his chest."

"Big guy? Skinny?"

"He was slight. That's all I can remember." Cam ran a hand over the table's battered wooden surface, scratched and marred with carved initials, which made it oddly out of style with the rest of the room. She traced one set of letters with her finger. But she couldn't bring up any more details about the man.

"Did he get into a vehicle?" the detective asked. "Or had he gotten out of one?"

"Neither. I mean, not that I saw."

"After you saw him, what did you do?"

"I took the flats into the greenhouse. I remember thinking that nobody was there. That's how it felt, or sounded, maybe. I called for Nicole a couple of times, but she didn't respond. So I took my seedlings to the back and set them on her worktable."

"Did you see the body at that time?"

"No. I mean, yes, a few seconds later I did. I'd sent her a text and turned to go when I heard her phone ping beyond the set of shelves."

"Please describe the shelves."

"They're just shelves. Like a plastic shelving unit about five feet tall, maybe ten feet long, a foot deep. Without a back, you know, so you can see through it. She used them for supplies, tools, what have you."

"Go on."

"Nicole always wore black and red. Every single time I saw her. When I went to see if that was her phone, I saw a flash of red. Usually there's nothing red in a greenhouse unless you have ripe tomatoes or peppers, and it's way too early in the season for that. Packaging for soil amendments and such don't often have red on them, either. So I went to look."

"And found her."

Cam nodded as she traveled in her mind once again back to that horrific scene. She felt seasick anew. It was a good thing her breakfast of peanut butter on toast had been hours ago.

"Out loud for the recording, please," Ruth said gently.

"Yes, I found her."

"Please describe every detail you can remember." Ivan narrowed his eyes at Cam.

She told him about the position of the body. About Nicole's shirt. About the slurry.

"Was any part of Ms. Kingsbury touching this slurry?"

"I don't think so. The level was pretty low. Unless her right hand was. I don't remember."

"What else?"

Cam told him about the rosary beads and what they looked like. "Oh, and a few of the beads seemed to be missing. Right, Ruthie?" *Oops.* Maybe she shouldn't have used her friend's nickname for the recording. Too late now.

"That's correct," Ruth said.

Ivan checked his notes. "And you touched her neck to see if you could detect a pulse."

"Yes. I couldn't feel one. I backed away and called nine-one-one. Ruth and Chief Frost arrived shortly after that."

"You didn't touch anything else?"

"No."

"Did your mother, Debra Flaherty, know the victim personally?"

Cam stared at him. This meeting had just veered from being a straightforward statement to a grilling about Cam's mom.

"Ms. Flaherty?" Ivan gazed at her with what looked like ice in his eyes.

"I don't think she knew Nicole, no."

"Professor Flaherty apparently spent some time in the greenhouse earlier."

"I wasn't there," Cam said. She lowered her hands to her lap and gripped one with the other to prevent them from revealing her nervousness.

"Did she tell you what she talked with the victim about?"

"No." Her mom hadn't even told her what she told Ruth in her interview. Maybe later today Cam could convince Deb to open up and talk with her about the questioning.

"Does your mother have a history of demonstrating for causes?" he asked.

"Not when I was living at home, she didn't." Cam shut her mouth. She was about to tell him what her father had said about Deb's more recent activities. Not a good idea. Let them ferret it out if they thought it was pertinent. Or ask Mom herself.

"When did Professor Flaherty arrive in Westbury?"

Why all these questions? Was her mom really in trouble? "She and my father flew in some days ago. They are each Professor Flaherty, actually. They rented a car at the airport and drove up here."

"I see. Do you have anything else to add?" Ivan clicked his pen shut and open, shut and open.

Oh. She should tell him about the text message. "I sent Nicole a text right before I found her. I was going to write her a note but decided to text, instead."

"Yes, you mentioned that." He peered at the legal pad again. "What did you write?"

"Just that I had left the seedlings."

"Did you also apologize for the protest? Are you sure you weren't also involved in organizing the demonstration? Perhaps you and your mother conspired together to put Ms. Kingsbury out of business."

"No. No!" Cam exclaimed. "That isn't what I meant at all." They must have already reviewed Nicole's phone. He knew what she had texted.

Ivan stared at her. Cam glanced up at Ruth, who looked sympathetic but remained silent.

"I felt bad for her that people I knew were demonstrating. That's all it was."

He let out an audible breath as if chiding her for not telling the truth. "You're sure about that?"

"Yes." Cam crossed her arms. "Of course I am. And we weren't in competition at all. I have a thriving business. If anything, I was helping Nicole get hers off the ground. I hoped she'd succeed."

"Do you have anything else you'd like to add?"

Meeting Orson Page flashed into her brain. "Maybe. Last night I was at Moran Manor with—"

"Moran Manor?" Ivan sounded like he'd run out of patience.

"Hang on a sec, Detective." *Geez*. He had a lot of nerve to get short with her. "You asked if there was anything else. The least you can do is hear me out."

He tapped the fingers of his right hand against the table in a *buh-bam, buh-bam, buh-bam* rhythm. "Go ahead."

"My parents and I were eating dinner at the assisted living residence in town with my great-uncle and his woman friend.

I happened to speak with an Orson Page. He runs a hydroponics greenhouse in Salisbury called Fresh Page. He didn't seem too happy about Nicole's business."

"Did you talk with Mr. Page about finding her body?"

"That didn't come up. And he didn't appear to know she was dead."

"This interview is concluded. Thank you for your time. I remind you not to speak to the public about what you saw." He slid a business card across the table. "I will be your contact person for this investigation, Ms. Flaherty. If you think of anything else, please contact me. Not Detective Pappas. Is that clear?"

Cam stood. "Couldn't be more clear. I hope you sort out this case sooner rather than later." She nearly crumpled the card in her fist.

"So do we, Ms. Flaherty."

Chapter 8

Cam pulled out onto Main Street right behind Simone Koyama's antique red work truck. A round red light blinked from the left rear corner of the truck's bed, signaling a turn into Sim's auto repair shop, which was almost directly across the street from the greenhouse. Cam hadn't visited with her friend in a while, so she pulled in to SK Foreign Auto after Sim. Cam needed to get back to her volunteers, but she could spare a few minutes to say hello. And maybe it would get the bad taste of being grilled by Ivan out of her mouth. Or at least the unsettled feeling he'd left her with.

The mechanic jumped down from the high cab and sauntered over to Cam. "How's it going, farmer girl?" She fistbumped Cam through the open window of Cam's truck, her dark hair both shorter and spikier than the last time Cam had seen her. The smile slid off Sim's face. "Did you hear about the death over at the greenhouse?" She pointed down the road in the direction of the greenhouse a quarter mile away.

"I did." The small-town gossip mill apparently didn't yet include Cam's role in the death. She switched off the engine and cleared her throat. "I was the one who found her." *Oops.* Was that saying too much? Too late now.

"Really? Wicked nasty. She was Bobby's cousin, you know." Sim and Bobby had been good friends before Cam met either of them. Sim wrinkled her nose, the silver ring in her nostril scrunching up, too. "You okay?"

"I guess. I just came from being questioned at the station."

"That's no fun. I speak from experience."

"I know." Sim had been questioned about Bobby's mother's murder in the fall, a woman everybody knew Sim didn't get along with. "Did you know my parents are here visiting?" Cam asked.

"Get out. I thought they like never came to see you."

"They're here now. And my own mom was demonstrating against Nicole's business when I found the body," Cam said. "I can't get her to talk about it, either."

"Give her time, girlfriend. Maybe she's just upset about the whole thing."

"Maybe. So what have you been up to lately? Business been good?"

"Yeah, steady." Sim mock-played a pair of air drumsticks. "Had a couple of good gigs on the weekend. And I, uh, might have a new girlfriend." She blushed. "She's pretty cool."

Cam smiled. She wondered if Sim had met the new prospect during one of her band's shows. "Name?"

"Oh, no, you don't. I don't want to jinx it. If we last, you'll meet her, for sure."

"I'd like that. I'd better get back to the farm. I have volunteers working, plus my parents, you know, probably want to see me." Her dad, anyway. Cam's gaze lit on a silver Mercedes with Florida plates parked at the side of the lot. "Nice wheels.

Did somebody drive that all the way up here and then it broke down?"

"Pretty much. I don't know what the dude's business is, but he left it here a couple of days ago and got himself an Uber to a car rental place." Sim shook her head. "He's one of those guys who kind of thinks the world owes him, ya dig?"

Cam flashed on the dark-haired guy she'd seen near the greenhouse. "Is he slight? Dark hair?"

"No way. This one's thick, blond, and balding. Why?"

"It's nothing."

"He wanted all kinds of recommendations for local places to eat and drink before he left, too."

"What did you tell him?" Cam asked.

"The usual. The Grog. Throwback Brewery. The Market. You know."

"I would have said the same. I should get going. Come on out to the farm when you get a chance."

"Pretty busy sched. You bringing the 'rents to the parade Monday?"

"The what?"

"The Memorial Day parade. Only the biggest happening in town for the year."

"That's a great idea," Cam said. "I forgot all about it. They aren't leaving until Tuesday. And I'll bet you're driving Ruby in it, right?"

Sim's truck was a classic 1948 Chevy, with rounded surfaces, a big silver grill, and shiny chrome bumpers. She'd added seat belts and kept the inspection up to date, and it was the vehicle she took out on service calls.

Sim grinned. "Of course. Ruby's already stocked up on candy to throw to the kids."

* * *

By the time the volunteers left, it was one o'clock and Cam was famished. They'd had a productive morning, finishing all the tasks she'd assigned them and then some. It really helped to have experienced volunteers like Alexandra and Felicity on the team. While Cam was out they'd taken the initiative to get some additional planting under way. Her dad was nowhere to be found, but at least the hens were clean and happy, and two full flats of clean eggs nestled in the barn fridge.

Trudging toward her antique yellow saltbox of a farmhouse, Cam swallowed and cleared her throat, which felt scratchy. If that was a spring cold brewing, she didn't want any part of it. *I don't have time to get sick.* On the chore list for this afternoon was some serious crop watering, since the sky remained cloudless. But first it was time for lunch. She pulled open the back door to find her father about to come out, his arms laden with a big tray full of sandwiches, a bowl of potato chips, and a pitcher of lemonade.

"Whoa. Let me hold the door for you." She took a step back and let him out.

"I didn't think you'd mind if I fixed us some lunch," he called over his shoulder as he made his way to the picnic table under the big maple in the back yard.

"Not at all. I'm going to wash up and I'll be right out," Cam answered. Smiling to herself, she headed toward the powder room tucked under the stairs. Her dad had always liked fixing lunch. She peered into the living room and waved at her mother.

"Hey, Mom."

Deb sat curled up on the couch, feet on the coffee table, typing on a laptop in her lap while talking to someone on the cell phone tucked under her ear. She glanced briefly at Cam.

"We're eating outside," Cam said. She gestured with a thumb over her shoulder.

"Got it." Deb focused on her computer again.

Cam frowned. Too busy to eat lunch with her seldom-seen daughter, even after what had happened yesterday. *Oh well.*

A couple of minutes later Cam sat at the table outside. "Thanks, Daddy. This is perfect."

He beamed and poured her a glass of lemonade. "Cheers. I figured you were probably going back out to work, or I'd have poured us beers."

"Cheers. And you're right." She took a bite of her sandwich, two pieces of multigrain bread loaded with turkey slices, lettuce leaves, and a hint of garlic. "You've outdone yourself," she mumbled, stuffing the end of a piece of lettuce into the corner of her mouth. "What's the garlic taste? It's delicious."

"I just whipped up a roasted garlic spread with cream cheese and a bit of sour cream. Thought it would go perfect with the smoked turkey breast."

"It does. It's heaven, Daddy. Thank you." Cam washed down a bite with lemonade. "Did Mom already eat?"

William raised his eyebrows and looked at her over the top of his glasses. "Your mother seems to have some urgent work to do. She's barely said a word to me all morning."

Cam wrinkled her brow. Deb hadn't spoken to her all morning, either. Preston ambled toward the table. He reared up and rubbed first his head and then his whole body along the end of the bench where Cam sat. He put his front paws on it, mewing in his tiny voice.

"He's an awfully big fellow to have such a little voice," William said.

"I know. Isn't it funny? Here, Preston." She drew a scrap of meat out of her sandwich and fed it to him. "That's all, now, Mr. P."

She gazed around the yard. She'd found time to mow the grass before her parents had arrived, but at this time of year it grew so fast it almost needed cutting again. The herb garden on the other side of the driveway was in full swing, too, with all the clumps of perennials filling out in several shades of green bordering on gray. Spiky chives lived next to spreading thyme, with a big variegated sage watching over the narrow, brilliant green leaves of the tarragon. The barn and the greenhouse were behind them, with the fields stretching out toward the back. Such an orderly, healthy scene was at odds with Cam finding a fellow farmer dead. She didn't quite know how to reconcile it.

"Did Mom say anything to you about—?" Cam asked.

William lifted his chin and pointed.

"Did I say anything about what?" Deb said from behind Cam. She took a seat next to her.

"Hey, Mom. Hungry?"

"I am." Cam's mom helped herself to half a sandwich and a handful of chips. "It sounds like you want to know if I talked with your father about my interview with the local police."

"Exactly," Cam said.

"The answer is no." Her mom took a big bite of sandwich.

Great. Cam didn't know how to talk with her mom about difficult or important matters. They never had, and she didn't have the tools.

For a few moments the only sounds were the crunch of potato chips, the cheep of a flock of sparrows busily flitting in and out of the lilac bushes near the house, and the occasional car whooshing by on the rural road.

She had to try. "I just wanted to know how it went," Cam ventured. "What the police asked you. What you told them. We don't exactly talk or visit very often."

Deb raised her eyebrows and pressed her lips together.

Cam realized her words had sounded like an accusation, but she was as guilty of not reaching out as her parents were.

"You probably don't know, either of you, that I have been involved in solving several murders during the past year," Cam went on.

"We know about that poor fellow in your hoophouse a year ago," William said. "And then your barn burning down."

Deb nodded. "That must have been very scary for you. Especially after being trapped in that fire when you were little."

This was new. "You can say that again." Her mom had almost never referred to the terrifying incident Cam had been through when she was six. "And I've been involved in other murders. I even thought Albert was a target last winter. It turns out I'm kind of good at figuring out who the killers have been."

"Do you mean you've been acting as a private investigator? Or a consultant to Detective Pappas?" Cam's mom lifted one eyebrow.

"Not exactly. Either someone has asked me to help, like when a poultry farmer was murdered a couple of months ago and his daughter wanted me to look into the crime." The daughter probably regretted asking for Cam's help after the killer was discovered, but she didn't need to go into that with her parents. "Or someone I know was falsely accused, like my carpenter last fall. Or a person I loved was in danger, like in the winter with Great-Uncle Albert."

"I'm proud of you, honey." William's eyes were bright. "But I hope you don't put yourself in danger."

"Thanks, Daddy. I try not to." Cam blew out a breath. "What I'm saying, Mom, is that I would hope you'd share information with me." Cam turned and gazed at her mother, but Deb kept looking at William across the table.

"Fine. Here's what I told them, and it's the truth." She

sipped lemonade before going on. "I spent half an hour yesterday morning trying to get that woman to see some reason."

"That woman being Nicole Kingsbury."

"Right. She shouldn't have been calling a product organic that wasn't grown in the earth, and I told her so. I was a bit reluctant, since she didn't seem to be feeling well, but I had to say it."

"What do you mean, she wasn't feeling well?" Cam asked. "How did you know?"

"She was kind of pale, and kept her hand on her stomach like it hurt."

"And it wasn't the flu or something?" Cam asked.

"I don't really know." Deb shrugged.

"Did you tell the police about her not feeling well?" Cam leaned forward.

"No, why should I?"

"Everything about the victim before she dies could be important. You should call Ivan and tell him."

"Fine." Deb waved her hand in irritation. "Whatever."

"How did Nicole react to your confrontation, Deb?" William asked.

"She didn't like it. She didn't agree. But we were respectful with each other, and of course I didn't kill her." She faced Cam. "That's what I told the police."

"Felicity knew you had gone into the greenhouse. Did anyone see you come out?" Cam needed to ask Felicity next time she saw her.

Deb rolled her eyes. "I will not sit here and be interrogated by my own daughter."

What? Had Cam's question merited that kind of response?

Cam's mom stood. "Thank you for the lunch, Bill." She walked with a brisk step toward the back steps, half-eaten sandwich in one hand, head held high.

Cam sank her head into her hands. "I don't know why I even try."

"It's who she is, Cammie. It's who she's always been and always will be."

She lifted her head as she heard the screen door clap shut behind her mother. "Why did you guys have me? Mom is the least maternal person I've ever met. Did she want to be a mother?"

William gazed at the house as if he were gazing into the past. "We were very much in love. We still are, even if that seems odd to you. And we both wanted a child." He returned his focus to Cam. "I'm sorry if it's been hard for you, sweetheart. You're right, she's not very maternal. But she does love you, in her own way. You must know that."

A bluebird swooped past before alighting on the birdhouse Cam had erected where her property bordered the neighbor's meadow. The sun flashed on the brilliant blue of his wings, a stroke of beauty in contrast with the petty cares of humans.

"Cam!" A girl's voice reached the tomato field where Cam was setting up a sprinkler several hours later.

Cam turned to see Ellie Kosloski jogging toward her, her long legs maintaining a smooth stride, her white-blond ponytail bobbing.

"Hey, Ellie, nice to see you. School just get out for the day?"

"Pretty much. How's the season going?" She squatted and ran her fingers over the nearest tomato transplant. Ellie, a Girl Scout and one of Cam's favorite farm volunteers, was finishing ninth grade.

"Dry, that's how. I hope we get some rain, but until we do, it's me and hoses and hoping the well doesn't go dry."

"Maybe you should dig a pond." Ellie cocked her head.

"That's a pretty big expense. And I'd need a pump, too,"

Cam said. "I think the long-range forecast talked about rain next week. So my crops just have to make it until then."

Ellie frowned, thin lines appearing in the pale skin of her forehead. "I hope it doesn't rain on Monday for the parade. Our scout troop is marching. Well, we're helping the little girls stay in line, the Daisies and the Brownies."

"Nice." Cam had met Ellie a year ago when the girl was working on her locavore badge for Girl Scouts. Ellie had managed to recruit some other ninth graders into the service-minded high school troop, no mean feat for that age. "How's track going?"

"Wicked awesome. I came over to work, but I also wanted to invite you to our meet tomorrow afternoon. It's the last one of the year, and it's a home meet."

Cam thought for a second. "Of course I'll come."

Ellie's face lit up. "Triton has some pretty fast girls, but I might have a chance of winning. I'm in the mile. It seems so short, though, after cross-country." She grinned. "I just, like, run all out. It's sort of fun." Ellie had grown nearly four inches during the year, most of it in her legs.

"You'll do great."

"So, Cam, the news was all over school today. They said you found a dead body and that your mom might have murdered Ms. Kingsbury. Your mom?"

Cam swore. She glanced at Ellie, sure the mild curse wasn't anything she hadn't heard before. "Of course my mother didn't kill Nicole. But she and my dad are visiting, and my mother somehow got involved in picketing the hydroponics greenhouse." Cam shook her head. "I'll introduce you to them both before you leave."

Ellie narrowed her eyes. "I'm going to ask around at school tomorrow if anybody knew Ms. Kingsbury or who she hung out with. Maybe I can find some clues."

"You don't need to do that," Cam said. "You really shouldn't be getting involved in a murder case, anyway. And Detective Hobbs is working the investigation. I doubt he wants help from a student." *Doubt* was a real understatement. Ivan would blow his top if he found out a ninth grader was sleuthing.

"Why isn't Mr. Pappas investigating?" Ellie studied Cam. "It must be because of him and you going out."

"That's right." Cam gave a little laugh. She was going to miss the overnights with Pete, the times they snatched from their busy lives to talk, snuggle, and have intimate interludes. She wondered when he'd even be able to call her. "And because my mother spent some time alone in the greenhouse with Nicole the morning she was killed."

"So that's why the kids are saying she killed Ms. Kingsbury. I get it."

"Maybe you can let them know she didn't, okay?" Cam headed for the post where the water spigot was attached. "How's the job at Moran Manor?"

"I wanted to talk with you about that. I think you should hire me to work here after school gets out. We only have three more weeks until vacation." Ellie's young face looked hopeful and excited at the same time. "I'm kind of tired of working with old folks. I mean, they're sweet and everything. But some of them, you know, kind of smell bad. And anyway, I'd rather be growing vegetables."

Cam set her hands on her hips and beamed. "I can't think of anyone I'd rather hire. But we'll have to check it out with your parents. Farming's really hard work. I work in both hot sun and pouring rain. There's bugs, mosquitoes—"

"I kno-o-o-w." Ellie stretched out the final vowel. "That stuff doesn't scare me. And you know I'm strong, and I love the work."

"Of course you are, and you do. It's just that volunteering is different than working a job. How old are you now?"

"I just turned fifteen last week."

"And I missed it? I'm so sorry. Happy birthday, late." *Darn.* She'd have to make a calendar reminder for next year. "I'll need to check the rules for hiring minors. I don't know if they cap the hours you can work or anything. But I'm sure we can work something out. If your mom and dad say you can do it."

"They will. That's so cool. I can't wait!" Ellie bounced on her hot pink sneakers as if she was on a trampoline. "Thanks, Cam." She gave her a quick hug. "What should I work on now?"

Cam thought for a moment. "I have a flat of pepper starts you can plant out. They're on the ground next to the hoop-house."

"I'm on it." Ellie jogged away.

After she switched on the water, Cam watched the arc of the sprinkler wave gracefully back and forth across the rows of ankle-high tomato plants. The water reached to the lettuces and other direct-seeded crops. She could almost hear them singing with delight at the much-needed moisture.

Cam was pretty delighted at the prospect of working with Ellie, too, and wished she'd thought of it herself. Funny, a year ago when Ellie asked if she could shadow Cam to complete the requirements for her badge, Cam had been nervous about hanging out with a child. She'd never spent time around kids and was such a loner she hadn't really wanted company as she worked. Now she was glad of it, especially from such a breath-of-fresh-air teenager like Ellie. The girl worked hard, showed up on time, and never displayed the sullen, rude behavior of some of her peers.

"Where do you want me to plant these, Cam?" Ellie asked,

appearing at Cam's side, holding the flat with forty-eight healthy little Lunchbox pepper seedlings. "Your dad said he'll help."

Cam turned to see William standing next to Ellie. They both held trowels, and William had a flat in his arms, too.

"So you met," Cam said. "That's great."

"He said he was coming out to work," Ellie said, smiling up at Cam's father.

"If you'll let me plant, that is," he said. "I promise not to pull up anything."

Cam laughed. "Go ahead. I trust Ellie to supervise you. The seedlings can go in that far row." Cam pointed. "The soil should be loose and ready. Thanks, you guys."

Inhaling the delicious smell of newly wet dirt, she watched as they trudged away together, William almost a foot taller than Ellie. With helpers like them, Cam might get through this crazy season after all.

By six o'clock, Ellie had gone home on her bicycle and William had headed back to the house, saying it was time for a cocktail with Deb. Under Ellie's supervision, he'd managed not to reverse any plantings, and it had looked like the two of them enjoyed each other's company as they worked.

Two hours still remained until sunset, but Cam was done working. Her head hurt and now her throat felt thick. She needed to go in, find one of her herbal cold remedies, drink something medicinal. And figure out what to do about dinner with her parents. Having houseguests was a real burden. When she was alone, Cam just heated up leftovers or downed a bowl of cereal if she didn't feel like cooking.

Postponing the inevitable, she sank onto the bench next to the barn for a minute. The slats of wood were warm and smooth against the backs of her knees. She hadn't been wearing shorts to work last year at this time, but these warm temperatures demanded it. Of course the way New England weather went, this hot, dry May probably meant June would be cold and rainy.

She pulled out her phone and stared at it, dying to call Pete. But he didn't want to hear from her, or if he did, he wasn't allowed to. She admired his integrity. Except at times like this. Instead she pressed Bobby's number. He'd been so upset at the news about Nicole, and at the prospect of having to deal with his cousin's ex-husband, too.

After six rings she was about to disconnect when he answered, breathless.

"Bobby, it's Cam. I wanted to see how you're doing."

"I've been better. A lot better." He laughed, dry and mirthless. "Just returned from being grilled by the cops. They don't even let you grieve."

"I'm so sorry. Did they say how she died, exactly?"

"They wouldn't tell me, but they said it didn't appear to be by natural causes. How do they know that?"

"I'm not the person to ask," she said.

"They kept asking the same questions, over and over. As if they thought I was lying about something!"

"What kinds of questions?"

"Where I was yesterday, for one thing. That one was easy. I'm renovating an antique house in Amesbury, down in the Point Shore area. With two other guys. We were there all day long."

"That's good, at least."

"And of course the detective wanted to know if I had any problems with Nicole, or if I knew anyone who did. Cam, you'd met her. She was sweet, wasn't she? Who would have problems with her? Besides Rudin, that is."

Cam wouldn't have described Nicole as sweet, exactly.

More edgy, but certainly not offensive or the kind of person who rubbed others the wrong way. But then she hadn't really known her except to do a few rounds of business.

"Have you talked to the ex?" Cam asked.

"I left him a message. He hasn't called back."

Cam flashed on the Florida plates at Sim's garage. "Bobby, what does this Rudin look like?"

"Like a fireplug. Thick, with a nose that looks like it was broken at least once."

"Blond and balding?"

"How did you know?"

"I saw a car with Florida plates at Sim's shop today. She described the owner as looking just like that."

He swore. "Rudin is here?"

"I guess. She said he drove here, but the vehicle had problems, so he left it with her and got a rental car."

Bobby whistled. "Somebody better tell Detective Hobbs to find him."

"For sure." Cam thought. "I can leave him a message to check out Rudin Kingsbury."

"No," Bobby said. "His last name is Brunelle. Nicole kept her maiden name."

"Good to know. I'll tell Ivan. He made it very clear to me that he is the lead on this case."

Bobby barked out a short laugh again. "Too bad your guy Pete isn't investigating this. He's all business, but he's a lot nicer than this Ivan dude."

"Pete can't."

"Huh? Why not?"

Cam explained about Deb's involvement. She gazed at the barn, beyond which stood the house, where she was going to have to deal with her mother. She'd been acting funny since the death. Her mom had never been the warm and fuzzy type, but Cam couldn't figure out why Deb refused to talk about what had happened. She let out a breath.

"You don't see your folks much, do you? You never talk about them."

"It's a long story," Cam said. "But yeah, I don't see them much." She fell silent for a moment, wondering how she and her mom and dad had fallen into a pattern of rare visits. Was it the geographic distance, or something more? "How's your aunt doing?"

"Devastated, of course. I'm going over to see her now."

"Let me know if there's anything I can do for either of you, please."

He thanked her and disconnected. Cam sat still for another couple of minutes. She wished her mom wasn't involved in the case. Because that would mean she could call Pete, hang out with him, talk with him about it. She scratched at a spot of mud on her knee

A breeze picked up, fluffing the leaves on the old oak behind the barn like a teenager fixing her hair. A cloud blotted out the slanting sunlight. Cam sniffed. Let it be rain coming. Let it be rain.

Chapter 9

An hour later Cam faced her parents across a table at The Market. It was an upscale restaurant in Newburyport owned by Jake Ericsson, the chef she'd gone out with the year before. She often sold produce to him, and it was one of the nicest restaurants the region had to offer.

Dark pink napkins were folded on the pink tablecloths, and white votive candles flickered in jelly jars next to a single pink carnation in a bud vase. Large matted photographs of colorful vegetables and farm scenes decorated the brick walls. She even saw a shot of her own asparagus field in May. The picture had been taken from a few inches off the ground, the narrow foot-high spears marching off into the distance like skinny green soldiers. Had Jake himself taken it last year?

Cam felt herself melting into her chair, relaxing after the long day of work and worry. The second sip of a chilled Vouvray didn't hurt, either. After her father had suggested they all go out to dinner, she'd agreed to let him drive them in the rental car, and she planned to have as much wine as she wanted. It soothed both her scratchy throat and her edgy nerves. Her mom actually seemed to be relaxing, too.

A waitress in a crisp white shirt and long black half-apron brought a basket of crusty sliced sourdough and a little mound of butter in the shape of a tulip.

"All set to order?" she asked.

Cam glanced up from the menu. "I'll have the sautéed scallops with braised spinach." It was one of the chef's specialties.

William ordered the roasted chicken with herbed potatoes, and Deb the brown rice vegetable risotto.

"I'll have the mixed greens salad, too," Cam said. Interesting. At the bottom of the menu it said herbs were grown by Fresh Page Hydroponics. Orson Page was everywhere.

"Split the spring rolls, honey?" William asked Deb.

"They're very good," Cam said.

"Why not?" Deb said. "I'm quite fond of them."

"You got it," the waitress said, collecting our menus.

Deb sipped the martini she'd ordered. "This is a lovely place. You said you know the owner?" she asked Cam.

"Yes. We dated for a while last summer." How much did she want to go into her history with Jake? "He's a brilliant chef." And a mercurial and jealous lover, she didn't add. "He had to go back to Sweden to straighten out his immigration status, but he found a good replacement chef for the kitchen."

"Will we have any of your crops in our dinner tonight?" William asked. He sipped his seltzer.

"No, it's too early. I'll be lucky if I have enough for my shareholders next week. But later in the summer you would." Cam wrinkled her nose. "Shoot, I forgot to call the detective. Mind if I make a quick call?"

"Cameron, what in the world are you calling the police about?" Deb's face turned stormy. "Can't you simply let them do their job without your interference?"

Cam's shoulders dropped. The pleasant air of their outing was gone. She should have simply excused herself and made the call in the hallway to the restrooms. "Mom, I talked with my friend Bobby Burr this afternoon, Nicole's cousin. I need to tell Ivan that Nicole's ex-husband is in town." She spoke slowly to make sure her message came across loud and clear. "I saw his car at my friend's auto repair shop. That's all."

Deb waved her hand and looked away. "Do what you must."

"I'll be right back." Cam stood. She made her way toward the hallway. The restroom doors were beyond the swinging door to the kitchen. As she passed the kitchen door, she heard the clatter of pans and dishes, the chatter of the cooks and waitstaff. She headed to the quieter end of the hall, found Ivan's card in her bag, and tapped the number into her phone. She heaved a sigh of gratitude when it went straight to voice mail.

After she identified herself, she said, "Detective, I think you might want to check out a car with Florida plates parked at SK Foreign Auto in Westbury." She told him about Rudin and what Bobby had said. She disconnected but remained leaning against the wall. How could she get her mom to open up to her? Would she ever crack Deb's shell? Cam understood shells, for sure. Hers had been a lot thicker a year ago. Maybe that was why she recognized her mother's self-protective shield better than she ever had. To Cam, Deb's now seemed more brittle than it had been.

The door to the kitchen swung out. Cam stared as a man hurried toward her. Half a foot taller than Cam, he wore black-checked pants and a black chef's tunic with a multicolored skull cap not quite covering his dark blond hair. She cleared her throat.

Jake Ericsson widened his eyes. "Cam! I didn't know you were here." He smiled and opened his arms. A shadow passed over his face, and he dropped them.

"And I didn't know you were back. How are you? Did you

get everything worked out?" She didn't know if she should hug him, shake hands, or do nothing. She chose the last. Their relationship had been intensely romantic but also insanely turbulent.

"I'm all legal now." He nodded slowly. "Just got back last week. I was going to call you, but . . ." His voice trailed off.

"I'm glad you're all squared away, then. I'm here with my parents." She kept her tone light. "Had to bring them to the best restaurant around."

"The elusive academics. I'll come out and say hello later. If you want me to, that is." His voice was tentative.

"Of course. We're friends, aren't we?"

He gazed at her. "Are we?" He glanced around and said in a low voice, "I had some counseling about my issues with anger while I was home. I learned a lot. Ways to cope, that kind of thing."

"I'm glad." She hoped what he'd learned would stick.

"I'm sorry for last year," he went on. "I wanted you to know that."

"Thank you." She had moved on, and he knew it, but she could tell the apology was heartfelt. "I'm glad you're back."

He gave himself a little shake. "I am, too."

Cam extended her arms. "Give me a hug, Lurch. I need to get back to the table." Last summer she'd affectionately called him that nickname because of his size, and he'd always loved it.

He laughed but leaned over to embrace her gently and briefly. "Go then. *Bon appétit.*"

Their plates sat empty except for a stray bite of spinach on Cam's and a coin of carrot on Deb's. Cam's father pushed back his chair a little.

"That was splendid, honey. The chicken was perfect." He patted his stomach.

"Mmm. I haven't eaten so much in a long time." Deb smiled.

Deb had eased back into cordiality during the course of the meal. Her martini followed by a glass of red wine might have had something to do with it. Cam was feeling no pain, either, having finished two and a half glasses of wine. She'd savored every bite of the nutty sweetness of the scallops, the savory spinach, and a scrumptious Hasselback potato, its thin crisp slices full of melted butter.

The waitress cleared the table. "Coffee and dessert for you tonight?" she asked.

Cam glanced at her parents. "Decaf espresso for me. And we might as well see a dessert menu. Right?"

"Absolutely," William said.

Deb and William put in their coffee orders, and the waitress left after handing them a couple of small menus.

"What's good for dessert here?" Deb asked.

"Everything," Cam said. "Let's see what they have."

"I like the sound of that chocolate-raspberry cake," Deb said, pointing to the menu.

"Sounds good to me," William said. "Cammie, tomorrow we're going to get out of your hair and take ourselves on a junket, if you don't mind. We thought we'd drive up the coast, check out Portsmouth, take in some of the Maine beaches."

"That's fine, of course."

"Could you leave the farm for a day and come with us?" Deb asked.

Whoa. That was a change of direction. "Thanks, Mom. I'd love to, but I'm afraid I just have too much work to do at this time of year to take a whole day off. But maybe Sunday afternoon we can do something fun together." Cam sipped the last of her wine and set the glass down.

William excused himself to go to the men's room. Cam casually glanced at a couple across the room. She'd seen the woman earlier in her line of sight, but the man had been hidden behind her dad. Cam's eyes widened. She'd seen this guy before. Was he who she thought he was? She narrowed her gaze. Yes. It was the slight, dark-haired man she'd seen in the parking lot. Right before she found Nicole dead.

She leaned over toward Deb. "Mom, don't make it obvious, but when you get a chance, can you look at the man sitting behind you?" She kept her voice low. "He's sort of slender, not too tall."

Deb frowned but made a pretense of examining the pictures on the walls. "I love the close-ups of the produce, don't you?" She used a normal voice, twisting in her chair to follow the wall around behind her. She faced Cam again and narrowed her eyes. "I saw him near the greenhouse," she whispered.

William returned. "Who was?" he asked with a quizzical smile. "And why are you whispering?"

Before William sat, Cam thought she saw the man glance up. "Dad." Cam made a quiet-down gesture, patting the air with a flat hand. "We'll tell you later."

The waitress arrived with their coffees. Cam caught something in her peripheral vision, and looked up to see Jake right behind the waitress. He held three plates of desserts. He smiled, but Cam thought it looked like a nervous version of his normal high-power beam.

"Courtesy of the chef," he said with a little bow. "Which would be me."

Cam introduced everyone.

Her father stood and shook Jake's hand. "Very glad to make

your acquaintance," William said. "Cameron has told us what a marvelous chef you are."

Jake said, "Oh, boy," but his smile grew a little broader. "It's very nice to meet you both."

"I must say, our meal was excellent," William went on as he sat again. "Prime quality. You should open a branch of your restaurant in New York City."

"I agree," Deb said. "You could compete with the best of them."

"Thank you both. I'm glad you enjoyed the meal." He set down the desserts in the middle of the table. "I brought you the earthquake cake, with three kinds of organic chocolate, filled with raspberry ganache. The apple crisp with local fruit is topped with a vanilla bean ice cream. And *Ostkaka*, or Swedish cheesecake, topped with strawberries and crème fraîche. My specialty."

"My goodness," Deb said. "We'll have to roll home."

"Enjoy. I need to be getting back into the kitchen now." He gave another little bow and turned to go.

Cam stood. "Can I ask you one thing, Jake?"

His eyebrows pulled together in the middle. "Sure."

She followed him back toward the hall. She lowered her voice again. "Behind our table is a slight, dark-haired man at a table with a woman. Would you have any idea who he is?" She glanced back. The man's hand covered the woman's in what looked like an affectionate gesture.

Jake shifted his eyes and looked at Cam again. "I do. His name is Carlos Griffith. He lives here in town. He's been a regular in the dining room since I opened, he and his wife. I was glad to see they were still coming when I returned."

"Thanks."

"Why do you want to know?"

"It's just, um, he looks like somebody else I know." She wasn't going to go into the whole story now, and Jake didn't seem to have heard about her role in the death. "Thanks for the desserts."

Jake leaned down and planted a light kiss on Cam's cheek. "Don't be a stranger now."

"You got it."

Chapter 10

Cam stared bleary-eyed at the seed shelf in the barn at eight the next morning and sniffled. Her cold was still almost at bay, maybe because she'd been chugging zinc and another herbal cold remedy every time she thought of it. But farmers didn't have the luxury of sleeping late in May or any of the growing months, for that matter, and she'd already been on the job for a couple of hours. She needed to direct seed the bush beans, start another couple of flats of lettuce, and weed the turnips. For starters.

She drained her coffee and set the mug on the table behind her. After she poured the bean seeds from the packet into a small plastic bucket, she added a little water and the black powdery inoculant that would boost the nitrogen-fixing capability of the beans. Grabbing a hoe, she trudged to the rows she'd already tilled and raked smooth. She peered at the sky, which glowered a gunmetal gray. Not as nice a day for her parents' junket as yesterday, especially as it was finally seasonably cool. It would be much better running weather for the track meet this afternoon, though. Cam had run cross-country and long track events in high school, just like Ellie did now.

Spectators might be shivering, but for the athletes today's weather would provide a comfortable temperature in which to compete.

As she hoed open a shallow furrow, she thought about seeing Jake again. She'd half expected to feel a spark of attraction, because it had been so strong between them last summer and fall. She hadn't, though. His behavior from before had killed it. She'd never felt physically threatened by him, thank goodness, but she'd cut off their relationship when his irrational jealousy had morphed into controlling behavior. He had so many positive traits, though, so much that was likable. Good for him for getting help with his dark side. She hoped they could still work together on a business level, and be friends, too.

Jake had identified the man from the parking lot as Carlos Griffith. Had Griffith known Nicole, been in the greenhouse talking with her? Or was he in the area to do business with the neighboring insurance company? She could Google him when she took a break later. She grimaced. She should report in to Ivan again about that name. She hated to seem like she was bugging him, but he would want to follow up on anybody seen in the vicinity. When she reached the end of the row, she set the hoe down and called him.

"Pappas here," Pete's voice said.

"Pete?" Cam squawked. "Did I dial your number instead of Ivan's?" Hearing his voice sent her heart into overdrive.

"Good morning," Pete said. "Hang on a sec, would you?"

Cam waited, smoothing down the end of the row with the toe of her boot. She missed the guy, plain and simple.

"Hey, hon." Pete's voice was low and husky. "Ivan's otherwise occupied, but he left his phone on the desk. I saw your ID so I picked up. Don't worry, I'm outside alone. But I can't talk long."

"I miss you."

He laughed. "Same here, sugar, same here. But you didn't call Ivan to tell him you missed me."

"Of course not. Are you following the investigation?"

"I'm working on it. Just not the parts involving you or your mother."

"I told Ivan I'd seen a slight, dark-haired man near the green-house that afternoon. Before I found Nicole." At a movement in the sky, she glanced up to see a turkey vulture soaring overhead, tipping the wings it held in a dihedral angle.

"Yes. I read the report."

"Last night I saw him in The Market restaurant in New-buryport."

"Jake Ericsson's place," Pete said.

"Right. Jake's back from Sweden, as it turns out. He came out to meet my parents and—"

"You've been in touch with him?"

Cam took the phone away from her ear for a second and stared at it. "Are you jealous?"

He made a *tsk*-ing sound. "No, Cam, I'm not jealous. Believe it or not, I am secure about your affection."

She laughed. "Good, because you should be."

"It was a simple question. For which I'm still expecting an answer."

"No, I haven't been in touch with him. I took my parents out for a nice meal last night, and I was surprised to see that Jake is back. Anyway, he said the guy I saw is named Carlos Griffith. He and his wife live in Newburyport and are regulars at the restaurant."

"Very interesting. Thanks for passing that along. I'll add it to the board."

"The board?"

"The wall in the case room where we post all kinds of

things about the investigation. Pictures, names, maps, anything we think will help."

"Wow. Just like on TV."

"Yeah, sort of." Pete laughed his deep laugh, the one that always got Cam's body senses on alert in the most stimulating of ways.

"Hey, gotta run," Pete went on. "You stay out of trouble, okay?"

"Will do. Love you."

"Love you, too."

Even during times like this, when she and Pete had a forced separation, she still felt the solid warmth of his love. It was a new experience for her, and one she found surprisingly comforting. She'd been self-sufficient for so long she hadn't expected a relationship to be so fulfilling, so satisfying.

Cam disconnected and walked slowly, smiling, down the row, dropping beans into the furrow about two inches apart. It was approximate. If two went in at the same time, she didn't bother to reach down and separate them. Beans liked company. Herself, she was glad for a morning alone with her crops and the out of doors, gray sky or not. No difficult people, no stubborn mysteries.

Cam knocked on the door of Bobby's home, a small building that sat behind a big antique house. The wide Merrimack River sparkled beyond Bobby's place in the early afternoon sunshine. She'd been inside once before. He'd renovated an old carriage house into a spacious one-room apartment, with handcrafted wooden paneling, a bank of windows facing the river, and simple colorful decor touches.

His truck wasn't parked in front, however, so her chances of finding him were slim. She'd decided to stop by on her way to

Ellie's track meet, hoping to learn more about Nicole and maybe about her elusive ex-husband.

When Bobby didn't come to the door, Cam perched on a chair under an old oak in the yard and called him instead.

After he connected and they greeted each other, he said, "What's up?"

"I stopped by your house but you're not here."

"Sorry, Cam. I'm still working in Amesbury. Big job, lots of pressure to finish it on schedule."

"I want to learn more about Nicole and Rudin. This murder is bothering me big-time." Cam heard the high-pitched whine of a power saw in the background of the call.

"Huh. Funny you should ask. Hang on a minute." When Bobby came back on the line, the noise behind him was gone. "Yeah, so Rudin called me this morning. He stopped by the job site a little while ago."

Interesting. "What did he want?"

"He wanted to talk about Nickie with somebody who also knew her. Who also loved her, is what he said."

"So he cared about her," Cam said.

"He sure seemed to. He said he had pleaded with her not to divorce him, that he wanted to fix what they'd had, go to counseling together, the works. He really seemed broken up about losing her, both in the marriage and now to death."

"That sounds like a different sort of man than the one you described when you first talked to me about him. You'd said, what, that he was a controlling type?"

"Right. Of course, he seemed nicer in the earlier days of their relationship. I was at their wedding, and Nickie was happy with him. He adored her, too."

"Did you believe him today?" Cam asked.

Bobby waited a moment before speaking. "He was very convincing." He paused again. "Actually, I did believe him. In recent years I'd only heard what Nickie told me. What he said today doesn't change that she was unhappy with him."

"I'm sure it doesn't."

"And you know, we can never know what really goes on inside a relationship. So, yeah, I think he is devastated by losing her."

Chapter 11

Where in the world was Ellie? Cam milled among the spectators on the grass next to the high school track at two that afternoon. She couldn't spy Ellie's dad, either. The girl's mom rarely went out to events like this. Her MS kept her confined to a wheelchair, which didn't play well with a grassy field.

Many dozens of teens in the various uniforms of their schools occupied the area in the center of the track and warmed up in clumps on the other side. Westbury's colors were green and white, but that didn't help Cam locate Ellie, since almost all the girls in those colors were also slim and wore ponytails. A half dozen boys jogged slowly around the outside lane of the track. A group in red and white sat in a circle, stretching in unison to the instruction of a girl in a red headband. A couple of girls in orange held long poles and repeatedly raced up to the beginning of the area in front of the high bar, stopping before vaulting themselves up and over onto the big landing pillow. All the activity looked chaotic, but Cam knew from her own high school track days that they had a schedule, timers, and league observers.

A coach with a bullhorn announced that the boys' mile would begin in five minutes. Good. Maybe the girls' mile would be next. Cam strolled down along the track until she neared the finish line. The sky was still gray, but the temperature had warmed to the seventies. Not very good running weather, as it turned out. She felt a tug at her elbow and looked down to see two farm volunteers who had ended up becoming good friends with Cam and with each other.

"Lucinda, Felicity!" Cam exclaimed. "What are you both doing here?" She sat on the ground in front of them.

Lucinda grinned from where she sat in a portable camp chair. "Hey, *fazendeira*. I could ask you the same thing." Her Brazilian friend always called Cam by the word for farmer in Portuguese.

Felicity piped up from her chair next to Lucinda's. "Lucinda said she was coming, and I didn't have anything else to do this afternoon. I thought it'd be fun to watch some young people again." She'd retired from teaching high school English at Westbury High not long ago.

Cam smiled at both of them. "And I'm here because Ellie's running the mile for Westbury."

"Cool," Lucinda said. "My niece already did the long jump and she's in one other event. Maybe it's the mile, too. She goes to Ipswich High, so she's wearing orange."

"That's right, I forgot your brother and his family are in Ipswich now. And your mom moved here, too, right?" Cam asked.

"Sure did. *Mãe* doesn't speak a word of English, but that doesn't stop her." Lucinda's brown eyes sparkled and her black hair curled in a cap all over her head, a new shorter do for her than previously.

"What grade is your niece in?"

"Tenth. Her mama had to work, so I said I'd come watch her."

"Smart of you to bring a chair," Cam said, pushing up to standing so her legs wouldn't cramp. Fighting off a cold as she was, she didn't want to get a damp rear end from sitting on the ground.

Lucinda pointed to a cylindrical green bag on the grass. "I got another one. Thought *Mãe* was coming, but she decided to go play bingo with her friends instead."

"Thanks." Cam extracted the chair and unfolded it. She sat and sneezed three times in succession into her elbow.

"Bless you," Felicity said.

Lucinda said something that sounded like "Sow-oo-gee" after each sneeze.

"What does that mean?" Cam retrieved a tissue from her bag.

"It means 'I wish you health.'"

"Thanks. I need it."

Two girls in Westbury uniforms jogged by. "Hey, Ms. Slavin," one called. After she detoured over to give Felicity a high five, her friend did, too.

"Go get 'em, girls," Felicity said as they jogged off. "I had both of them in the creative writing club a couple of years ago. One's a poet, one was writing a dystopian novel. Dystopia is big with the kids these days." She watched the runners with wistful smile.

"Sounds like you miss being around teenagers," Cam said. She wasn't surprised that the cheery Felicity had a close relationship with her students.

"I do."

Several dozen boys, two or three in each of the ten uniform colors, positioned themselves in at the starting line, one behind the other by school. Cam remembered from her own track days that the top runner from each school took the initial lead in front of his teammates. A few guys jogged in place with knees coming up nearly to their shoulders. An extra-skinny kid in a crimson and gold uniform with an intent look on his face shook his shoulders, hips, feet.

Cam widened her eyes and smiled when she saw Ellie's boyfriend, Vince Fisher, in green and white in front of the other two boys wearing the same uniform. Senior Vince had had a tough time in the fall, and Cam was glad to see him participating in track in his last season at Westbury. When the couch announced, "On your marks," the boys all half crouched, leaning over with one foot forward and the ball of the other foot anchored in the track behind them.

And they were off. Classmates cheered, and cries like "Tigers rule!" and "You can do it, Brandon!" rang out. When Cam heard a familiar voice call out, "Go, Vince!" she finally spotted Ellie, almost directly across the track from her. Ellie faced away from Cam, her blond ponytail bobbing as she followed the progress around the track with her face and body. When the pack came around again, Vince was in third place. Ellie jumped up and down. "You got it, Vince!" she shouted.

Cam waved and caught Ellie's attention. The girl's eyes flew wide open and her mouth widened in a smile. She waved back, and then focused on the race again.

Three more laps and it was the home stretch. Vince was even with the guy in blue and white, sprinting for the finish. When Cam jumped to her feet, Lucinda did, too. "Yay, Vince!" Cam called through cupped hands. He put on a final burst of speed and finished one stride ahead of his competitor.

A cheer went up from the parents on the sidelines and from Vince's classmates. He staggered to the infield and stood panting, hands on his knees. Ellie ran over to him and gave him a high five when he stood again. The bullhorn blared, "Vince Fisher wins for Westbury in four minutes twenty-eight seconds. Girls' mile is in five minutes. Girls' mile, please assemble." Vince gave Ellie a quick hug before she set out on a warm-up jog around the track.

"That was a great race, wasn't it?" Cam said to her friends.

"Vince is fast," Felicity said

"And more important, determined," Cam added. "So much of running is mind work."

"He deserves a win after what happened to his family last year, no?" Lucinda looked over at Cam with a sad expression.

"For sure," Cam said. "He seems to be doing really well. Ellie said he's been accepted to UMass Amherst. He has a running scholarship and he wants to study agricultural science."

"So before the next race starts, give me the lowdown on what happened Thursday," Lucinda said in low voice. "Felicity told me you found the body."

"You mean in the greenhouse?" Cam asked, even though she knew that was exactly what her friend meant. When Lucinda nodded, Cam outlined the events once again. She described finding Nicole, Deb's involvement, and being questioned by Ivan Hobbs. "Right, Felicity?" Ivan had said not to talk about it, but Felicity had already told Lucinda, so it couldn't hurt.

"Right. The detective was really interested in the part about your mom going in and talking with Nicole."

"And I saw this guy in the parking lot hurry by me before I went in. He might have come out of the greenhouse." Cam frowned.

Lucinda rubbed her hands together. "He was the murderer?"

"I have no idea," Cam said. "Felicity, did you see him? Slight, dark hair?"

"No, I don't think I did."

Cam flashed on last night's dinner. "You both might be interested in this. Jake's back."

"Jake?" Felicity's eyebrows flew up nearly to her hairline. "You okay with that?"

Cam laughed. "I am. The spark is gone and that's fine with me. But get this, the man I saw near the greenhouse was in the restaurant. Jake told me his name is Carlos Griffith."

"Get out. No," Lucinda said, her dark eyebrows now knitting together. "I know him. He's half Brazilian."

Cam opened her mouth to speak when from the bullhorn she heard, "Girls' mile. On your marks."

The group of girls behind the starting line jockeyed for position, then settled into their stances. The girls' race seemed to feature only one or two from each school.

Lucinda pointed. She called out to her niece. An athletic, dark-haired girl in orange singlet and shorts tossed her head in our direction with a big smile. She sank into her stance, right next to Ellie.

"Go, Ellie!" Cam shouted, giving Lucinda a friendly elbow.

"Maybe they'll tie," Felicity offered.

The girls set off around the track. Classmates and parents filled the air cheering for them.

"Lucinda, I need to talk with you more about this Carlos guy," Cam said as the girls rounded the first bend. "Do you want to go for a beer after we're done here? Felicity, can you join us?"

"You got it," Lucinda said.

"I'd love to join you," Felicity chimed in.

They watched as the girls ran their laps. Neither Ellie nor Lucinda's niece ended up winning, although Ellie squeezed into third place. The two girls shook hands afterward. Ellie slung an arm around the other girl's shoulder, and they walked back toward their respective teams.

"*São amigas*," Lucinda said. "Looks like they might be friends."

"Nice," Felicity said.

"How about that beer?" Lucinda stood and packed up her chair.

Cam fist-bumped her. "Thought you'd never ask."

Chapter 12

The three women settled into a booth at the Grog in New-buryport at four o'clock. Westbury's only stab at a pub was the House of Pizza, and its alcohol offerings were pretty slim. After they'd each ordered glasses of draft beer, Cam stretched her legs out and yawned.

"Hey, the day is still early, *fazendeira*. What, you need a nap or something?"

"I'm just tired. You know farmers get up early. Plus, having my parents around is kind of exhausting." Cam pulled a wry smile. "I told them I was too busy to go off exploring New Hampshire and Maine with them today. And yet here I am at a pub well before dinnertime."

"They can't see you from Maine, right?" Felicity asked.

"Exactly." Cam laughed. "So the kids did pretty well today, didn't they?"

"Sure. My niece had already won her long jump event," Lucinda said. "I don't think she cares so much about the mile. Good that Ellie placed and Vince won. He did awesome."

"Ellie has three more years to work on her form and her speed," Cam said. "She's going to miss Vince when he goes away to school in the fall. But she's too young to get tied down to someone."

The waiter set their beers down on coasters. The women clinked their glasses. Cam's cold remedies seemed to be working, so she didn't feel that bad about going out drinking two days in a row.

"I got hitched to my high school *namorado*, my sweetheart, back in Salvador." Lucinda sipped her beer and gazed at Cam over the top of the glass.

"Wait, El Salvador? But you're Brazilian," Felicity said.

"Not *El* Salvador." Lucinda laughed. "Salvador is the capital of the state of Bahia in Brazil. It's on the ocean, and it's gorgeous."

"Aha. But I didn't know you were married before. I don't think you ever told us. What happened?" Felicity asked.

"I didn't know, either," Cam said. Lucinda definitely wasn't married now.

Lucinda traced a line through the condensation on the outside of her glass. She raised her eyes. "He ended up being wicked mean. He beat me so bad I lost a baby." She raised her shoulders and let them down with her breath. "Already ten years ago now. I had to escape to here."

"He abused you." Cam stared at her, covering her friend's hand with her own. "How awful."

"I was almost four months pregnant. I had him arrested, but his family, they were everywhere. I was so afraid. So I came here. Now I don't know if I'll ever have children."

Cam didn't know what to say. "I'm so sorry, my friend. But you must have guys interested in you." She'd be surprised if there weren't. Lucinda was smart, energetic, and attractive. She was at least five years older than Cam's own thirty-three, but that was still young enough to start a family.

"Do you have anybody special lately?" Felicity asked.

Lucinda squeezed one eye shut and half grinned. "Maybe. *Mas é cedo ainda*." She laughed. "It's too early to tell you girls about him."

Funny. That was the same thing Sim had said. Maybe love was in the air this spring.

"Really?" Felicity asked. "That's good news, anyway."

"Definitely." Cam smiled at Lucinda. "Now, what can you tell me about this Carlos Griffith?"

Lucinda sipped her beer. "I met him through somebody. Lemme think who. I know his mother is Brazilian but he grew up here. Like maybe in Portsmouth."

The New Hampshire seacoast town was thirty miles north. "What would he be doing in Westbury?"

"I think he lives in Newburyport. And he's kind of big into being a Catholic. I mean, he has a regular job. He doesn't work for the church or anything. But he's a lector and a lay minister. So he could have been at Saint Ann's. I saw him at Mass there a couple of times."

"Do you know what his job is?" Felicity asked.

"Something with money. Taxes, maybe. Or insurance."

That must have been why Carlos had been in the parking lot that the greenhouse shared with the insurance agency. Unless his visit was connected with Nicole's rosary beads.

After they finished their beers, Lucinda blushed. "I gotta go. I have to get ready for a date."

Felicity gave her a thumbs-up. "Can you drop me at my car at the high school?"

"Of course," Lucinda said.

The three women exchanged hugs on the sidewalk outside the restaurant. Felicity and Lucinda headed for the municipal parking lot. Cam walked slowly in the opposite direction to her truck, musing about Carlos Griffith. It felt like he was a key to this mystery. She was thinking so hard the toe of her sneaker caught on brick sticking up out of the old sidewalk and she nearly crashed to the ground, rescuing herself only by grabbing a nearby lamppost.

She arrived where she'd parked and climbed into the cab of her truck. Instead of turning on the engine, she pulled her phone out. Jake had said Carlos lived in Newburyport. Maybe she could at least drive by. She didn't have a reason in the world to visit him, but she felt an urge to know more about the man. She ran a search.

Bingo. His wasn't a particularly common name. His name and street popped up in a news article about the city council, where Carlos had apparently offered public comment. The article said his home was on Bromfield Street, a wide thoroughfare that led from High Street down to the water of the wide Merrimack River, where it headed for the Atlantic Ocean a few miles east. She checked the search results again, but the house address didn't show up anywhere. Bromfield was only a few blocks from here. It couldn't hurt to just drive down his street. Could it?

She turned onto Water Street, and a quarter mile along took another right onto Bromfield. The houses were mostly antiques, looking as if they'd been constructed in the eighteenth and nineteenth centuries. Many were built right up to the sidewalk and had narrow profiles with the front door on the right, while several others were large boxes with a row of smaller windows on the third floor, probably servants' quarters, Cam thought. Newburyport had been a thriving port in the seventeen and eighteen hundreds, hosting clipper ships and whaling boats, and was where the Coast Guard was founded.

Glancing from left to right, Cam rolled down the street at not much above twenty miles per hour, but she didn't see any sign of Carlos. It was a silly venture, really. He could be any-

where. Indoors watching the Red Sox. In his backyard gardening or enjoying a drink with friends on a patio. Cruising on a
sailboat. Dining out with his wife again.

From the direction of High Street she spied two figures on
the sidewalk coming toward her. The smaller of the two
walked a good-size dog trotting on a leash. Cam narrowed her
eyes as the gap decreased between them and her. If she was
not mistaken, that was, in fact, Carlos Griffith. With only a few
houses between them, she saw that the smaller of the pair was
a dark-haired girl of eleven or twelve wearing shorts and a
light jacket in Newburyport's colors of crimson and gold. So
Carlos had a daughter. The two laughed about something as
the golden retriever pulled at the leash.

Cam passed them and arrived at busy High Street, where
the ship captains had built mansions complete with widow's
walks. Carlos Griffith looked every bit the picture of a happy
family man. So what was his connection with Nicole Kingsbury?

By six o'clock Cam was home and had the chickens all
tucked in for the night. Cam's mother had texted that they
wouldn't be back until nine or ten, so Cam nuked some left-
over pasta and settled in at the kitchen table with a glass of
red and the local newspaper. Her eyes perked up at headline
below the fold.

LOCAL BUSINESSWOMAN'S DEATH DEEMED HOMICIDE

So the news was out. She read the article closely, but all it
said was that State Police Detective Ivan Hobbs was following
up every lead. It didn't mention the cause of death or Cam,
thank goodness, only that a local resident discovered Kingsbury unresponsive in the Seacoast Fresh Hydroponics green-

house. It did, however, feature a picture of the sign-holding protesters on the sidewalk, all of whom were named. Cam groaned. Her mom would probably want to cut it out and save it. The story ended with a plea for anyone with information about the victim or anyone who had been in the vicinity of the greenhouse on Thursday to please contact the police.

Cam finished eating and headed to her laptop. Maybe Google could help with information about Carlos Griffith. Or Rudin Brunelle, Nicole's ex, for that matter.

She couldn't find much else on Carlos Griffith. His name was associated with a Catholic retreat center in Rowley. He held an insurance license. He apparently was a runner, because he'd finished eighth in his age class in the Yankee Homecoming ten-miler last summer. Lucinda thought maybe she'd seen him at St. Ann's, the Westbury Catholic Church. And Cam had seen he was a father and a dog owner.

She rapped her fingers on the desk. What was the name of the insurance agency next to the greenhouse? Huntington. That was it. Perhaps Carlos worked for them. She found their Web site, but he wasn't listed as one of the agents. A Helen Fisher was, though. Vince's mother.

Cam thought, taking a sip of wine. She could go over to the agency on Monday and ask Helen if Carlos had been in. Her gaze fell on the wall calendar. No, she couldn't. Monday was Memorial Day. But she and Helen had met last fall after Howard Fisher's death. It would probably be all right to call her. Or to call Vince and congratulate him. He sometimes volunteered on the farm with Ellie, and he'd been a big help last winter after a killer had attacked Pete and Cam. She found his number on her phone.

"Vince, it's Cam Flaherty. I saw you win that race today and wanted to congratulate you."

"Thanks, Cam. I'm pretty chuffed about it."

"You sure are fast. You looked like you really wanted the win."

He laughed. "Got that right." He said something to someone else. "Ellie's here at the house. Just told her it was you on the phone."

"Tell her hi. Listen, does your mom happen to be there? I have a question I wanted to ask her."

"Sure. Just a second."

Cam heard him yell, "Ma!" and a minute later Helen came on the line.

After they exchanged greetings, Helen said, "What can I help you with?"

"You work at Huntington Insurance in town, don't you?"

"Yes, I do."

"I wondered if you've had dealings with a man named Carlos Griffith? I think he's in insurance, too."

"Carlos is one of our agents. He just started with us recently. I don't know him well, but he seems to be settling in. I was assigned to help him get up to speed. Did you need some insurance, Cam?"

"No, I'm all set." Cam pondered how much to tell Helen, deciding on nothing for now. "A friend was asking about him, that's all. Hey, did you see Vince run today? He was a speed demon."

"I'm so sorry I missed the race. My boss had something urgent he said only I was good enough to deal with."

Cam could hear the disappointment in Helen's voice. "I know you're very proud of how hard Vince has worked on his running," Cam said.

"I certainly am. Hold on a second." A moment later Helen went on in a low voice. "I wanted to get out of earshot of the kids. Cam, what do you know about the death in town? Our office is right next to that greenhouse. It's just awful what happened. I hear you found the body of that poor woman, too. Nicole Kingsbury, the hydroponic farmer."

"I did. And it is awful. Did you know her?"

"I chatted with her a few times when we met each other in the parking lot."

"Have the police been in to interview you?" Cam asked.

"An Officer Hobbs did. At least he didn't make me go down to the station. He stopped into the office to ask if anyone knew Nicole."

"I've had some conversations with him, too."

"He's not a very nice man, is he?"

Cam laughed. "I'm sure he's perfectly nice." *Maybe.* "He certainly takes his job seriously. And really, that's the kind of law enforcement officer we need."

"He was asking me all kinds of questions, like—" Helen yelled away from the phone, "What?" After a moment she came back on. "Shoot, Cam. Dinner's burning. I have to run. I'll call you later."

Cam told her to go rescue her dinner and disconnected the call. So Carlos worked right here in Westbury yards away from Nicole's new home and business. He was active in the Catholic Church. Had he known Nicole? Worse, had he been the affair that was connected with her divorce?

Chapter 13

Cam pushed open the screen door ten minutes later to let in Pete and his husky mix, Dasha, along with some cool night air. She bent down and rubbed Dasha's head before accepting a kiss from Pete. A long luscious kiss, as it turned out. He'd called her after she'd finished talking with Helen and asked if she'd dog-sit. Naturally she'd said yes. She'd grown fond of Dasha over the past months, a bit to her surprise. They'd never had a dog when she was growing up.

"Mmm," she said when she and Pete separated.

"Mmm is right. And you're rescuing me again," he said. "I can't believe I'm called off to a different suspicious death, this time in Salem."

The seacoast city, a forty-minute drive south, was the county seat and a sometimes-troubled town. "I'm always happy to take Dasha. You know that." Cam smiled at Pete, whose eyebrows were dark over deep brown eyes, his open-collared blue shirt crisp under a navy blazer. She knew the jacket hid his shoulder holster, and that didn't bother her. "Can you sit down for a minute?"

"I can't. It's already eight o'clock and they wanted me down there an hour ago, but I had to touch base with Ivan about the situation here. I hope this new case isn't a complicated one."

Preston wandered in from the living room. He halted when he saw Dasha and stared. Dasha's tail whapped the floor over and over. He always wanted to play with Preston, and the cat would have nothing of it. He wasn't upset by Dasha's visits anymore, but he gave the dog a wide berth on the way to his dry food bowl in the kitchen.

Pete glanced around. "Where are your parents?"

"They went up to Maine today. They'll be back late tonight."

"Wish I could take advantage of that." He slipped his arm around her waist and pulled her in close.

"I wish you could, too," she murmured into his shoulder. She cleared her throat and pushed back a little. "Before you go, can you tell me anything about the investigation into Nicole's death?"

"Not really." Pete frowned. "Still trying to locate the ex. Thanks for the tip about him being in town."

"Do rental cars have trackers on them?"

"Some do. A few years ago a big public outcry went up about car agencies secretly tracking renters, and lots of them took out the devices. But we'll find him. Or Ivan will, that is."

"I found out that guy Carlos Griffith works at Huntington Insurance. Right next door to the greenhouse. And he's an active Catholic."

"Griffith. The man you saw in the parking lot. That's certainly a plausible reason for him to be in the vicinity of the greenhouse that day. But where did you learn that? You're not—"

Cam held up her hand. "I just happened to be talking with Vince Fisher's mom, Helen." Cam crossed her fingers at the little white lie, *just happened to be*. "Lucinda knows Carlos, sort of, because he's half Brazilian. She said she thought he was in insurance. So I asked Helen. That's all."

"And you're talking about the death with all your friends, is that what you're telling me?" He still frowned, but the look in his eyes was soft.

"They asked me—separately, of course—what was going on. In a town this size, everybody knew I'd found Nicole's body way before the news actually came out."

"I'm sure Ivan or one of the local officers would have tracked down Griffith's occupation sooner or later, if they haven't already."

"Did Bobby Burr tell you or Ivan that Nicole's divorce was caused in part because of an affair she had with someone she met at a Catholic retreat?"

"I'd have to check with Ivan," Pete said. "I would hope Burr would have shared that information with us."

"I was just wondering if Carlos was the man. And if he was . . ."

"Cam. We're checking all the angles. We appreciate alert citizens like you passing along information. But please leave the investigating to us, to Ivan."

"As long as the angles don't include my mom. Much as I have my difficulties with her, I know she wouldn't kill anyone. She's way too cerebral for that."

"I certainly hope she didn't."

Cam cleared her throat. "Do you know the cause of death yet?" She doubted he'd tell her, but it was worth a try.

Pete gazed at her with an expression mixing tenderness with exasperation. He knelt and hugged Dasha, who gave him a sloppy cheek kiss. Pete stood. "I'm outta here. I'll call you tomorrow."

"Stay safe," Cam called as he walked down the back stairs.

"You too, honey. You too."

* * *

Cam adjusted the spray of water from the sprinkler the next morning. Yesterday's clouds were gone, and the sun had already been up for almost an hour at six o'clock. This was the best time to water. The thirsty plants would have water to use for growing during the daylight hours. If she watered later, the heat of the day could evaporate half the spray before it even reached the plants. And she didn't run the risk of introducing mildew, always a chance with evening watering.

Her parents had arrived home at ten last night and promptly gone to bed. Cam wasn't sure they'd even seen Dasha sleeping on his bed in the corner of the kitchen. He was now keeping her company out here. He'd spent plenty of time with her on the farm over the last eight months when Pete had had to work long hours on homicide cases. By now Cam knew the smart, sweet-tempered dog wouldn't run off into the woods in back or chase a car on the road. It was fine to have him off leash.

Despite Pete's admonishment, she'd spent some time after he left last night looking for information on Rudin Brunelle, Nicole's ex-husband. Cam had discovered he was a pharmacologist in the Miami area, working in a pharmaceuticals lab. He apparently also played the violin in a community orchestra and had bought a three-bedroom house five years ago. All of which the police surely knew by now. But who he was, how he thought, where he grew up—none of that was easily available simply through a Google search. She could ask Bobby. He obviously knew Rudin to a certain extent, but he definitely didn't like his cousin's husband, and that would color what Bobby said about him.

It was interesting that nobody had yet been able to locate Rudin in the Newburyport–Westbury area. Sim must have given the police Rudin's cell number, and the rental agency would have disclosed the plate number of the car. Or would the police have even known which agency to contact? Rudin might not have told Sim which rental car place he was going to. With an all-points bulletin, or whatever that kind of alert was called, wouldn't some officer somewhere have seen the car and reported it? Cam hadn't thought to ask Bobby if Rudin had told him where he was staying.

As Cam trudged out to the chicken coop, a red flicker hammered relentlessly at a dead branch. Thoughts about Nicole's case poked just as insistently at her brain. She assumed that Ivan and company had searched Nicole's house. Maybe they'd found clues among her belongings about who she was and how she thought. Did she drink soda or beer? Was she a vegetarian or a committed carnivore, a picky eater or a lover of the smells and tastes of good food? Did she keep her house tidy and clean or lean more toward the hurricane style of housekeeping? Most important, Cam wondered if they'd found any clues to who'd killed her.

After she let the hens out for the day, Cam busied herself with tending the seedlings in the hoophouse for an hour until her stomach informed her it was time for breakfast. She called Dasha and made her way to the house, walking in to alluring smells and delicious sounds of popping and sizzling. William stood with his back to her at the stove stirring something in a pan.

"Good morning, Daddy," Cam said. She handed Dasha a biscuit and listened to him crunch it while she went to her father. A pile of grated cheese sat on a board next to the stove, and frothy beaten eggs waited in a stainless steel bowl. William sautéed sliced mushrooms and onions in a skillet. A fresh pot of coffee only added to the tantalizing aromas. "Looks like you're making an omelet. Got enough for me, too?" she asked.

"Hi, sweetie. Of course I have enough." He slid the softened golden onions and mushrooms onto a plate and wiped the pan clean with a paper towel. After the chunk of butter he added had melted, he gently poured in the eggs and lifted the handle, turning the pan to swirl the eggs out to the edges.

"Can you set the table but bring the plates to me?" He turned away from the stove and had his mouth open to go on, but when he saw Dasha in the corner he set his fists on his waist. "Is that a dog?"

Cam laughed. "Yes, it's a dog. Did you think he was a hippo, or maybe a flamingo?" She washed her hands at the kitchen sink.

"Not funny, Cameron. Where did it come from?"

"It's a he, and his name is Dasha. He's Pete's dog. I often take care of him here when Pete is out on a case, like he is now." At the mention of his name, Dasha perked up, looked at both of them, then took the rest of his biscuit into the living room to finish. "Dasha is a real sweetheart."

When Cam's windup ladybug timer dinged from the windowsill, William swore softly. He turned back to the stove. He bent over and used pot holders to pull out a covered pan from the oven.

"Hash brown casserole." After William set it on the back of the stove, he worked on the omelet until all the fillings were added and he'd folded it over. Without looking at Cam, he said, "Please bring me plates, then call your mother for breakfast. But she won't be happy."

"Why not?" Cam grabbed silverware and place mats. She set the table in the adjoining room, which connected to the kitchen by a wide, doorless space. She selected three plates and set them on the counter next to William. "Doesn't Mom eat breakfast?"

Her mother appeared in the other doorway to the kitchen wearing a long-sleeved, red Indiana University T-shirt with khaki shorts and bare feet. "Of course I eat breakfast. What won't I be happy about?"

Dasha padded back in, his toenails clicking on the wide pine floor, and sprawled next to Cam.

"Is that a dog?" Deb's eyes widened. "In the house?"

Chapter 14

Cam stared at her. "Mom, what's wrong with a dog in the house?"

"I don't like dogs, and they don't belong in the house." She folded her arms, her nostrils flared, her lips pressed into a thin line.

"He's very well-behaved dog," Cam said, bewildered. Why was her mom reacting like this? "His name is Dasha. Don't you want to meet him?"

"No. Either he goes out or I do."

Cam frowned. "What do you mean?"

"She means can you please tie him up outside, honey," William said in a soft voice. "Your mother had a—"

"William, please. That's not necessary."

William faced Cam, his eyes pleading with her, his hands full with omelet-laden plates. "Cam?"

"Geez. All right. But only because it's nice weather. And you're going to have to explain this phobia to me. I'm not a kid you need to hide things from anymore." She grabbed Dasha's leash and called him.

Dasha looked up and whapped his tail on the floor a few times.

"Dasha, come," Cam repeated.

He stood and trotted over to her. She clipped the leash to his collar and walked him out to the barn.

"What's up with my mother?" she asked him as she found a long length of clothesline. "Telling me what to do in my own house. She's got a lot of nerve."

Dasha didn't answer. Cam tied the rope to the maple tree in the yard and secured the leash to the rope. She didn't mind him being off leash when she was outside, but it seemed safer to tie him up while she was in the house. If anything happened to him, Pete would be devastated. She would be, too.

"Sorry, bud." She scratched him between the ears. "We'll go for a long walk later, okay?"

He yipped his agreement and sat in the shade, tongue out, watching as she headed back to the house.

Her parents were already eating as Cam poured a cup of coffee in the kitchen and slid into her chair at the table. "Thanks for cooking."

"My pleasure." William looked sidelong at his wife, but she didn't look up from her plate.

They ate in silence, the only sounds the clinks of forks on plates. Deb avoided Cam's gaze, too. The potatoes were crisp and cheesy, the omelet perfect. The atmosphere in the room, not so much.

Cam spoke. "Did you guys have a good time yesterday?" She was determined to get to the bottom of her mother's reaction, but it was probably wiser to let the mood calm down for a while first.

"Oh, yes," William said, looking relieved at the change in topic. "We popped into a couple of Maine beaches on our way

105

north. Old Orchard was very charming, wasn't it, dear?" He patted Deb's hand.

"Very." Deb ate her last bite of omelet and sat back in her chair.

"And then we spent quite some time in Portland," William went on. "Lunch at a brewpub, the afternoon in the Portland Museum of Art. And dinner and a stroll in Portsmouth on our way back. Very much a New England experience."

"I'm glad," Cam said. "I haven't been up to Portland in a while." She scraped up the last bit of potatoes. "That was delicious, Daddy."

Deb looked at Cam. "I've been thinking about poor Nicole. She really didn't seem well that morning when I was talking with her. I wonder what it was."

Now she's talking about the death? Cam's head reeled from the whiplash, but she didn't want to ignore this opening.

"I'd never seen her like that before," Deb went on.

"Wait. You knew her before?" Cam wrinkled her nose. "Where? Not here. You just got here."

"Remember we spent a sabbatical year at Miami University a few years ago?" Deb asked. "Along with my teaching and research, I volunteered in a rehabilitation facility in the area, a place for people recovering from surgery and injuries. I gave talks about our travels and such."

Her mom continued to surprise. Volunteering had never been part of her life when Cam was growing up.

"Nicole had been in a bad car accident. Even though she was fifteen years younger than I am, we became friendly. That's why, when I heard she was the greenhouse owner, I thought I could persuade her to change her growing practices."

"But Mom, why didn't you want to talk with me about her? And did you tell the police you'd known her?"

"I just didn't want to get into it, all right? And no, I didn't tell them. If they knew we were acquainted prior, I might be a more plausible suspect."

William shook his head. "I told her she needed to come clean. But she refused."

"You have to." Cam focused all her attention on her mother. "You didn't kill her. You didn't have any reason to want her dead. You need to call Ivan right now and tell him."

Deb shook her head. "It's not like anything bad happened between us in Florida."

"He'll find out and it will look much, much worse for you." Cam couldn't believe her extra-intelligent mother was being so stupid about this.

"They won't find out," she said. "Who would tell them?"

Me, that's who.

"Well," her father said in a bright tone. "What fun thing shall we do today? How about a walk on the beach later?"

Cam waited a moment before speaking. Her mother withholding information from the authorities was serious. But Cam couldn't do anything about it now, and her father clearly wanted to change the subject. "Sure," she said. "And I'll take you to a very cool brewpub after. The owners buy some of my produce. The food they serve is really good, as is the beer. We can sit outside."

Twenty minutes later Cam checked the clock. Nine o'clock. She'd done the breakfast dishes while her parents read the Sunday paper in the living room. They'd all agreed to go to the beach in the early afternoon. Cam still needed to press her mother about why she felt so strongly about dogs, but first she had more work to do outside. And she wanted to follow up with Helen, too, since she'd been about to tell Cam something on the phone last night. She didn't know if Helen was a churchgoer, but if not, Cam could take Dasha out for a walk and pop by for a visit at the same time. The Fisher farm was not far through the woods from Attic Hill Farm.

"I'm heading out back to work," she called to Deb and William.

"Do you want help?" William asked

"I'm good, thanks." She popped her phone into her back pocket. Outside she untied and unleashed Dasha and ran him a bowl of water in the barn. "You might have to sleep out here for a couple of nights," she told him.

He ignored her, sloppily lapping up the water as if he'd been in the desert for a week. She called Helen, who said she'd be home at eleven and would be happy for a quick visit. Cam resolved to take a lesson from Dasha and ignore the cares of the world for a couple of hours.

Helen handed Cam a glass of iced coffee and sank with her own glass into a lawn chair opposite Cam. They sat under a big oak in the front yard of Helen's white farmhouse. Pink and purple petunias spilled over blue window boxes that matched the trim on the house. Dasha sat in a sphinx pose next to Cam, having slurped up the water Helen had brought him.

"Thanks." Cam asked. Her T-shirt was damp around the neck from the exertion of the walk, and she was glad she'd changed into denim shorts before heading out. She sipped the sweet, cold milky coffee. "This is perfect. It's another warm day, isn't it?"

"I'll say." Helen raised her eyebrows. "How are your crops doing?" She stretched her Capri-clad legs out in front of her and crossed them at the ankles, one of which was adorned with a small tattoo of a butterfly.

"It's going to be iffy for some of them. I can't seem to water them enough. How about your farm? Are you still keeping pigs?" Last fall had been a tough time for this family, and their pigs had suffered. Cam caught a whiff of freshly cut grass in the air but none of the stench that keeping swine usually brought.

Helen's smile was a sad one. "We only have the two now. Vince is too busy to spend much time with them, and he'll be off to college in the fall. I don't mind the work, and continuing the farm keeps us in the agricultural tax bracket. But I have to get one slaughtered soon, or we won't appear to be a working farm, and I'll need to get a piglet to replace him."

Cam touched the cool glass to her cheek. "I'll buy some meat from you if you're selling. You can't beat slow-roasted pork."

"It's a deal. I'll let you know."

Cam's gaze fell on the barn to the side of the house. It was freshly painted and no longer sagged. "Looks like you had some work done on the barn."

"Yes. It was either that or tear it down." Helen took a sip of coffee, cradling the glass in both hands. "So I was telling you about all the questions the detective asked me."

Cam nodded with what she hoped was an encouraging look.

"He kept asking me what I'd seen," Helen said. "Did I see anybody going in or out of the greenhouse that day? Did I ever see anyone except Ms. Kingsbury go into the house behind? How long had Carlos been with us? And so on."

"What did you tell him?" At a little noise she glanced down at Dasha, who was now asleep on his side. He was having doggie dreams, complete with quick a movement of one of his feet and a faint whimper.

"It's true that my desk is right next to the front window of our offices. I like it that way, even though it can be a little bit distracting." She ran a quick hand through her chin-length sandy hair, hair the same color as Vince's. "So I saw the woman with the ponytail go into the greenhouse."

The woman with the ponytail. *My mom.*

Helen continued, "I never saw anybody but Nicole come or go from her house, but of course I'm only in the office from eight-thirty to five."

"What about Carlos?" Cam asked. A couple of crows squawked from high in the oak. With a rustle of leaves a hawk flew out from the canopy. With a few beats of its wings it arrived on the peak of the barn roof and perched there, erect and haughty.

"That's the thing. I'd been in a meeting with our boss in the back. When I came back to my desk, I saw Carlos in the parking lot right near the greenhouse. He was staring at the door, then he hurried toward our building. I saw you looking at him before you went in."

"You do see everything, don't you?"

Helen laughed. "Almost. Anyway, I didn't feel I could ask Carlos if he'd been in the greenhouse. But I told the detective everything I just told you."

"Good." Unlike Mom, at least some people told the police the truth. "Did you ever happen to see a kind of stocky man go in the greenhouse?" She thought back to Sim's description. "Balding, thickset, with short blond hair?"

Helen's eyes widened. "I did.

So Rudin not only left his car at Sim's but also went to see Nicole. That could be important. Or it could be an innocent visit from a divorced husband curious about Nicole's new business.

"Let's see, what day was that?" Helen asked. "That poor woman died on Thursday, right?"

"Right."

"Then it must have been Wednesday, because I leave work at three that day every week to visit my mother in the nursing

home. The stocky man was coming out of the greenhouse as I
left our building."

"Can you do me a favor and let Detective Hobbs know
that?"

"Sure. But who is this guy?"

"I think he's Nicole's ex-husband, Rudin Brunelle. I haven't
met him myself, but that's apparently what he looks like."

"That's interesting. So he was probably the first person the
police wanted to talk to. Isn't that what they say in the cop
shows, that they suspect spouses before anyone else?"

A small bell dinged in the distance. Ellie and Vince appeared down the driveway on bicycles, racing each other toward the house and laughing. The finish looked like a tie to
Cam when they pulled to a stop, cheeks flushed, hair flying.
The sight of two healthy, happy teenagers with zero involvement in a suspicious death had never been so welcome.

Chapter 15

"We have time. Do you mind if we stop in to see Fresh Page Hydroponics on the way to the beach?" Cam asked from the back seat of her parents' rental car. They'd set out at two o'clock for Rye on the New Hampshire coast, but passing through Salisbury was on the way, mostly. She was curious about Orson Page. He'd said he'd never met Nicole, but that seemed odd, not to have checked out the competition, even introduced himself to her. "Orson said to come for a visit."

"It's fine. Just give me directions," William said.

"Great. Another nonorganic hydroponics farm," Deb grumbled.

Ten minutes later they'd found the place in a scenic spot on Ferry Road. The greenhouse, boasting a Fresh Page Hydroponics sign on the road, was clearly visible behind an old colonial farmhouse.

William turned in and drove past the house, which featured a new-looking wheelchair ramp of pressure-treated lumber that zigzagged up to the side door. He parked next to the greenhouse. It was bigger than Nicole's, and older. The sign above the door matched the one on the road but was faded and slightly off-kilter. A piece of the plastic that enclosed the structure flapped at the corner, and the rest of the covering was yellowed and dirty. Cam was surprised Orson didn't have the sides rolled up in this heat. Maybe it was okay for a hydroponics greenhouse to be hot inside.

Cam opened the car door. "Do you want to see, too?" she asked her parents.

"I do," her father said.

"I'll wait here." Deb pulled out her phone. "I have no interest whatsoever in supporting such a venture."

"As you wish," Cam said as she climbed out.

"Leave your door open for air, would you?" Deb called after her.

William followed Cam to the door of the greenhouse. "Think it's okay to just go in?" he asked.

"Sure." Cam pulled open the door, which squealed a rusty-hinge complaint. "Hello? Orson?" she called out. Long rows of what looked like house gutters—dingy, white, square-edged pipes—stretched in front of her, unlike the new, bright white, round pipes in Nicole's greenhouse. The bright green herbs in Orson's didn't seem to care their containers were old. Most of the healthy-looking crops seemed to be basil, but she also spied parsley and cilantro, and some others toward the back she couldn't identify.

"This is some outfit," William said. He brushed his hand over the closest basil plant and sniffed. "Ah, takes me back to Ethiopia."

"Basil in Ethiopia?" Cam asked.

"It was colonized by the Italians, you know. They grow basil everywhere there."

The door creaked open behind them. "Hello, there." Orson stood in the entrance. "What do you think?" Once again he wore a denim work shirt with sleeves too short for his long arms.

Cam greeted him. "The plants look happy."

"Sure are."

"Do you start all your own seedlings, too?" Cam asked. It was a lot of work for one person.

"Yup." Orson pointed toward the back. "I do it down at the end, plus I have a smaller hoophouse out behind, just for the starts. My business model requires frequent cutting and re-planting. So far it's working."

"And now your new competition is gone, too." William looked calmly at Orson, eye to eye since they were about the same height.

Cam shot a glance at her father. Was he also thinking Orson could have killed Nicole to eliminate the competition?

"What's that?" Orson shifted his feet. "You mean that new lady in Westbury? I heard on the news she'd expired. Shame. I don't think she was too old."

"I wonder what they're going to do with all that new equipment," William said.

"Search me," Orson said. "She had quite the fancy setup in her place. Maybe they'll sell it off cheap. I could use some new pipes, myself."

Orson had said at Moran Manor he'd never met Nicole. But he'd seen the inside of her greenhouse? "Did you help her get set up?" Cam asked.

"No." He shifted his eyes away from Cam's gaze. "She never asked me. I just meant it must be all new. You know, I haven't seen much of a market for used hydroponic equipment. Even mine was new once." He gazed over his crops, his shoulders sloping, the big grin nowhere to be seen. "Now, with my wife laid up? I don't have any money to spare for sprucing up the place."

* * *

"See, I told you it was worth the drive." She and her parents stepped onto the sand from the metered parking lot at Jenness Beach in Rye and walked toward the water. Cam pointed at the flat beach stretching out on both sides, the waves rising up and breaking with hypnotic regularity, the array of gulls sitting in silence as if they were meditating Buddhists. Plenty of beachgoers occupied towels and chairs, and a few umbrellas dotted the expanse. In August this beach was packed with families and sun worshippers. A half-dozen black-clad surfers floated astride their boards, waiting for the next big swell. It was still early in the season, and Cam knew from experience the water was way too cold for swimming without a wet suit.

Deb's face lit up as she looked left and right. She plopped down on the sand and tore off her sneakers and socks. "I'm going for a run." She threaded her ponytail through the Red Sox cap Cam had lent her and set off toward the water.

Cam watched her mother jog away from them at the water's edge, her red T-shirt a bright spot growing smaller. William also sat and removed his socks and shoes. At least today he was wearing cargo shorts instead of irregularly chopped-off khakis. He slid his glasses into one of his sneakers and pulled his polo shirt off, folding it neatly on top of the shoes. His scrawny chest was so pale it looked like he hadn't been shirtless outdoors in decades.

"I'm going in." He stood and slid the shorts down to reveal a faded bathing suit.

"Daddy, the water is way too cold. You'll die if you go in."

"I can't be at the ocean without going in." He beamed, spreading his elbows wide as he took in a noisy inhale and made fists of determination. He took off for the water on his long, skinny legs.

Cam shook her head. "I'll be right here with the towels." She spread a blue beach towel the color of the sky next to the shoes and clothes and sat with her feet in the sand. She slid off her flip-flops, leaned back on her hands, and wiggled her calves and toes in the warm grains, glad she'd changed into a swingy short skirt for the outing. But her mind dwelt on her conversation with Helen. Once the kids had arrived, they'd chatted with Ellie and Vince, and then Cam had walked Dasha back to her farm. She assumed Ivan would follow up on Helen's having seen Rudin coming out of the greenhouse. And she'd seen Carlos near the door to the greenhouse, too. Had he been inside?

A tern swooped over her head and toward the water. The small, white bird with a black head flew parallel to the surface for a moment. It paused, beating its pointed wings, then dive-bombed straight into the water. With a furious flap of wings, it came up again carrying a tiny, wriggling fish in its beak.

Her thoughts strayed to what her mom had said about knowing Nicole. How could she convince Deb to tell Ivan? It was serious business to withhold that kind of information from an investigation. Maybe Deb was so used to being a successful professor she thought she could decide what was important and what wasn't. Cam thought about Orson. Surely his remark about Nicole's equipment was innocent. Or was it? She'd have to remember to let Ivan know. But not now. Her phone was in the car and she was leaving it there.

Cam traced a circle in the sand with her finger. A boy and a girl dashed by laughing, veering past Cam's towel and spraying up sand from their feet, full of the same happy innocence as Ellie's and Vince's. An innocence not involved in death.

William still stood at water's edge, the water running up and around his feet before it washed out again. His ankles had to be numb by now, Cam thought. She watched as he threw his elbows out again and marched straight in. When a wave caught him at waist level, he stretched his arms to the side but kept pushing forward. A high breaker loomed in front of him. He dove into the curl.

Her father surfaced and shook his head fast. Cam laughed as he jogged back toward shore, lifting his bony knees in a kind of leaping run. She grabbed a towel and hurried toward him.

"Here." She extended the towel a moment later, standing a couple of feet from the water. "Cold enough for you?"

"Thank you, Cameron." He rubbed his face before wrapping the towel around his thin shoulders. "It was bracing." He was still beaming. "Positively bracing."

"You're a better man than me. I can barely stand it even in August."

Cam's mother ran up from the opposite direction than where she'd headed. "I see you found the saltwater irresistible." Breathing hard, she smiled at William.

"Wait," Cam said. "How'd you . . ." She frowned and looked right and left.

"I reached the end and then ran past to the other end." Deb pointed.

"I must have missed you," Cam said.

"I need a bit of a cooldown. Walk with me?" Deb asked, looking at Cam.

"Okay." This kind of offer wasn't like her mom, but Cam wasn't about to pass up the chance to walk and talk.

"I plan to lie on the warm sand," William said. "You girls have a nice stroll."

Cam and Deb walked in silence for a minute. They detoured around a toddler girl squatting with her bucket and shovel, a pink ruffle not quite covering her little diapered tush as she shoveled sand with great concentration. A suited-up teenage surfer, board under one arm, ran across their path and

117

into the water, her board attached to a cord leading to a cuff fastened around her ankle.

A white-haired woman approached with a curly little dog on a leash.

"They let dogs on a public beach?" Deb's voice rose.

"I think it's because it's before Memorial Day. Just. Or maybe they don't and she's flaunting the rules."

It was a very long leash, and the woman didn't reel in the dog to her side, so it ran toward Cam and Deb. The woman smiled and waved.

"Dog owners," Cam's mom said in a harsh whisper. "They expect everyone to want to talk to their little darling."

The dog gazed up at them, panting, almost pleading to be petted. Deb steered Cam in a wide berth around it, casting a dirty look at the owner.

"Why do you hate dogs so much, Mom?" Cam asked, keeping her voice casual.

Deb walked so long without answering that Cam thought she wasn't going to. When they reached a tumble of giant rocks separating Jenness from the next beach to the south, Deb perched on the edge of a boulder and gazed out to sea. Cam sat on the dry sand next to her, resting her arms on bent knees.

"I don't hate them, Cameron. I had a very bad experience with a dog when I was a teenager. I'm terrified of it happening again."

This might be the first vulnerable thing her mom had ever said to Cam. She glanced up at Deb. "You going to tell me what happened?"

Deb stared at the waves. "I was out running by myself. A big dog came racing up to me. It sank its teeth into my leg." She tugged up the hem of her left shorts leg. A ragged scar marred her outer thigh near the underwear line.

"Mom, that's awful."

A shiver ran through Deb. "I was terrified. I couldn't make it let go. I whacked it and yelled. The beast was growling and pulling at me." Her voice trembled. She brought her hand to cover her mouth. "Finally a man driving by stopped and hit the dog with something, made it let go."

"I had no idea. It must have been so scary." Cam stood and wrapped her arms around her mother, something she never would have done a year ago. She felt her mother's slender shoulders shudder, as if still experiencing the attack from forty years earlier. "It's okay, Mom. It's in the past."

"I know. But it doesn't feel that way," her mom whispered.

"I don't blame you for not liking dogs," Cam said, pulling back but keeping one hand on Deb's shoulder. "I have fears from my childhood, too."

Deb squared her shoulders and turned to gaze at Cam. "From the fire," she murmured.

Cam nodded. "I can't stand it when I hear sirens in the distance or smell smoke in the air. It's stupid, because people in New England love to burn their leaves in the fall and heat with wood stoves in the winter."

"It's not stupid. I still feel responsible for that situation, Cam."

"You do?" Cam asked. Her mother had never said anything of the kind.

"It was that irresponsible babysitter. We were so desperate to go out, your father and me, I hired a teenager I hadn't fully vetted." Deb's eyes drooped, and she pressed her lips together in an expression of regret. "I hope you'll forgive me."

"Of course," Cam said. "I'm just glad we're talking."

By five o'clock a hungry Cam and her parents were seated at a round, wrought iron table on the patio outside the Throwback Brewery. Umbrellas in bright reds and blues kept the sun off and matched a dozen Adirondack chairs arranged in seating clusters. Big, red sliding doors at the end of the whitewashed barn that housed the brewery were wide open. Cam loved the place. And since Sim had recommended it to Rudin, there was a chance he'd be here on a nice Sunday afternoon, too.

A young woman in a black brewery hoodie brought a tray with the beers they'd ordered. IT'S LOCAL was written on the front of her sweatshirt above the logo of a slatted wheel like a windmill.

Cam thanked her. "Is Annette around?" She'd arranged to sell her produce with one of the two women who owned and ran the brewery.

"Sure. I'll ask her to stop by your table when she has time."

"Great. You got the porter, right, Daddy?" Cam asked as the waitperson left.

He nodded as he sipped from a glass full of a dark brew. "Mmm, smoky."

"Love Me Long Time Pilsner," Deb said. "What a fun name."

Cam tasted her hoppy brew. "Hopstruck is a perfect name for an IPA. And it's the right temperature. Lots of places serve it too cold." She pointed to a structure with lines hanging from twenty-foot-high pipes. "Did you see they're growing some of their own hops?"

"Hops grow that tall?" William asked.

"They do. See, the plants are already climbing up those lines."

"Do they have to replant them every year?" Deb asked.

"No, they're perennials. And once the hop plant gets established, it has such a strong root system it's been known to crack pipes when somebody plants it too close to a house."

The three sat, sipping, observing other dining customers

come and go. Two twenty-something couples arrived and sat in the Adirondack chairs. A family of five departed, the father cradling a fat-bellied growler with the brewery logo painted in white letters on the dark glass. The scent of fresh-mown grass mixed with the aroma of grilled meat emanating from the restaurant.

Deb was seated across from Cam, legs stretched out, one hand in the pocket of her shorts. She seemed more relaxed than she had since her arrival. Cam wondered if it would be psychobabble to think Deb's talking about her fears had let her release some tension. But Cam was a former software engineer turned farmer, so she didn't really have a clue. She was simply glad the lines in her mother's forehead had smoothed out and her laugh was closer to the surface.

After the waitperson came back and took their food orders, Cam said to her parents, "So tomorrow's a big day in Westbury. You're not going to want to miss the Memorial Day parade."

"I'll bet it's just like the one in Otsego where I grew up," William said, his face alight. "The veterans lead off, and all the children's organizations march. Does the whole town turn out to watch like they do in Michigan?"

"They sure do," Cam said. "It's exactly as you said. Scouts, ball teams, 4-H—they all walk in the parade. Plus the high school marching band, antique vehicles, the works. Last year a guy even drove his riding lawn mower, all decorated in red, white, and blue. The town fire trucks bring up the rear, and at the end all the kids get to pile on for a ride back to the fire station for free ice cream."

"That sounds a little dangerous," Deb said.

"Kind of, yes. Teenagers hang off the outside. But the firefighters drive slowly."

"We'll certainly go and watch, won't we, hon?" William squeezed Deb's hand.

"Of course."

A couple made their way from the parking lot down the path toward the seating area. They took the only open table, a couple of yards from where Cam and her parents sat.

Cam's friend Annette, a wiry, petite woman in her forties, approached the table with a tray full of food. "Let's see, you had the black bean burger," she said to Deb as she set it down.

"I'm the hamburger," William said.

"And Cam must be the poutine with the kale and couscous salad on the side," Annette said to Cam. "How are you?"

"Great to see you, Annette." Cam smiled and introduced her to her parents.

They exchanged greetings and pleasantries. "It's not just my brewery," Annette said. "My business partner Nicole and I run it together."

"But you're the brewer, aren't you?" Cam asked.

"I'm in charge of brewing, that's true. I hope you enjoy your meal as much as we like using Cam's greens and other vegetables later in the season," Annette said. "Are you all still good with your drinks?"

"I think so," Cam answered.

"I'll take another," William said. "Since my wife is driving home. The stout this time, I think. I like beer I can almost chew."

"You got it." Annette moved on to the newcomers.

"Bon appetit," Deb said.

Cam heard the man at the next table tell Annette, "We're visiting from Florida."

Cam had extracted a fat french fry from the delicious morass of gravy and cheese curds. She stopped her hand halfway to her mouth and looked across the table past her mother. The woman of the couple, in profile to Cam, was striking, with almond-shaped eyes and a low ponytail of shiny black hair stretching halfway down her back. She wore a summery sheath dress in magenta that lit up her tanned skin. From the back Cam could see the man with her had a squat, square head, half bald, with thin blond hair. Was this Rudin Brunelle? Had her bet paid off? He sure looked like how Sim had described Nicole's ex-husband.

Cam ate her fry and kept watching. The couple ordered a flight of beer samples, which the waitperson brought back a couple of minutes later—four small glasses full of different-colored beers resting in an arched wire holder.

"Did you want to order food, too?" the waitperson asked.

The man shook his head. "Just drinking for now."

The woman tasted one of the beers and passed the glass to the man as they murmured to each other. Cam couldn't quite make out the words.

"Cam?" William waved his hand in front of her face. "I asked you a question."

Cam startled. She dragged her focus away from the couple. "I'm sorry, what?"

"I asked how your dinner was."

"It's delicious. Did you know this is the national dish of Québec?"

"You don't say."

"You can have it." Deb wrinkled her nose. "Why spoil perfectly good fries with gravy?"

Cam focused on her meal. She asked her parents about their upcoming trip to Brazil. They chatted until their plates were empty. After Deb excused herself to go to the restroom, Cam glanced up to see the woman at the next table pull out her phone. The man grabbed it out of her hand, and she stood, nostrils flaring. Her high-heeled black sandals showed off toenails in an eggplant shade.

"Rudin, give that back to me this instant."

Cam froze. It was him, all right.

He held the phone just out of the woman's reach. "No phones at the table. Isn't that your rule?" he taunted her.

The woman reached across the table for the phone. As she grabbed for it, she lost her balance on those stiletto heels. She tipped to the side, knocking over one of the wire chairs. The glasses in the holder took an actual flight, too, rolling on the table, splashing what beer was left in them. Cam jumped up and hurried to the woman's side, where she sprawled on the ground.

"Are you all right?" Cam asked, extending a hand.

The woman accepted it and boosted herself with her other hand until she sat in her chair again. She rubbed the elbow she'd fallen on. Rudin hadn't stood. He sat leaning back with his arms folded across his chest. The woman glared at him for a second before looking up at Cam.

"Thank you. I'm Geneva. Geneva Flores." She held out a slender hand also displaying expertly manicured nails.

"Cam Flaherty." They shook hands. "Is your elbow okay?"

"Yes, thanks," Geneva said. "This is my 'friend,' Rudin Brunelle." Geneva surrounded "friend" in finger quotes.

"Nice to meet you," Cam said to him. What did Geneva mean with the finger quotes? That they weren't really friends, or were more than friends?

He kept his arms folded and nodded without speaking.

"I'm sorry about the death of your ex-wife," Cam said.

He sat up straight, setting his forearms on the table. "How do you know who I am?" His pale green eyes were wide over ruddy cheeks, the lashes so light Cam could hardly see them.

How much to tell him? "I'm a farmer, and I'd been starting some seedlings for her."

William piped up from the other table. "Cam found the poor woman dead."

Rudin twisted in his chair with a "who the heck is this guy?" look on his face.

"William Flaherty. Cam's father." William stuck out his hand.

Rudin shook it. He returned his gaze to Cam. "You found Nicole dead in the greenhouse?"

"I'm afraid so," Cam said. "We're all so sad about it. She had high hopes for her business."

"Terrible news." Geneva shook her head with a somber expression on her face.

Rudin blinked. "Yes, of course. It's very sad. She and I were separated, but naturally I didn't wish her ill. I'm curious, how did you know I was her ex?" Rudin asked.

Separated? Not divorced? "Apparently the police have been looking for you. I'd heard your name."

He raised his eyebrows and let them drop. "I'm on vacation. Maybe they don't have my cell number."

Or maybe you haven't been answering it. "Where are you staying while you're here?" Cam asked. She kept her voice light. Casual. Interested.

Rudin didn't speak. Geneva glanced at him. Cam caught the slightest shake of a head from Rudin.

"We found the sweetest Airbnb," she said with smile.

Cam's mom approached from the building.

"I paid the bill inside and . . ." Her voice trailed off as her line of sight landed on Rudin and Geneva. Deb stared at Geneva, who stared back.

"Thanks, Mom," Cam said, glancing from her mother to Geneva. What was going on?

An almost imperceptible look passed over Geneva's face. Was it alarm or malice? Cam couldn't tell, and it was gone as quickly as it had appeared.

Deb faced Cam. "Shall we get going?"

Cam cleared her throat. "Sure. Enjoy your drinks," she said to the couple. She headed with her parents toward the parking lot. Turning back, Cam said, "You might want to contact the Westbury police department, Rudin. They really do want to talk with you."

Chapter 16

Still in the Throwback Brewery parking lot, Deb twisted in the driver's seat to look at Cam in the back of the rental car. "I saw that man near the greenhouse, Cam. Who is he?"

So that was why that look had appeared on her mom's face when she came out of the building. Except she'd been staring at Geneva, not at Rudin. "You did?" Cam asked.

"Yes. At least I think I did. Who is he? Do you know him?"

"He's Nicole's ex-husband, Rudin Brunelle."

"The plot thickens." William spoke in a deep, dramatic voice. "As they say."

"Nicole's former husband. That's very interesting," Deb said. "Very."

"Why?" Cam asked. "What was he doing when you saw him?"

"It was when we first got to the greenhouse that morning, your friend Felicity and me. Before I went in to speak with Nicole."

"Wait," Cam said. "Tell me that later. I have an idea. Let's pull out of here but only drive to the end of the block. I want to see their license plate number."

"Don't you think the police already have that, from the rental car place?" William asked.

"Let's just do it. Please," Cam urged. "Maybe they don't have it."

Deb started the car.

Cam directed her out of the lot. "Turn left and pull into that lot." She pointed to a gas station on the corner with busy Route 1. "We can sit here and wait for them to leave." She really should text Ivan right now and tell him she'd seen Rudin. But if she could include a license plate number, so much the better.

"This could take a while," Deb said, but she did as Cam requested. She backed into a parking spot so they faced the corner and rolled down the windows before shutting off the engine. The whoosh and thrum of traffic on the state route was constant. People coming home from the beaches, heading out to Sunday dinner, picking up groceries for the week, shopping at the outlets in no-sales-tax New Hampshire.

"Perfect, Mom. This way we'll see them whether they turn north or south."

"Are we going to give chase? Tail them?" William sounded delighted at the prospect.

"No, Bill, we are not." Deb rolled her eyes at her husband. "Right, Cam?"

Cam considered that idea. While it held a certain appeal, following Rudin and Geneva would be foolhardy and maybe dangerous. "Right. We're going to phone in the make of the car and the license plate number, maybe send the police a picture, and then go home." She unbuckled her seat belt and moved into the middle of the backseat so she'd have a better view.

After a few minutes of the three of them watching every car that passed and listening to the *ding-ding* of cars pulling up to the gas pumps, William spoke up. "What if they ordered a meal at the brewery? We could be here for an hour."

"Rudin said they were just drinking," Cam said.

"Well, I'm going inside to use the facilities. Don't blink, girls, you might miss them." William climbed out and headed for the convenience store.

Deb drummed her fingers on the steering wheel.

Cam pulled out her phone and activated the camera so she'd be ready. "You acted like you recognized Geneva, Mom. Do you know her?"

"She reminded me of someone else." Deb looked straight out the front window.

"While we have time, tell me about seeing Rudin that morning."

"I didn't think anything of it at the time. But I saw a man come out of that little house behind the greenhouse. I'm pretty sure it was Rudin, now that I know who he is."

Nicole's house. Cam hoped her mom wouldn't bite her head off like she had a couple of days ago, but she had to ask. "Did you tell the police?"

"No. They never asked me about the house. And I didn't know what the ex looked like at the time."

"I assume you're willing to tell them when I call in the license plate?'

"Yes, I suppose," Deb said.

"Wait, Mom. You knew Nicole in the rehab place. You never met her husband?"

"No. She said he was working a lot. I'm sure he visited in the evenings, but he never came while I was there."

William ambled toward the car. He stood outside the passenger door and stretched his arms to the sky. He leaned his forearms on the open window and stuck his head inside. "Not yet?"

"Nope," Cam answered.

A red convertible with the top down sped down the block from the brewery and screeched to a halt at the stop sign just beyond the gas station.

"I see them," Deb whispered.

Rudin drove, with Geneva in the passenger seat. The directional signal blinked on the left side like a metronome. Cross traffic on Route 1 was heavy. As they waited to turn, Cam tried to snap a picture of the license plate, but she was too much to the side of the car. Another car pulled up behind the convertible.

"Daddy, here." She shoved the phone at him. "You know how to use a phone camera, right? Try to get around the back. Quick!"

He took the phone and straightened, but whacked his head as he did. He swore as he stood. He'd taken two steps toward the road and lifted the phone in front of him when Geneva turned her head. Cam watched as her eyes widened. She pulled on Rudin's sleeve and pointed at William. Rudin glanced over. The car behind honked. Rudin looked forward again at a gap in the cars and accelerated into the turn with a squeal of tires. Geneva kept her eyes on Cam's father until the red car disappeared around a bend.

Chapter 17

"No, Ivan, we weren't following them," Cam said into her cell phone for the second time. "We just happened to be in the same place at the same time, at the Throwback Brewery in North Hampton. We'd arrived first, and then Rudin showed up." She watched the woods on the side of Route 95 speed by as her mother drove south toward Massachusetts. "In fact, we specifically did not follow them."

"Did you catch the make of the car, the plate number?" Ivan asked.

Cam read out the license plate number from the receipt she'd scribbled it on after the convertible drove away. "You didn't already have it from the rental car agency?"

Ivan sighed. "Make of the car?"

"It was a red convertible, but I don't know what kind."

"Mustang," William chimed in.

Cam pressed the speaker icon. "Say it again, Dad."

"The car was a Mustang," he repeated.

"I might have a picture on my phone," Cam said. "I'll check after I disconnect and send it to you if it's any good."

"Please do," Ivan said.

"And Rudin was with a woman named Geneva Flores," Cam said. "Long black hair, attractive, maybe thirty-five, maybe forty. They're staying in an Airbnb somewhere."

"And you learned that how?" Ivan kept his words short and terse.

"It just came up in conversation." Cam crossed her fingers, something she was making quite a practice of this week.

"Anything else I need to know?" he asked.

"My mother has something to add." Cam handed the phone up to her father, who held it up in the direction of her mom. The closed windows kept the noise of the highway at bay, so her voice should be audible. This small rental sedan definitely wasn't a Mustang, but it still had a new-car smell. Cam, seated behind William, stretched her feet into the space behind Deb's seat. She wasn't exactly built for the back seat of an economy vehicle.

"Yes, Professor Flaherty?" Ivan said.

"I saw that man, this Brunelle guy, coming out of the small house behind the greenhouse that morning right after I arrived." Deb kept her eyes on the road and steered left through the E-ZPass lane of the toll station.

"Why didn't you tell us that in the initial interview?" Ivan asked.

"I didn't know who he was. I didn't even know that was Nicole's house. I'm telling you now."

"Was he walking openly? Or moving like he was trying to hide?"

Cam watched her mom from the back seat. She seemed to be calmly driving and talking, but her hands gripped the steering wheel so hard her knuckles were shiny with spots of white.

"He came out of the house. I didn't see him crouch or move

suddenly or anything. And I don't know where he went. I was busy setting up our signs. He must have driven away."

Cam narrowed her eyes at her mom. Wouldn't she have seen a red convertible drive away? The stress in her hands made it seem like Deb was still hiding something. *Oh, Mom. Please don't.*

"Did you see the Flores woman, too?" Ivan asked.

"No. I'd never seen her before today," Deb said.

"Thank you. Might you have any other detail you forgot to share?" Ivan pronounced "forgot" like he didn't believe it.

Deb waited a beat before she answered. "No."

"I trust you'll be around in case of further questions," Ivan said. "All of you, I mean."

Deb and William exchanged a glance.

"I'll be around, of course," Cam said in a rush. "By the way, have you checked out Orson Page yet? I told you about him, the guy who runs a hydroponics greenhouse in Salisbury, Fresh Page. Nicole presented new competition for him, the only competition, really."

"And you think a business owner is going to murder someone to eliminate competition." Ivan's voice dripped scorn.

He had a lot of nerve. "Not my job to think about it. You asked if I had any other detail and I'm telling you one. We visited Orson's greenhouse earlier this afternoon. He said he'd never met Nicole and hadn't been in her greenhouse, but he described her all-new equipment. It seemed odd to me. You could at least check out his alibi."

"Thank you," Ivan said. "I guess."

You're not welcome. "Can I get into Nicole's greenhouse to retrieve my seedlings?" Cam asked. "They need water by now, and I'd hate to have them die."

"Contact the local police. I'll tell them to let you in."

"Thanks."

"And you, Professor?" Ivan pressed. "Anything else?"

Deb cleared her throat. "My husband and I have airline tickets to leave on Tuesday. We're traveling to a research site in Brazil."

Ivan's barely contained frustration came through loud and clear. "That might not be possible, ma'am. I'll be in touch." He disconnected the call.

"They can't keep us here," Deb exclaimed. "Right?"

"I don't believe he can force us to stay," William said. "Not unless they arrest you. Which would be absurd."

Cam watched as her mother stole another look at William. Deb's gaze lingered on him until she looked back at the road in front of them. She steered the car over the beautiful, new John Greenleaf Whittier Bridge that crossed the wide Merrimack River, the structure's pale blue arches gleaming graceful in the late-day sun.

Ivan would need cause, evidence, to arrest Deb. Surely he didn't have that. Or did he?

Chapter 18

At the farm, Cam first grabbed Dasha's bed and filled his dinner bowl. She headed for the barn and let the dog out, leaving his bed in a corner near some hay bales. He ran to a tree to relieve himself, then trotted back to Cam.

"How you doing, big guy?" She rubbed his head and received a kiss on the hand in return. "Sorry about having to stay in the barn. It's only until Tuesday." Or whenever Pete came to pick up Dasha. *Pete*. She hadn't heard from him all day. That was kind of unusual, especially when she had his dog. He must be busy with the case in Salem.

She secured the chickens in the coop. She headed into the hoophouse to water her seedlings in the soft, early evening light as Dasha sat and observed. The gentle spray from the watering wand arched over the table to wet the infant plants. Watering was definitely meditative for Cam. Watching the spray calmed and cleaned her jangled thoughts. Smelling the wet soil reassured her that life continues, that despite the apparent murder of a fellow grower, the cycle of growth was universal and never-ending.

Despite her attraction to sleuthing, her job was to nourish her plants, big and small. Ivan's job was to sort out who killed Nicole Kingsbury. Thinking about Nicole, though, reminded Cam of what Bobby had said yesterday. Rudin had claimed to be broken up about losing his wife. So why was he already with another woman, and a gorgeous one, at that? He could have been lying to Bobby—but why?

As she watered, Cam remembered the flats of basil she'd brought to Nicole. She needed to call the station and make sure she could get into the greenhouse and pick up her flats. Cam turned off the hose and connected with the Westbury police, asking for Ruth. Miracle of miracles, she was at the station. She came on the line.

"Ruthie, Ivan said I could go into the greenhouse and get my seedlings. I was on my way to deliver a couple of flats to Nicole when I found her dead, and I wanted to bring those home."

"Sure," Ruth said. "I'll meet you at the greenhouse in twenty?"

Cam thanked her and disconnected. "Come on, Dasha. It's back to the hotel for you." He followed her to the barn but stopped short of the door. He planted his feet and barked into the twilight. He looked at Cam and barked again.

"What is it?" She looked all around. The sun had descended behind the row of trees to the west, but some light lingered. "Is it a coyote, or a fox?" She'd seen both on the property, one reason she made sure her chicken girls were snug inside every night. She didn't hear a rustling or any sign of predators. No living shadows lurked behind the trees or headed for the coop—not that she could detect, anyway.

Dasha barked again, then let out a long howl. Cam shivered as she knelt next to him and stroked his head. Beyond the barn to the east she glimpsed a silver orb rising. It was full tonight. Maybe Dasha's inner wolf was calling to him to salute the moon.

"Come on, Dash. Let's go in." She persuaded him to follow her into the barn, where she topped up his water before locking him in. She headed for the house, pausing in the backyard. The warm light from inside the farmhouse beckoned, but Dasha was still barking in the barn. Why? Could there be a human predator nearby? If someone was hanging around, she couldn't do anything about it. She'd put good locks on the barn earlier in the year, so Dasha was safe in there. She had good locks on the house, too. She wasn't going to call the cops with no proof that an intruder had in fact invaded her space.

Cam popped her head into the house. "Daddy, Mom? I'm going into town to get my seedlings."

William emerged from the living room, newspaper in hand. "Your mother has already gone up, said she was going to do some work in bed." He raised a shoulder and dropped it. "She's like that. I'll come with you, if it's all right." He reached out and laid a hand on Cam's shoulder. "I hate the thought of leaving so soon. I'm enjoying our visit, sweetie."

Whoa. Another confidence from a long-distant parent, another expression of affection. Another shake to her snowglobe world, albeit a welcome one. "Me too, Daddy." Cam grabbed her truck keys. "Come on, then. It's been a long day." After her father followed her out, Cam made sure the door was locked.

As they drove down the hill, William said, "What was Dasha barking about in the barn?"

"I don't know. Something seems to have spooked him. He was howling at the moon for a minute, but now he's just barking."

"He probably misses being in the house."

"That could be." Cam steered them past the town ball fields. "So Mom talked about her issue with dogs as we walked today. I never knew."

"Yes, she was pretty scarred by that incident—and not just on her leg. I've urged her to seek counseling over the years, but she says she'd rather simply stay away from canines altogether."

"You always said we couldn't have a dog for a pet because you and Mom traveled every summer. It made sense."

"Your mother was not interested in telling you about her fears. I'm sorry, honey."

"Now that I think about it," Cam said, "I remember her always avoiding dogs when we'd be out walking anywhere. I didn't feel afraid of dogs, but her feelings must have rubbed off on me. I was never interested in getting a dog, and Dasha's really the first one I've gotten to know well."

Cam turned left onto Main Street. A quarter mile down the road she pulled into the greenhouse parking lot and turned off the engine. She didn't see a cruiser anywhere, so Ruth must not have arrived yet. A wide strip of yellow tape stretched across the greenhouse door at the end facing the street, proclaiming CRIME SCENE—DO NOT CROSS in convincingly stern black letters. Cam climbed out of the truck and walked to the back end of the greenhouse. The cottage behind was dark. The moonlight revealed an identical strip of tape across the front door to the house. Had a crime been committed in the house, too?

Her father stood beside her. He glanced back at the street and at the house again. He ambled out to the sidewalk and stood under a streetlight.

"Come here, Cameron." He beckoned to her.

Cam took one last look at the house, then joined her father. "What is it?"

He pointed toward the back. "You can't see the house from here. It's blocked by the greenhouse. And with the insurance company right next door, this is the only exit from the parking lot."

Cam looked across to the insurance company building twenty feet away. It didn't have a wide profile on the street but instead stretched away toward the back, with the main door halfway down. She glanced past the greenhouse. Daddy was right. She couldn't see the house from here.

"Are you saying that Mom couldn't have missed a red convertible leaving the parking lot?"

He nodded slowly.

"He could have parked somewhere else and walked."

"I don't peg that man as a walker, Cam."

"I think I agree. Anyway, Mom couldn't have seen Rudin from here."

"Exactly."

"But if she'd parked back in the lot, she would have had a view of the house."

"We'll have to ask her that." William frowned.

Cam thought about that first day. "No, that won't work. That day when Nicole was killed, Felicity told Ruth they had all parked across the street. Probably because this is a private lot and they didn't want to get in trouble for using it."

"Your mother has admitted she went into the greenhouse and talked with Nicole."

"Yes. But she told Ivan she saw Rudin when she first arrived. Something's not right, Daddy."

"The question is, can we convince your mother to tell us what she's hiding. I'm not optimistic about that."

Ruth pulled up a few minutes later in a small SUV while Cam and William stood next to the rental car in the greenhouse parking lot. Ruth, clad in civilian clothes, emerged and hugged Cam.

"I was just going off shift," Ruth said "I have to get home and see my girlies."

Ruth's fraternal-twin daughters, age six, were favorites of Cam's. They were as different as could be in temperament and appearance, but both were sweet and smart and fun to be around.

"I'll be quick," Cam said. "The kids are with your mom?" Ruth's troubled husband had left during the previous year, and despite surfacing last winter had not rejoined Ruth and the girls.

"Yes, bless her sainted heart. If she didn't live nearby and wasn't willing to watch the twins after school and when I have to work on weekends, I don't know what I'd do."

"You're lucky to have her." Cam introduced her father and Ruth.

"Please call me William," he said to Ruth. "We met many years ago, of course, when we picked Cammie up from the farm at the end of summer one year. The two of you had been swimming, and she didn't want to come home. I'm glad you're still friends."

Ruth cocked her head. "I can almost remember that. It was a long time ago."

Cam wrinkled her nose. She couldn't recall that scene.

Ruth held up a zippered plastic bag holding a key. "You want in?" She walked to the back door of the greenhouse, which was also protected by crime scene tape, and detached the tape on one side.

Cam touched her friend's elbow. "Was a crime committed in the house, too?" She pointed toward the cottage. The illumination from the streetlight barely reached back to where they stood, but the rising moon cast its cold eye on the small one-story abode and the yellow tape across its front door.

"Detective Hobbs insisted on the tape on that door. As far as I know, no crime was committed in there. But I suppose an overabundance of caution never hurt anyone." She unlocked the door, pulled it open, and flipped on the light switch. "After you."

The bright overhead lights lit up the interior like a movie set. Cam felt like tiptoeing in, except who did she think she was being quiet for? Nicole was long gone. Cam paused inside. Behind her William cleared his throat.

"Where did you find her?" he whispered.

"Back in that corner," Cam whispered in return. She pointed past the long rows of white pipes. Seeing them, new and hopeful, was a stark contrast to Orson's faded, older, no doubt leakier system. In here, though, the ventilation fan no longer hummed. The pump for the irrigation must have been turned off, too. The already planted seedlings drooped sad and wilted.

"Um, folks, we don't have to whisper," Ruth said in a normal voice.

"You're right." Cam laughed nervously. "Thanks for letting us in, Ruthie. So do you know if they've made any progress finding Nicole's killer?"

"I don't know. It wouldn't be," Ruth paused to make finger quotes, "'following procedure' for Ivan to inform me of the status." She pulled a wry smile. "And Cam, I'm sorry, but I do have to return the key and head for home. I promised the kiddleywinks I'd be home to tuck them in, and bedtime is upon us."

"Of course." Cam took a deep breath. She headed for the other end of the structure. For the planting tables. For the vat of slurry. *No, don't go there*, she scolded herself. She was here to pick up her flats and take them home. She arrived at the table to see her basil seedlings drooping, too. She could revive them with water and TLC. Cam glanced briefly over at the vat, but that space now sat empty. They must have emptied it and taken it for evidence. Now that she looked more closely, she could see traces of fingerprint powder, and small, yellow numbered markers like tiny road signs on the ground and on the shelves near where the vat had been. The police had done their work. With any luck they'd find their villain.

As she slid the first flat onto her forearm, something fell to the floor. Cam stared at it, a stretchy piece of a rubbery material less than an inch wide and about eight inches long. She called out, "Ruth? Can you come back here, please?" She carefully laid the flat back on the table but in a different spot.

A moment later Ruth, at Cam's side, asked, "What is it?"

Cam pointed. "There."

Ruth knelt, examining the object without touching it.

"When I picked up the flat from this spot here"—Cam indicated the place on the table—"that thing fell to the floor, like it was tucked under it, or even hidden. I left it on the ground where it fell."

"It looks like a tourniquet," William said. "Like what they use around your arm when you get blood drawn. We're always getting tested for one tropical disease or another after we return home from our various sojourns abroad."

A tourniquet? Cam couldn't think of a single use in a greenhouse, hydroponic or otherwise, for such a thing.

"I think it could very well be a tourniquet." Ruth stood. "Good catch, Cam. I'll call in the team." She twisted her mouth. "And now I'll never get home."

"I'm sorry. I just thought—"

"You did the right thing. I'll ask you both to leave now, though, all right?" She turned away, pressing buttons on her cell phone.

"Wait. Can I still take my flats?" Cam asked.

Ruth frowned. "I guess. Ivan will come get them back if he needs them."

Chapter 19

Cam and her father settled into her living room with mugs of steaming peppermint tea after Cam left the flats in her hoophouse with a good dose of water. She'd feed them with a dose of compost tea tomorrow to hit up the stressed baby plants with needed nutrients. She heard a knock at the door and glanced at the clock on the mantel.

"Who's here at eight-thirty?" she asked. A sudden rush of fear flooded her. She stared at her father. "What if it's—"

"Cammie," he said gently. "Do you think a murderer is going to politely knock at your door?"

"I guess not." She laughed but could hear the nerves in her voice as she set her tea down and went to the door. She switched on the porch light and spied Pete through the door's glass inset. *Whew*. She unlocked and pulled open the door.

"Hey, stranger," he said, wearing a chagrined smile.

"Hey, yourself." Cam stepped back to let him in. "Looks like you've been working." He wore slightly rumpled detective clothes, not his usual Sunday faded jeans.

He kissed her lightly before running a hand through his

dark hair, which had acquired a few new streaks of silver. "I sure have."

"Come on in." She gestured toward the living room. "My dad and I were just having tea. Want some?"

"Sure, thanks." He looked around, tilted his head, and frowned. "Where's my boy?"

"I'm afraid he's in the barn."

"The barn? Was he bad?"

"My mother has a real problem with dogs that I wasn't aware of when you first brought Dasha over. She's terrified of them. But he's comfortable out there. He has his bed, food, and water."

"I understand. Anyway, I'll take him home with me tonight."

"That you, Peter?" Cam's dad appeared in the doorway to the living room. He held out his hand to Pete, who shook it.

"Me in the flesh," Pete said. "Good to see you again, sir."

"You guys go sit down," Cam said. "I'll get Pete some tea."

"I saw an intriguing bottle of Ipswich spiced rum in your liquor cupboard, Cameron," William said. "I think a taste of that in our tea might be just the ticket."

Cam smiled. "Help yourself."

A minute later she handed Pete his mug and sat at the end of the couch facing him, curling her feet up. William stepped over and poured a splash of rum into Cam's mug and his own.

"Detective?" he asked, proffering the bottle.

"Only a splash." Pete extended his mug. "It's been a long day and I still have to drive home."

Darn it. How much nicer it would be if he could settle in for the night. With her. But having him stay might feel awkward with her parents there, even if he could.

William doled out a little rum to Pete before sinking into the easy chair.

"How's the Salem case going?" Cam asked.

"It turned out to be a gang shooting. Nasty business, but we caught a lucky break and nabbed the guy who did it."

"And you must be off duty now or you wouldn't be having rum, I daresay." William regarded Pete over the top of his glasses.

"That's right."

Cam sipped her tea, letting the warmth of the alcohol spread its calm from the inside of her body outward. "Too bad Nicole's death isn't such a neat package."

"So I hear." Pete cleared his throat. "I also caught wind of a couple of new pieces of information today. Ivan has been sending me updates."

William glanced toward the second floor. "I'll be right back." He headed for the stairs.

Pete stroked Cam's foot and smiled at her. "I'm sure Ivan and his team will have this wrapped up soon. Then you and I can get back to normal."

"I can't wait. For so many reasons." His hand on her foot was comforting, but also an alluring reminder of what else his hands did when she was alone with him. Her cheeks warmed as she told him about their trip to the beach and their dinner at the brewery.

"I'll take you to Throwback next chance we get," she said. "Food's great, beer's excellent, and it's a fun setting."

"Sounds like a plan."

"And we ran into Nicole's ex there today, too," Cam said.

"You're kidding me."

"Nope." Cam outlined their interaction and told him they had duly informed Ivan.

"Did you just possibly know Brunelle was going to be at Throwback and that's why you took your folks there?"

"Of course not. Sim did tell me she'd given Rudin that brewery as one of several good places to eat. But it really was only chance that they showed up at the same time as us." Which was true. Pete raised one eyebrow but didn't challenge her on what she'd said. *Whew again.*

William returned. "Deb's sound asleep. I didn't want to talk behind her back. But I imagine you heard that my wife told the detective she saw the ex-husband coming out of Ms. Kingsbury's house." He glanced at Cam and back at Pete.

Should he be telling Pete that? Cam shrugged mentally. Too late now.

"The thing is, we're not sure she could have seen him unless she had some other business back behind the greenhouse," he went on. "I feel like Deb is hiding something, but I don't know what it is or why she would."

"Do you know?" Pete asked Cam.

She shook her head. "Not a clue. I wish I did know."

"You probably shouldn't have told me that," Pete said to Cam's dad. "On the other hand, Ivan is thorough. He'll follow up with her."

"We found the oddest thing in the greenhouse tonight," Cam said. "Ruth let us in, with Ivan's permission, so I could retrieve the two flats of seedlings I'd taken to Nicole. When I picked up the first one, a stretchy band had been underneath it on the table. It fell to the ground."

"A band like a tourniquet," William added.

"I can't think of any use for something like that in a greenhouse," Cam said.

Pete sipped his tea. He set the mug on the coffee table, his expression serious. "Nicole could have misplaced a tourniquet near her planting supplies if she was shooting up. If she was injecting drugs."

147

Cam inhaled a sharp breath. *Really?* Nicole, an addict? "You mean like heroin?"

He nodded slowly. "Like heroin. Or cocaine. Actually very few drugs can't be injected."

"But Nicole was . . ." Cam's voice trailed off.

"You might be surprised at who's an addict, Cam." Pete's tone was soft. "They don't all look like a homeless person sleeping on the street. And heroin is a brutal habit to kick."

The moon was tracking for heaven when Cam and Pete strolled out to the barn hand in hand at nine o'clock. They paused to gaze up at the disk the color of a shiny new dime. A narrow cloud floated over it like on a Halloween greeting card. Cam almost expected to see a black figure on a broom fly across the moon's surface.

"You had quite a day," Pete said.

"That's for sure," Cam murmured. "So do you really think Nicole might have been an addict?"

"I don't know. It would certainly complicate things. People on drugs operate in a different world than we do." Pete squeezed her hand. "Her killer could have been a dealer she didn't pay, or a fellow addict who couldn't afford to buy what she had."

Cam faced Pete. "That guy Carlos Griffith. Maybe he was also into drugs. Maybe that was why he had gone to see her."

"It's possible."

"I don't really know how a person acts when they're on drugs like that. The few times I was with Nicole, she was sort of speedy, moving with nervous energy."

"That's a helpful piece of information. I'll let Ivan know. But what about this secret of your mother's? I don't like it that she's still hedging her story."

"I don't either, Pete. She was honest with me this afternoon about her issue with dogs. For the first time. I hope she'll keep talking to me from her heart." A great horned owl called its low, mournful *whoo-whoo-whoo* from the woods as if it, too, wanted Deb to come clean.

"I'd like to know what she's hiding. And you can bet Ivan does, too." They walked another couple of paces. He stopped and faced her. "Your mom. Do you have any evidence that would lead you to believe she's using?"

"Mom? Drugs? No way. She's a super-straight arrow, Pete. Really." *Mom, a heroin addict? No way.*

"But you haven't lived with her for a long time. How would you know?"

Cam let out a breath. "She's been here for a week and I haven't seen any signs of drugs. But you're right. I left for college about fifteen years ago, and I never lived at home after that. I only visited during vacations. Listen, I'll ask my dad. He would know. They're very close."

"All right. Keep me in the loop?"

"Of course."

Dasha barked from inside the barn. Pete laughed. "He knows I'm here. Coming, buddy," he called to the dog.

Cam unlocked the door and slid it open to Dasha's eager greeting. She flicked on the light switch inside as Pete knelt, burying his head in Dasha's fur for a moment. He straightened when Dasha alerted. Ears forward, tail straight out, the dog stared out the open door into the darkness.

"What is it, Dash?" Pete asked in a terse voice. Frowning, he kept his hand on the dog's collar. "Cam, leash?"

She grabbed the leash off the hook where she'd hung it and handed it to him, watching as he clipped the leash's connector to Dasha's collar.

"He barked at something a couple of hours earlier, after we

returned from the brewery," Cam whispered. "I thought he was howling at the full moon, but maybe he knew something was out there."

"If it's an animal predator, I don't want my dog racing off to his death." Pete rolled the strap around his wrist twice.

Cam shuddered.

"But a human would be a worse threat," Pete continued.

Dasha growled a low, guttural sound. Cam could swear he narrowed his eyes.

Pete thrust the leash into her hands. "Take him, please. Stay in here. Got your cell?

When she shook her head, he handed her his phone. "If I'm not back in five, call it in."

"Okay, but I'm sure it's nothing."

He took her face in both hands. "I love you."

Her eyes widened. "I love you, too." He really thought a threat could be outside, and he was protecting her. And Dasha.

He took a step for the door. "Wait," Cam called. She grabbed the flashlight she kept near the door and handed it to him. "In case you go around the back. The motion detector lights will go on in front here. Be careful."

"I will." Pete rumbled the sliding door shut behind him.

Cam sank onto an upended milk crate and stroked Dasha's head, holding his leash in her other hand. The dog stared at the door, but he sat on his haunches and seemed to calm down somewhat. What could be out there? It must be an animal, because surely no person would've been lurking since seven o'clock, when Dasha had barked earlier. She checked the time on the phone. It had only been one minute. It felt like an hour. Was Pete still wearing his weapon? They'd had a very close call right here in this barn last January when a murderer had come after them, and Pete had left his gun in his car.

Dasha came to the rescue that time. Maybe Pete should have taken the dog out with him.

She stood. "I can't sit down, Dasha." She walked with him to the rear of the barn and back, over and over. All her senses were on alert. She could smell the rough-grained wood of the walls, the motor oil in her old tiller, Dasha's breath. Her palm sensed every thread of the embroidered leash. She heard Dasha's nails clicking on the wooden floor. She tasted the acrid flavor of her own nerves. She saw the specks of dirt on the tines of her pitchfork and a few spilled seeds on her planting table, each one as clear as if they were under a magnifying glass.

Every time they neared the door, the dog strained toward it. Cam checked the time on Pete's phone again. It had been four and a half minutes. Her heart pounded. Dasha barked. This time he refused to leave the door.

A man yelled outside. *Pete?* She grabbed the door handle. It stuck an inch into its tracks even as she heard another yell. Frantic, she shoved it closed again. She forced herself to slow down and slide it with more care until it opened wide.

She gasped. In the yard about ten yards away, in the shadows cast by the moonlight, Pete and Carlos Griffith grappled on the ground.

Chapter 20

Dasha strained at the leash. "Pete!" Cam ran toward the two men. Her heart thudded against her ribs. The motion detector lights flamed to life.

"Stay back, Cam," Pete yelled.

She halted and gripped Dasha's leash. "Sit, Dasha," she commanded, but he stayed on his feet, quivering to join his master. She pulled out the phone to hit nine-one-one when Pete wrestled Carlos face down on the ground. Pete set a knee on his back and twisted one of Carlos's arms behind him.

Carlos turned his head to the side. "I didn't do anything," he said in a rasping voice.

"You were trespassing on this property." Pete called out, "Dasha, come."

Cam let go of the leash and Dasha streaked toward Pete. Her hands were almost numb from the adrenaline of the moment, but her heart rate began to slow. Pete was all right.

"Sit, Dash," Pete commanded. He released Carlos's arm and patted him down. Carlos wore a long-sleeved shirt tucked into jeans, with nowhere obvious to hide a weapon. Pete stood. "This dog is trained to attack on my command."

It was true. Cam had seen Dasha in action last winter. Pete had trained him well. But what was Carlos doing on her property at night?

"Roll over and sit up." Pete watched Carlos carefully as he maneuvered himself to sitting with his arms on his raised knees.

Carlos's face glistened with sweat. He patted his right pants pocket. His eyes widened, and his hand was about to go into the pocket.

"Freeze," Pete commanded. "Keep your hands on your knees where I can see them."

Carlos seemed to sag with despair, but he did as Pete said. What did he need from his pocket that was so important? It didn't look like he had room for a gun in there, and anyway, Pete had checked for a weapon.

"Cam, can you get cuffs from my car? Driver's side door pocket. Not locked."

Cam gave the two a wide berth on her way to the car. She tossed the handcuffs to Pete from a couple of yards away.

Pete drew Carlos's hands behind him and clicked on the cuffs. "Now tell us what you were doing out here," Pete demanded.

"I heard that this woman was snooping around about Nicole's death." He gestured with his head in Cam's direction. "I know she saw me that afternoon." Carlos swallowed. "I wanted to tell her I'm innocent. I never hurt Nicole, not physically, anyway."

Cam shot a glance at Pete. "What do you mean?" she called out to Carlos.

He didn't answer.

"That's a funny way to get a message to someone." Pete glared at him. "Poking around outside in the dark on a Sunday night. Why didn't you just knock on the door?"

"I was afraid . . ." Carlos's voice trailed off.

"Afraid of what?" Pete barked out.

"I was going to talk to her, to Nicole. I went into the green-house but . . ."

"But what?" Cam asked.

He blinked several times, and a tic beat fast at the corner of his mouth. "I don't think I should say anything else." Carlos clamped his mouth shut.

"Was she still alive when you saw her?" Cam stared at Carlos.

He stared back at her with the same haunted eyes as last week. He shook his head slowly but didn't speak. Cam narrowed her eyes at him. She couldn't figure out if he was shaking his head because he'd found Nicole dead or because he was refusing to speak.

"You can tell the lead detective all about it. Let's go." Pete took a few steps toward Cam, but he kept his eyes on Carlos. "Sorry. I'll call you tomorrow."

"Are you still taking Dasha?" She reached out and handed him his phone.

"Yes. I'll call in a cruiser and keep this idiot in my car while I wait for them. Why don't you lock up the barn and head back to the house."

"Okay." She was willing to bet Nicole had been dead and Carlos saw her that way. At least that was his story if Cam had interpreted his head shaking correctly. But was it true? And if it was, why hadn't he called the police himself? Maybe he was afraid of being accused of the murder. Or maybe Nicole was his former lover and he was devastated by seeing her dead. Or maybe he'd killed her himself.

She watched as Pete took Carlos's arm and helped him stand, keeping Dasha next to his other side. She turned off the interior barn light and locked the door behind her, glad the moon made it easy to navigate through the area beyond the barn's lights to the house. The driveway light illuminated Pete ushering Carlos into the back seat of the car. He closed the door, clicking the locks shut, and made his call, still holding Dasha's leash. He beckoned to Cam where she stood at the back steps.

She walked to his side. "What was he doing when you found him?" she asked in a whisper. "It's scary that he tracked me down."

"The fool was crouching behind the house. I don't believe a word of his story about why he was here. We'll do a more thorough search in the morning." He shook his head.

"What do you think he meant, he never hurt Nicole physically?" A siren keened in the distance.

"No clue, unless he was mean to her otherwise."

"So maybe he was the affair," Cam mused. "And he cut it off because he had to go back to his wife, and doing that hurt Nicole emotionally. If he saw her dead but didn't report it, he might have been afraid he'd be accused of killing her."

"That makes sense."

"Or maybe he did kill her. He'd definitely be afraid of being accused."

The siren grew near. A moment later a black Westbury Police cruiser pulled into the driveway, lights flashing. Two officers jumped out. The male officer hurried to Pete.

"Cam, you can go in," Pete said to her, squeezing her hand. He turned to the male officer. "I found the suspect trespassing. Ms. Flaherty was not involved."

"Yes, Detective." The male officer's respect for Pete was obvious on his face.

Cam moved toward the steps to the back door. She paused on the landing, watching them transfer Carlos to the back seat of the cruiser.

What had been Carlos's purpose? And if Dasha's earlier reaction this evening was any clue, he'd been on the property for a couple of hours. He'd tracked her down and had been sneaking around her house, which was too creepy by half. She shuddered, glad that threat was over. At least for tonight.

Chapter 21

Cam locked the door behind her, remembering when it seemed Preston had been taken by a predator in the woods. A human murderer had turned out to be the kidnapper, but she'd managed to rescue her cat in time to nurse him back to health. She'd been too late for the vandals who'd let her baby chicks die in March, enacting cruelty in the name of animal rights. The fox that had defended her own kit by breaking a rooster's neck at around the same time? That was at least the natural order of things, in Cam's mind. What a relief that Pete had found Carlos so she didn't have to spend the rest of the night in fear of a vandal, whether person or animal.

She sniffed and followed the tantalizing aroma to the kitchen. William stood at the counter buttering two pieces of whole-grain toast. Classical music floated in from the living room.

"You can't believe how good that smells," Cam said. What it smelled like was her childhood. Every night her father would make them both toast before bed. Their similar tall, thin frames gave them similar appetites, what Albert used to call Hollow Leg Syndrome. Cam couldn't help it if she was always hungry, especially growing up. And now she worked so hard physically she never had to worry about her weight, unlike some friends her age.

"Want some?" he asked. When Cam nodded, he popped two more pieces of bread into the toaster. He took one of the toasted pieces and handed her the plate with the other.

"I guess dinner was a while ago," she said, before crunching off the corner of her piece. He'd applied exactly the right amount of butter, now melted into the crispy crumbs.

William swallowed his bite. "What's up with the police outside? I was watching out the window until the toaster dinged."

"Pete found that guy Carlos snooping around the barn."

"Is that so? I didn't hear a thing. Because I was listening to music, I guess. What did the man hope to accomplish?"

"He wouldn't say. But Pete's going to be letting Ivan know all about it." She took another bite of toast, thinking as she chewed. "If Carlos killed Nicole, he seemed awfully mild mannered for a murderer. He didn't have a gun, and he looked terrified after Pete wrestled him down."

When the toaster dinged again, William extracted the next two pieces. As he buttered them, he said, "You certainly lead an exciting life, Cameron. Murders and prowlers and all what not."

"It's not by design, Daddy. This stuff just happens." She leaned an elbow on the counter and watched him. "Mom's still hiding something from us. From me, anyway. Do you know what it is?"

"No, honey. She's not telling me, either." He handed her another piece of toast.

"Has she ever had a problem with drugs? I mean, illegal ones?"

William stared at her. He laughed. "Are you kidding? She won't even take an aspirin. The woman lives a clean life. I'd have thought you'd know that."

"That's what I figured. But I haven't spent that much time with either of you for years. She could have changed. She's changed in other ways."

"Did Pete ask about Deb and drugs?" He tilted his head and frowned.

"Yes, but that's his job. That's how a detective's brain works. Always asking questions."

"You can tell him the answer to that one is a dead-end alley going nowhere." He finished the last bite, dusting off his hands on the sides of his pants.

Cam watched fondly. Her father, never even remotely a fashion plate, usually had light stains on the hips of his pants from that very habit.

"But what about this Page character?" he asked. "Think he would have murdered a woman he perceived as threatening his business?"

"I sure hope not, although he's clearly having money problems from the costs of his wife's care. But remember at the dinner with Albert? He said he'd never met Nicole. So why did he know about her all-new equipment?"

"I noticed the same thing," William said. "He tried to rescue himself. I suppose he could know what it looks like from catalogs and such. Regardless, I hope your Pete and colleagues check Page out. I find something a bit off about him."

"I do, too."

He yawned, not bothering to cover his mouth. "I'm going to bed, my dear. Catch you in the morning. We're going to that parade, right?"

"Yes. Have a good sleep, Daddy." Cam kissed her father on the cheek before he ambled out of the kitchen. She wasn't feeling at all sleepy, herself. She found her mug from earlier, made a fresh cup of lemon-ginger tea, and added a couple of glugs of rum. She took it to the couch and curled up in the corner. Preston jumped up and climbed onto the back of the couch behind her, purring into her ear. Her phone sat on the end table where she'd left it. Jake seemed to know Carlos pretty well. Perhaps he'd be willing to talk about him. Now that she and he were friends.

She tapped out a text.

Wondered if you'd talk with me more about Carlos Griffith. Call me?

She hit Send and waited a couple of minutes, but he didn't answer. He might still be winding down the dinner hours at the restaurant. Or he might not want much contact with her. Maybe he didn't really mean it when he'd told her not to be a stranger.

She still wanted to learn more about Carlos. She hadn't talked to Bobby in a few days. He might know something he'd be willing to share.

She pressed his number. After the call connected and they exchanged greetings, Cam said, "How are you doing, my friend?"

"Could be better. I spent half the day with my aunt. She's a mess because she can't understand why they won't release the body to her. She wants to arrange the wake and the funeral mass."

"I'm so sorry."

"But life goes on, doesn't it?" His voice was more subdued than usual. "And tonight's been good. Tell me how you're doing. How's the farm?"

"The farm's fine," Cam said. "And I'm all right, I guess. A lot is going on. You probably know the police haven't made an arrest in Nicole's case."

"Yeah. That's not helping my aunt cope, either."

"So I'm trying to figure out a few things. Maybe I can help."

"Why am I not surprised? You're being careful, right, Cam?" Bobby asked.

"Of course." She crossed her fingers. Again. "Listen, what do you know about the guy Nicole had an affair with?"

"I don't know much. They met at a weeklong Catholic retreat in Florida. A renew-your-faith kind of thing. He'd gone without his wife, and Nicole was without Rudin, of course. I guess Nicole and this dude just fell for each other."

"And then he went home to his wife and that was it?"

Bobby laughed. "Not exactly. They kept seeing each other on the sly for a while. It motivated Nicole to finally divorce her abusive husband."

"Rudin hit her?"

"No, but he was raking her over the coals psychologically. She'd had it and told him so."

That seemed to fit with how Rudin was acting toward Geneva at the brewery. "What about the new guy?" Cam asked.

"That was the problem. He decided he needed to go back to his wife. Broke Nicole's heart, but it also gave her freedom to do what she wanted." Bobby's voice creaked at the end. He made a squeaky noise, then fell silent. After a moment he sniffed. "I'm sorry. We were just so close, you know? Me and her. She'd moved up here, opened her business. Her life was looking up. And then, boom. She's dead."

"I know. It's awful. Bobby, do you know the name of the guy from the retreat?"

"No. She never told me, even though we shared all kinds of other stuff. Said she had to protect him."

"She never mentioned a Carlos? Carlos Griffith?"

"Carlos Griffith? I don't think so. Who is he?"

In the background Cam heard a woman's voice say, "Carlos?"

"Hang on a sec, Cam. Somebody here wants to talk to you."

A second later Lucinda came on the line. "*Fazendeira*, why you asking Bobby about Carlos?"

Cam's eyes flew wide. "Whoa. Let me recalibrate here. First of all, why are you at Bobby's?"

Lucinda laughed. "I'm gonna put you on speaker."

Cam heard the sound quality change.

"Remember I told you I might have somebody?" Lucinda asked.

"Sure. And it's Bobby?"

"Yup," Bobby chimed in. His voice made it clear he was smiling.

"I can't tell you how happy that makes me," Cam said, smiling herself. "You guys could have, like, told me, though."

"We were gonna," Lucinda said. "But what's this about Carlos?"

"You know Carlos, Luce?" Bobby asked.

Cam kept smiling. If Bobby had a nickname for Lucinda, clearly something good was under way.

"Yeah, like I told Cam. He's half Brazilian. And the Brazilian community around here, well, people know each other."

"Got it," he said.

"I was wondering if Carlos Griffith was the man Nicole Kingsbury had the affair with," Cam continued.

"Why him?" Bobby asked.

Cam ticked it off on her fingers. "One, I saw him outside the greenhouse that afternoon, right before I found Nicole dead. Two, he's apparently a devout Catholic like Nicole was. Three, he was prowling around outside my house tonight. After Pete caught him, Carlos said he'd heard I was asking questions. When we asked him, he said he wanted to tell me he was innocent and that he never hurt Nicole physically. So I did some simple addition and he turned up as the sum."

Bobby whistled. "It fits, doesn't it? When he left Nicole to go back to his wife, it would have hurt my cousin emotionally. That must be what he meant."

"I'll ask around," Lucinda said. "If he was *pegando* another woman—"

"Pegando?" Cam interrupted to ask.

Lucinda laughed. "You know, sleeping around. If he was doing that, somebody in the Brazilian community's gonna know."

"The thing is, if he wanted to talk to me, why didn't he just come to the door? Or e-mail me, or call me. I run a farm. It's not like I'm hard to find."

"And he's outside your house in the dark on a Sunday night, no less," Bobby agreed. "Something's fishy with him, for sure."

"Let me know if you hear anything, okay, Lucinda?" Cam said.

"You bet."

"See you at the parade tomorrow?" Lucinda asked.

Cam groaned. "Of course. I told my parents I'd take them. Except I only have a million things to do on the farm at the end of May."

"It'll be fun," Bobby said. "Tell you what, we'll come back with you after the parade and do some work, right, Luce?"

"Sure," she said. "It's a holiday. I miss working in the dirt." She had been one of Cam's most stalwart volunteers last year when Lucinda was cleaning houses on a flexible schedule. Now that she was a school librarian, her free time was more limited.

"That would be awesome. We can have a simple cookout, too. Good?" Cam asked.

"*Perfeito*," Lucinda said. "Perfect."

"See you tomorrow," Cam said. "You guys have fun, now." At the sound of Bobby's laugh, she disconnected. What could be more perfect than two of her favorite people becoming a couple? Besides solving the mystery of a murder, that is.

Chapter 22

"Good morning, chickens," Cam called as she unlatched the coop door at six the next morning. She'd forced herself to get up early so she could get a few hours of work in before heading downtown to the parade. "Come on out, girls. It's another beautiful day in paradise." And it was. The sun was just rising above the tree line, Baltimore orioles warbled their rich-throated mating calls, and the world smelled like growth and hope. Too bad a murderer still walked free.

Hillary strutted down the ramp into the fenced area, followed by Mama Dot, with the rest of the hens hopping, flapping, and otherwise rushing into the fresh air. They hummed their gargling clucks as they foraged for fresh insects. Cam tossed in a bag of wilted lettuce and a couple of apples that had gone mushy, and watched as the girls rushed in for the treat. She took her bucket around to the people door on the back, emerging five minutes later with the container full of multihued eggs. All this daylight really upped the hens' egg production, which had fallen off sharply during the short days of winter.

She headed for the barn and filled the bucket with water.

She grabbed the hoe with a blade shaped like a stirrup, plus a rake, and made for an area she'd tilled under last week. She needed to sow more bush beans, but the tilling had exposed a layer of weed seeds to the light, which resulted in a fresh crop of baby weeds she had to kill off before she planted.

As she drew the stirrup hoe through the top inch of soil, cutting the tender weeds from their roots, she thought again about Carlos. Why in the world had he been trespassing last night? She couldn't come up with a reason. And had they kept him in jail all night or let him go? Jake had never returned her text, so maybe he didn't want to talk, or didn't have any more information about Carlos. Too bad.

Her thoughts went back to earlier in the day. Had Ivan located Rudin and Geneva? If so, had he learned anything from them? Also, why had Nicole moved back north? To be near the man who had ended their affair? Maybe she'd hoped to rekindle it. Or maybe she just wanted to get as far away from Rudin as she could. Her brain roiled with questions.

Preston ambled up and sat on the dirt she'd just cleaned. "Hey, Mr. P," Cam said. "What do you know?"

He kept his thoughts to himself, gazing out at her through slitted lids.

After she finished the first bed, she remembered Pete had said they'd do a more thorough search of her property this morning. She ought to do her own search first. Maybe she could save them the trouble. She left her tools on the ground and hurried back to the house. Pete had found Carlos crouching behind it. But why?

Cam began at the corner of the house nearest the driveway. She walked slowly next to the south-facing back wall, examining the ground. She passed her gas grill and caught a glint of light from under it. But it was only an abandoned beer bottle, likely forgotten after one of her post work gatherings with her volunteers. Lilacs grew along the house, ones Marie had planted many years ago. A tall one bore cones of white flowers, another deep purple. Flowers from both were deeply fragrant, but their Mother's Day blooms had passed by now. Although Cam focused on the ground, she didn't see a thing out of place or strange. She passed under the kitchen window. She glanced in but didn't see either of her parents, and moved on.

She approached the next corner of the house. A flash of orange and black caught her eye, and she looked up at a high branch of the big sugar maple where one of the orioles had just landed. It groomed for a moment, then lifted its head and crooned out its song. When Cam looked down again, she spied a flash of color on the ground too. She'd had so many farm chores in October and November she hadn't done a great job of cleaning up last fall's leaves back here. Half hidden under a scuffle of yellow and brown leaves was a rosary. A rosary with a gold cross and tiny red beads dotted with black. A rosary exactly like Nicole's.

Chapter 23

She stared at the beads. Carlos must have dropped the rosary last night. *Yes.* After Pete had told him he could put his hands down, Carlos had patted his pocket and looked alarmed that something wasn't in there. He must have realized he'd dropped the beads outside. But Pete had already caught him. What would be so fearful about knowing he'd left his possession out here? Or maybe he needed the beads for comforting prayer and supplication in stressful times. Being nabbed for trespassing pretty much qualified as stressful.

Cam pressed the police department number and told them what she'd found. She added that she hadn't touched the rosary and that she'd be home for the next two hours if someone wanted to pick it up. She headed back to her weeding. The day was warming up, but a brisk breeze held the promise of rain later. Clouds scudded by like teenagers in a hurry to get to the beach to the east.

An hour later, she'd just returned the tools to the barn when a car door clunked shut in her driveway. By the time she arrived at the wide barn door, Ivan strode toward her.

"Good morning, Detective," Cam said, wiping her hands on her legs to brush off the dirt.

"Can't say it's a particularly good one." He grimaced. His eyes looked tired, and dark patches showed under them, in contrast with his customary crisp slacks and shirt, and his always neat hair. "You found a piece of evidence, I hear?"

"I did," she said. "Follow me. I'm pretty sure Carlos Griffith dropped it last night. You heard about Pete catching him, right?" Cam asked as she led him to the house and around to the corner where she'd found the beads.

"Detective Pappas filled me in, yes. We questioned Mr. Griffith for quite some time last night, but let him go on his own recognizance."

"Was he the man Nicole Kingsbury had the affair with?" Cam asked.

"Apparently. As you must know, that's not a crime we can prosecute, though."

"Do you think he murdered her?"

"We're not discussing that, Ms. Flaherty."

"Well, did Carlos at least say why he was snooping around here?"

"He did not enlighten us, no. Will you be pressing charges against him for the intrusion onto your property?"

"I don't know. Should I?"

Ivan let out a noisy sigh. "Perhaps you should consult with your lawyer about that."

They rounded the corner to the side, and Cam halted. "Right there. Half hidden by those leaves." She pointed.

Ivan snapped a couple of pictures with a small camera before lifting the rosary with the end of a pencil. "Hmm. Looks familiar." He turned it without touching it.

"I think it's identical to the one Nicole was holding," Cam said. "Except this one isn't missing any beads."

"I think you're right." He pulled out a paper evidence bag and slid in the rosary. "You didn't find anything else?" He blinked as he regarded Cam.

"No, but you're welcome to search. Did Pete also tell you what Carlos said last night?"

"That he never hurt her physically? Yes, he did." He cleared his throat. "Thank you for the tip about Mr. Brunelle's license plate and car model, by the way."

"You're welcome. Did you find him?"

"We were able to locate him and Ms. Flores last evening."

"Do you think he killed his ex-wife?" Cam knew she was asking too many questions, but she couldn't help herself. And so far Ivan was actually answering, even though he'd said he wasn't going to discuss the murder.

He cocked his head. "I will not be sharing our lines of investigation with you, Ms. Flaherty. That said, Mr. Brunelle and Ms. Flores are coming in to be interviewed this morning." He glanced at his watch and groaned. "In twenty minutes, as a matter of fact. I have to get back."

"What about Orson Page, the hydroponics guy?"

Ivan rubbed his forehead. "Working on that. Listen, I'll send someone else out here to do a more thorough search. But it might not be for a while. This blasted parade and the holiday are making a mess of officers' availability."

"No problem. They can come any time, and even if I'm not here. We're going to the parade, too." Her trip to the greenhouse last night popped up in her mind. "Did you also get the thing that showed up in the greenhouse last night? My dad said it might be a tourniquet."

"Yes." Ivan tapped one hand on the side of his thigh like he was eager to leave.

"Do you think Nicole was a drug addict?" Cam asked.

"We're looking into all angles, Ms. Flaherty." Ivan turned to go.

"Hey, good luck with the case," Cam called.

He raised a hand in thanks as he hurried away. At the same time Cam's phone buzzed. She checked it to see Jake's name and number on caller ID. She raised her eyebrows. He was up early for a chef.

"Good morning," she said after connecting.

"Got your text too late to call," he said in his deep voice. "You want to know more about Griffith? Like what he usually orders for dinner, or?"

"No, not that." Cam laughed. "It's just that he was here snooping around my barn last night."

She heard his sharp intake of breath.

"He didn't hurt you, did he?" Jake blurted.

"Not at all. Don't worry. The police dealt with him. I can't figure out why he was here, though."

"Why in the world would he be?"

"There's something you don't know. A local woman was murdered in Westbury last week—"

"I know," Jake said. "I saw it on the news."

"Carlos apparently had an affair with the victim."

"Really? Interesting. I have picked up on some tension between him and his wife since I've been back."

"Huh. The affair makes him involved in the murder case. And I was selling seedlings to the woman who was killed. In fact, I found her body. So I'm kind of involved, too." She'd leave it at that. It'd be too messy to explain why Deb was also part of it all.

"That's terrible," Jake said. "I mean that you found the dead woman. Do the police think Griffith killed her?"

"I don't know what they think. I just wondered if you knew

anything else about him that could help me understand why he was on my property last night. He wouldn't say."

"I can't help. I wish I could. I think he's in insurance, and I know he wears a crucifix on a chain around his neck. I'm usually too busy to talk much."

Cam was about to thank him and say good-bye when she flashed on the note about Fresh Page herbs she'd seen on the menu at Jake's restaurant. "Jake, what do you know about the guy who owns Fresh Page Farm, Orson Page?"

"Why? Jealous of the competition?" Jake laughed.

"No, that's not why I asked."

"Listen, Cam, I'm still committed to buying your stuff whenever you have enough ready to bring me."

"And I'm glad you still want my produce. I hoped you would. No, Orson is, was, a competitor to Nicole. And I'm a bit bothered by something he said."

"Page seems like an honest guy. My chef brought in his herbs while I was away, and they're good quality. The man himself is a little odd. But you know? I don't have to live with him. I just buy what he grows."

Chapter 24

By ten o'clock Cam had cleaned up and eaten a late break-fast. She now sat in the car with her parents as they drove toward town for the parade, a blue Red Sox cap on her head matching her team T-shirt.

"What time does the parade start, Cameron?" William asked.

"I think they set off from Maple Street at eleven sharp," Cam said. "But we need to park and meet up with Albert and Marilyn before Main Street gets closed off. Let's park behind the greenhouse. The lot is half hidden from the street, so maybe we'll find a spot." Albert had called Cam's cell while she was weeding and arranged that he and Marilyn would meet up with Cam and her parents to watch the parade to-gether.

"You want to be that close to where murder was committed, Cam?" Her mother, this time in the passenger seat, peered around into the back.

"Mom, a year ago a guy was killed in my own hoophouse. It's not like murder is catching." Or was it? This was the fifth violent death in a year Cam had been associated with in one way or another.

"Whatever," Deb said, but she didn't sound convinced.

They continued down Bachelor Street, passing gardens featuring rhododendrons in full, glorious blooms of light fuchsia and deep magenta, rows of purple bearded irises, and spirea bushes with their snowy cascades of blossoms. Cam never had time to cultivate a flower garden in the spring. Vegetables always took precedence. Luckily these flower-loving homeowners provided a visual treat for her every time she went into town.

"Turn left onto Main Street, Daddy."

"I remember the way, sweetheart. We went to the greenhouse just last night."

They swung left. The sidewalks were already filling up with residents in lawn chairs. Little kids holding American flags perched on the curbs, and bands of teenagers prowled here and there. A man in a tall Uncle Sam hat wheeled a cart full of flags, hats, cotton candy, and popcorn along the edge of the road.

"Where are we meeting Albert?" Deb asked.

"In front of Sim's shop. She said she'd rope off an area for us to sit but that she'd already rented out all the parking spaces."

"She won't be watching, too?" William asked.

"She's driving her antique truck in the parade. There, I see them." Sure enough, Albert and Marilyn already sat in prime viewing position, Albert in his wheelchair and Marilyn on the seat of her fancy red walker with a wide straw hat shading her face. Albert had had his foot amputated due to his diabetes several years earlier, which was why he'd had to stop farming. Cam lowered her window and waved as they passed. "Be with you in a minute," she called.

Her father pulled into the drive between the greenhouse and the insurance company where Helen and Carlos worked, and found a spot in the back. Rudin's rental convertible was parked near the house, today with its top up. Rudin and Geneva must have parked here and walked the short distance to the police station.

"See that?" William asked, pointing to the convertible.

"Ivan told me earlier that he was going to be interviewing them both this morning at the station."

Deb didn't comment. She climbed out of the car and closed her door with a touch more force than necessary. William exchanged a glance with Cam. He made his own way out, opened the trunk of the rental, and extracted their three lawn chairs.

When Cam exited the car she sniffed the unusually warm and muggy air. Beyond the aromas of people, popcorn, and a fragrant flower blooming somewhere, she detected the unmistakable smell of a rain cloud. This weather reminded her more of July than the end of spring. She scanned the sky. With any luck the rain would hold off for a couple of hours.

"Shall we cross?" Deb asked.

They made their way across Main Street to Albert and Marilyn, and exchanged greetings and kisses.

"Excited, Cammie?" Albert asked Cam. His green John Deere cap was pushed up on his forehead.

"Sure. Who doesn't love a good parade?" Cam smiled at him. She'd always found the sound of marching bands stirring despite the militaristic association. She pulled her chair open and set it next to Albert. William and Deb did the same on the other side of Marilyn.

Marilyn reached into a bag and pulled out a pink box of donut holes. "Snack, anybody?" she offered.

"Don't mind if I do," William said, reaching in and then pulling out three of the sugary orbs.

Deb shook her head. "No, thanks. I've been eating too much on this vacation as it is."

Cam took the box and found two chocolate donut holes, her

favorites. "Thanks. I have a big weakness for donuts in any form."

"I wish I could," Albert said. "But with diabetes it's a major no-no."

"I'll have one for you, dear." Marilyn smiled as she selected one covered in powdered sugar. As soon as she bit into it, the sugar drifted onto the royal blue sweatshirt she wore over a red polo shirt. She laughed and brushed it off. "Can't take me anywhere."

Albert leaned toward Cam. "Any news on the murder?" His blue eyes blinked with interest.

Alexandra and her sister strolled up, one blond, one dark haired. "Murder, you say?" Alexandra asked.

Cam greeted both of them and introduced the sisters to her parents and to Marilyn.

"Good news, Cam," Alexandra said. "DJ is coming home tomorrow." Her cheeks pinkened. She and DJ, a thoughtful and resourceful guy about Alexandra's age, had been seeing each other before he'd left at the beginning of March for a months-long meditation retreat.

"That's awesome," Cam said. "It hasn't been three months, though, has it?"

"No. He decided two and a half were enough. Plus, he has a job with his brother waiting for him here. So how's the murder case going?" Alexandra asked. "You got it solved yet, Cam?"

Deb frowned at the tall, young woman but didn't say anything.

"Not exactly. Pete caught a guy snooping around my barn last night, but he wasn't armed. He was a, uh, friend of the victim's."

"Did you call the authorities?" Albert slapped his knee. "Of course, Peter Pappas *is* an authority. That was a silly question."

"Yes, he called it in and they took Carlos away."

"You don't mean Carlos Griffith, do you?" Marilyn twisted a little to face Albert and Cam.

"I do," Cam said

"I couldn't help but overhear," Marilyn said. "Carlos is my insurance man. Does excellent work. Always prompt, and honest as far as I can make out. He prays a lot, but you can't really go wrong doing that in my book."

"Are you a Catholic, too, Marilyn?" Cam asked. She'd never talked religion with Albert's sweetheart.

Marilyn laughed. "No dear, not at all. If anything I'm a lapsed Presbyterian. I'm a Christian, certainly, but I haven't found any church that suits my needs. Except . . ." Her voice trailed off.

"Tell her about those Quakers, honey," Albert urged.

"I went across the river to the Friends church in Amesbury last week. Well, they call it a Meeting, more so. I'll tell you, sitting in silence with like-minded folks suited me. And it's a lovely historic building. I think I'll be going back. Maybe even get Albert here to come with me."

Albert beamed fondly at Marilyn. "I might just do that."

In the distance from the west came the thrumming of drums followed by the sound of horn instruments beginning a tune. A siren whooped into action.

"It's starting," William exclaimed. He checked his watch. "Eleven o'clock, right on time."

Alexandra fist-pumped the sky. "Love me a good parade. Catch you all later. We're meeting some friends." The two sisters hurried away down the sidewalk.

Cam looked up and down the wide street. The chatter quieted, and most faces turned toward the west end of town. A preschool-age girl marched in place next to her parents, lifting her knees high and waving her little flag above her head in time with her steps.

Glancing to her left, Cam saw her parents, who sat holding hands, chatting quietly. Across the street, though, two people walked along ignoring the entire spectacle. Rudin and Geneva, the latter in a fashionable white sun hat and matching dress, hurried away from the police station toward the greenhouse. They wove their way behind the crowds at the edge of the road and vanished behind a group of tall teenage boys.

The grand marshal, Westbury's oldest veteran, had led the parade driven in a convertible, waving a wizened hand. He was followed by the three selectmen, one of whom was a woman. A color guard of older vets followed carrying flags in belt holders. Cam was surprised to see her new subscriber Sue Biellik as the only woman among them, her hair peeking out from under her military hat.

"Sue!" Cam called, waving.

Sue glanced over, smiled and saluted with her free hand, then marched along. A collection of younger, fatigues-wearing veterans in their twenties and thirties came after the color guard. A farm wagon drawn by draft horses came next, with children in overalls throwing candy out from the wagon and a woman playing a ukulele atop a hay bale.

Now four women on horses approached, one of them a tall, congenial real estate agent with a ready smile whom Cam had seen around town. Their blue polo shirts and light pants all matched, and their helmets were decorated with stars. Red, white, and blue streamers flowed from the horses' manes and tails.

When the equestrians on their steeds passed, Rudin and Geneva reappeared across the way. He was gesturing with his hand, his face even redder than it had been at the brewery. Geneva shook her head with an angry movement. Cam checked, but her parents didn't seem to have seen the couple. Rudin and Geneva disappeared behind the crowd again.

After the equestrians came the high school marching band in green and white uniforms, playing the "Marine's Hymn." William sang along, "From the halls of Montezuma to the shores of Tripoli." Albert joined him, tapping his remaining foot. Deb rolled her eyes as she smiled indulgently.

The color and noise of the parade couldn't quite divert Cam's thoughts. Where had Rudin and Geneva gone? What were they arguing about? Something Ivan had said to them, probably, since they'd come from the police station.

"Look, I see Ellie." Albert pointed.

Sure enough, to the side of a dozen little girls in blue vests walked Ellie in a polo shirt and khakis with her green Girl Scout sash diagonally across her chest. Three girls in front of the group carried a banner reading WESTBURY DAISY SCOUTS. A woman with light brown hair and a big smile walked on the other side from Ellie wearing a green polka-dotted Girl Scout scarf knotted around her neck.

"Hey, Ellie," Cam called.

She glanced over, grinned, and waved.

"Let's hear it for Daisies!" William stood and clapped, setting off a round of clapping from other bystanders.

One of the Daisy Scouts holding the banner beamed and waved, making her end of the banner sag to the ground. Ellie swooped in and rescued it. A Westbury police officer riding slowly by on a black bicycle gave Ellie a high five.

A still-arguing Rudin and Geneva emerged from behind the crowd across the street again. Cam couldn't hear their words, but a woman with three small children looked at the couple with alarm and shepherded her charges in front of her and away from the irate couple. What Cam wouldn't have given to be standing within earshot on that side of the street. She watched as the two turned into the greenhouse parking lot and disappeared from view. Something had not gone well in their interview, that much was clear.

After several uniformed Little League teams passed by, the Veteran Fireman's Association Band approached playing "Yankee Doodle." Cam spied Vince in the back row of the band, a drum hanging from his shoulders and drumsticks with big padded ends in his hands.

"Did you know Vince played drums, Uncle Albert?" she asked

"Can't say that I did." Albert's eyes focused across the street in the gap after the band passed by. "Uh-oh." He pointed.

Cam looked to see Rudin at the wheel of the red convertible, now with its top down, and Geneva in the passenger seat. The car faced the street at the entrance to the parking lot. But three rows of people sat or stood in front of it. Rudin beeped the horn as about a dozen adult women in matching T-shirts and black stretchy shorts approached as part of the parade. Several volleyballs popped through the air between them. A young father at road's edge with a toddler boy on his shoulders turned to the car and waved his hand back and forth in a "No" gesture. Rudin beeped again. The man turned back to the parade, shaking his head, but the little boy kept making the same hand gesture.

What in heck was Rudin doing? Was he nuts?

"He can't just drive into the middle of a parade," Marilyn said, echoing Cam's thoughts. "Who is he, anyway?"

"He's the ex-husband of the woman who died in the greenhouse," William explained.

"My word." Marilyn shook her head.

Deb stared across at them, her eyes wide, her lips pressed together. Cam watched as her mom twisted in her seat to face William, almost as if she was hiding from Rudin and Geneva's view.

"He certainly can't drive out onto the road. What's he thinking?" Cam asked. What *was* he thinking? She stood to get a better view. Sim's shop signpost was anchored in a concrete pedestal behind them. Cam climbed onto the base, giving her two more feet of visibility.

Rudin edged closer to the crowd, pressing the horn. One of the volleyballers, a pretty woman with dark hair pulled back in a short ponytail, hit the ball back to her teammate, then pulled out a phone and thumbed it. A moment later a uniformed Ruth sped up on her police bicycle. She laid it down on the street and blew her whistle. The bystanders quieted. Ruth slid through the crowd until she stood tall in front of Rudin's car.

"Move back, sir," she called, holding both hands up, palms toward the car. She made a pushing movement in the air. "I need you to park the car in back. You're not going anywhere until the parade passes, which could be another half an hour at least."

Rudin glared at her. He threw his hands in the air. He jammed the car into reverse and backed up, not looking. He nearly took out the corner of the insurance building before he slowed and turned around.

Ruth stood with her fists on her hips until the car disappeared around the back of the building. The volleyball group moved on. Sim, driving her vintage truck, edged forward behind them at a crawl. She tossed handfuls of candy out the driver's side window and beeped the horn lightly when she saw Cam and family. Ruth retrieved her bike and, after Sim's truck moved on, she walked the bike across the road to where Cam stood.

"He had a lot of nerve trying to drive through the crowd and interrupt the parade," Cam said to her.

Ruth stood still with her hands on the handlebars, staring at the greenhouse. "I don't like this. He better not try that again or his ass'll be in jail in a New York minute."

Half an hour later, Rudin hadn't reappeared and Ruth cycled away. A clutch of Civil War reenactors marched by, Union soldiers in their blue uniforms plus women in wide, homespun skirts and several children in miniature versions of the grown-ups' costumes. One dark-haired, older woman was quite short and had a broad smile that could light up the darkest corner. She waved to each side of the road in turn and tossed candy out of a woven basket on her arm wherever she saw a child.

Cam's mom stood. "I'll be back." She headed off across the road.

"Where are you going?" William asked.

"I have to talk to Geneva."

"To Geneva Flores?" Cam asked. "Why?"

Deb shook her head and darted across just in time for a big, green antique tractor to avoid running her down. The farmer on the tractor glanced after Deb, scratched her head, and drove on. Deb hurried around the back of the greenhouse and disappeared from sight.

Cam stared at her father. "What's she doing?"

"I don't have the foggiest idea, dear," he said.

"Does Deb know this Geneva woman?" Albert asked.

"She seemed like she did when she saw Geneva at the brewery, but then Mom said Geneva only reminded her of someone she knew. I guess she could have been lying."

"Now, Cameron. You know your mother doesn't lie." William pressed his lips together and shook his head

Cam opened her mouth but shut it again without speaking. Her father's persistent, sunny view of his wife was all well and good. This week Deb didn't seem to be acting like the straight arrow William made her out to be.

"Do you think she's safe over there with that man, Cam?" Marilyn asked. "The spouse is always the first suspect in the mysteries I read." Her cheeks were pink as if with the excitement of a real-life mystery.

"I hope she's safe." Cam wanted to tell Marilyn it wasn't exciting in real life. Murder and its investigation were dangerous and confusing. Excitement wasn't part of the process. "Daddy, should I go after her?"

"She'll be fine," her father said, waving off the idea. "I don't think she'd appreciate our interfering in whatever she's up to."

Cam hoped that first part was true. The second part definitely was.

The weather, which had been pleasantly breezy, with clouds puffing over the midday sun, turned windy and darker. The spectators wearing sunglasses took them off. Sirens ramped into action and grew louder as the town's collection of fire trucks approached at a crawl, red lights rotating and strobing.

The first drops of rain splattered the dry pavement in big splotches. They were followed by more and more drops until the rain fell in a steady stream. A flurry of activity set up among the parade watchers. Some unfurled umbrellas, some packed up their chairs and hurried off, some just kept clapping for the fire engines and dashing out for candy. Marilyn opened a wide umbrella and held it over herself and Albert.

"I should have brought an umbrella, too," Cam said. And why hadn't she? Some farmer, neglecting the weather. She shook her head. Her T-shirt was now damp, as were her bare legs. She was glad she'd at least thought to wear a baseball cap.

"Voila!" William announced, producing a compact umbrella from somewhere. He opened it and motioned Cam to sit next to him where her mother had been.

She obliged. "Thanks, Daddy. Although I think the fire engines are the end of the parade."

Sure enough, after the hook and ladder went by, fourth in the lineup of the heavy, noisy rescue vehicles, that was it, except for a last police cruiser, also with lights and siren activated. Townspeople now filled the road, following the engines the quarter mile farther to the Training Field. Skateboarding teens led the pack, getting drenched in the process. The engines would turn around at the green and begin the process of ferrying youngsters back to the fire station for free ice cream.

"It's noon. Marilyn and I are going to get back to Moran Manor for lunch," Albert said. "Hope you find Deb safe and sound." He gazed across at the greenhouse, his bushy white eyebrows knit together.

"I hope so, too." Marilyn handed Albert the umbrella before she stood and went around to the back of her walker, ducking her head back under the umbrella's shelter.

Cam also focused across the street. She shivered from being wet, and from worry, too. "I'll go over and see what's up."

"I'll bring the chairs to the car," William said. "Meet you there." He also stood, setting the umbrella on the ground, and collapsed the first lawn chair.

"Bye." Cam kissed Albert's cheek and Marilyn's, too. "You guys go get dry. I'll call you later and fill you in."

"Sounds like a plan," Albert said.

Cam hurried across the street. She made her way behind the greenhouse. Were they inside? No, the police still had the tape up, so it must be locked. She didn't see anyone in the parking lot. Deb had to be in the cottage with Geneva and Rudin. The crime scene tape blocking the door to the house now hung flapping in the wind from one end. Cam was a few feet from the door when her mother burst out.

Deb's eyes were wide and her hair mussed. "He's dead!"

Chapter 25

"What? What are you talking about?" Cam stared at her mother. "Rudin is dead? In the house?"

Trembling, Deb said, "Yes, but . . ." She shook her head, fast. "It's . . . he's . . ." She couldn't finish her sentence. Mutely, she pointed inside the house and pulled at Cam's elbow.

"Wait a sec, Mom. Look at me." Cam yanked her mother's hand off her arm. "He died just now?" She pulled out her phone with her other hand and pressed nine-one-one for the second time in a week.

Deb nodded with fast little movements like a bobblehead.

"How? How did he die?" Cam asked as she waited for dispatch. She jabbed at the speaker icon.

"Is this an emergency?" the tinny voice of the dispatcher asked.

"Yes, a man needs urgent medical care," Cam said. "At the house behind the Seacoast Fresh greenhouse on Main Street in Westbury. Please hurry."

"What is the nature of the illness, miss?"

"Hang on." Cam looked at Deb, who just shook her head. "I haven't seen him. Someone who was with him said he might be dead." Cam cringed at how ridiculous that sounded. "Please get an ambulance over here ASAP." She disconnected.

Deb stood with her arms wrapped around herself, shivering in the rain.

"Come on," Cam said. "You're going to take me to Rudin. I need to see what happened."

"No!"

"What do you mean, no?"

"It's not Rudin."

Cam craned her neck at her mother. "What's not Rudin?"

"Rudin's not dead."

"You said he was!" This was turning into a twisted Three Stooges routine.

"No, I didn't. *He's* not dead. A different man is." Deb's eyes pleaded with Cam.

"A different man?" *What the heck?*

"Yes."

"Do you know who it is?"

"No, but he's that guy who was in Jake's restaurant that night, the one you told me to look at. The man Bill said was trespassing last night."

No. *Carlos Griffith!* Cam took an extra deep breath and let it out. "Are Rudin and Geneva in there with him?"

"Yes. You have to come see."

"Did one of them kill Carlos?"

Her mom stared at Cam as if she were a lunatic. "Of course not!"

"All right," Cam said, trying to make her calmest voice override her roiling insides. "Let's go see."

Deb turned on her heel and headed through the cottage door, which opened into a hallway. Cam paused for a second. The only sounds were the distant sirens at the Training Field and the murmur of the dissipating crowds. Where was the ambulance that should be speeding toward her, the cruiser full of investigating officers? Cam did a mental head slap. Blocked by hundreds of townspeople and their children, that's where. But how could the police department not have a team standing by in case of a real emergency?

Deb turned. "Hurry."

The scene in the kitchen at the back of the house looked like a vignette from an old crime movie, except for the clothes the actors were wearing. Rudin leaned back against a metal-edged kitchen counter, arms folded. Geneva sat at a small kitchen table painted in now-chipped light shades of green and blue to match the faded floral wallpaper. Cam's mom stood near the antique white stove, her hands clasped as if to control their trembling. All three stared at Carlos lying half on his side on the worn linoleum floor, his eyes focused on nothing. The open window above the sink let in faint sounds of the sirens and commotion from the Training Field mixed with the patter of the gentle rain.

Cam squatted and touched Carlos's neck. No pulse. His skin, still faintly warm, had lost its alive color and now held a yellowish tinge. Poor Carlos. How had he died? She didn't see blood anywhere. She stood, filled with sadness at his death.

"What are you doing here?" Geneva stared at Cam, eyes narrowed.

What are you *doing here*, Cam thought. Instead she said, "What happened?" His was the third body she'd seen in a year. Emotion rose up just like it had a year ago when she'd discovered the murder victim in her hoophouse, and like when she found Nicole only days earlier. No wonder Deb was so upset. Cam took a deep breath and tried to swallow down the tightness in her throat and a numb sensation all over. She only hoped his was a natural death, not a suspicious one.

Geneva and Rudin looked at each other. "He came in the back door," Rudin said. He gestured to the door at the rear of the kitchen, a lace curtain covering the window in the top portion. "Nicole must have given him a key. He said he was looking for something he'd left here. We had a disagreement. A few minutes ago he just fell down. Probably had a weak heart. I don't know."

"How long ago was this?"

Geneva pointed with her chin at Deb. "After she showed up."

"But that was like fifteen minutes ago," Cam said. "Not one of you thought to call nine-one-one?" What kind of idiots were they, her mom included? "Maybe he could have been saved."

"I felt for a pulse," Deb said, her voice trembling. "He was gone."

"Mom, was Carlos already here when you came in?" She hadn't seen Carlos from across the street, but he was employed at the insurance company. He could have come in early on the holiday to get work done and been in the office building well before the parade began. But what had he been looking for? Maybe a memento he'd given Nicole, or something as innocent as a razor or a book that he'd left behind.

Deb nodded. "And the three of them were definitely arguing."

"About what?" Cam asked. She'd have to wait until later to get her mom to reveal her own reason for joining them.

"In case you didn't know, that man was the reason Nicole divorced me." Rudin pointed at the body. "Two married people who claim to be religious having an affair. It was disgusting. And I told him as much."

Something felt very wrong about this story. According to Bobby, Rudin was abusive to Nicole and the affair was just the catalyst for her deciding to leave him, despite what Rudin had said about wanting to woo Nicole back. "Had you met him before?" Cam watched Rudin.

"No."

"You, Geneva?"

"None of your business."

"How did you two get in here, anyway?" Cam looked from Geneva to Rudin.

"What are you, president of the amateur police corps?" Rudin scoffed. "I happen to have a key my almost-ex-wife gave me, okay?"

Speaking of the police, where in the world were they? Cam made a quick decision. She pulled out her phone and pressed Pete's speed-dial number.

"Nosy," Geneva muttered.

Cam turned her back, but she didn't dare leave the room. "Pete, I'm in Nicole Kingsbury's house with my mother, Nicole's ex, and his friend Geneva Flores. Carlos Griffith is here, too. He's dead. I called nine-one-one, but they must all be tied up with the parade. Can you come?"

He swore. "I can't believe what you just said. But yes, I'll be there. I'm actually at the Westbury station. Don't let anyone leave." He disconnected.

"Everyone is to stay right here," Cam said to all of them. "A detective is on his way." A kitchen clock that was an ad for Gerber baby food ticked steadily forward without a care for the situation in the room. Deb stared at Carlos. Geneva rapped her perfect nails on the table. Rudin, frowning, paced a couple of steps, but the room wasn't big enough for him to get too far, especially with Carlos occupying square footage on the floor. Cam kept an eye on all three. If Rudin tried to leave, she doubted she'd be able to stop him. She was taller by a few inches, but his stocky, muscular body had a lot more power in it than her tall, thin one.

Exactly two sweeps of the minute hand later, Pete burst into the room from the hall, followed by Ivan, their hair and shoulders wet from the rain. The back door opened to an EMT carrying a red bag. He stopped short and looked at Ivan. Ivan held up a hand.

Pete looked at Ivan, too, and gestured. "It's your show."

Geneva examined the blood-red nails on her left hand. "Kind of crowded in here, isn't it?"

Chapter 26

Fifteen minutes later the wheels of justice were turning. Pete kept an eye on Cam, Deb, Geneva, and Rudin in the small front room. Ivan was supervising the examination of the kitchen by an understaffed crime scene team.

Geneva and Rudin occupied the short sofa in the living room. Cam perched on a hard chair, with Deb in the only upholstered chair. Nobody was talking. At a knock on the front door, Pete frowned.

"Everybody stay right where you are." He stepped into the hall.

From where she sat, Cam glimpsed him opening the door to her father.

"Pappas, what a surprise. I've been waiting for Cam in the car. Is she . . ." William, rain plastering his thin hair to his head, peered around Pete. "What a relief. There she is, and my wife, too." He gave a goofy wave. "What's going on, Detective?"

Pete sighed. "You can't come in. It's a possible crime scene."

"You don't say." William's eyes went wide.

"There was a death in the house," Pete said. "We're going to need to question all these folks. Ivan wants to do it down at the station, but it's going to be a few minutes. Why don't you go on home, sir. I'll call you to pick up Cam and Dr. Flaherty when we're through."

"A death? Who died?" William looked at Cam and then at Deb.

Pete had opened his mouth to speak, but Deb beat him to it. "That man we saw in the restaurant last week. Carlos Griffith."

"How did he die?" William asked.

"That's yet to be determined," Pete said. "Please, sir. Let me ask the questions. Did you see anyone go into or come out of this house this morning?"

"Can't say that I did. Only this one trying to run down a few dozen parade watchers in his fancy red convertible an hour or so ago." He pointed to Rudin.

Rudin folded his arms and examined the corner where two walls met the ceiling. Pete gazed at him.

"Ruth witnessed that, too, Pete," Cam said. "She made him go back into the parking lot. She'll know what time it happened. Daddy, you didn't see the detectives and the EMTs go into the house?" Wouldn't he have? Why hadn't he come looking for her earlier?

"No, I stayed on the other side of the street yakking with Albert and Marilyn in their car. She has some fascinating stories about growing up in the San Francisco area. I told her they'd be late for their lunch, but she just kept talking. I didn't cross over to this side until a couple of minutes ago."

"All right." Pete gestured toward the outside. "I'd like you to leave and go back to Cam's, sir. We'll call you later."

"I suppose," William said. "I'm sure my wife and daughter had nothing to do with this death, though, Detective."

"Thank you." Pete's face was getting tenser by the minute.

"See you, girls." William gave a little wave.

Cam waved back. Deb lowered her head to stare at her hands in her lap. Cam had never been more confused by her mother's actions. She must have had a good reason for leaving the parade and coming over here. She'd known Nicole in Florida. Maybe she'd met Geneva or Rudin in Florida, too, even though she'd said she hadn't. Cam thought back to the scene at the brewery and afterward. A strange look had come over Deb's face when she saw Geneva, but later Cam had thought it was because her mom had seen Rudin near the greenhouse. Deb had told the police she didn't know Geneva. Cam stared at her mother. She was lying

Chapter 27

Cam had been sitting on a hard wooden bench in the station lobby for an hour. Her stomach growled. Waiting to be questioned had not been her plan for the lunch hour, and those two donut holes seemed weeks ago. Ivan and Pete had taken the others—Deb, Geneva, and Rudin—into the inner reaches of the station. Deb hadn't even met Cam's eyes when she went with the detectives. Cam tapped her foot. She'd checked her texts and e-mails on her phone. She'd breezed through a few Facebook posts and read a couple of news articles on the Internet. Nothing had answered the question of what her mother knew and wasn't saying.

Ivan appeared at the door. "Ms. Flaherty?"

Cam rose and followed him through to a messy office. Stacks of paper filled the built-in bookshelf and covered the desk. A photo of Chief Frost shaking hands with the recently elected governor was the only framed item on the walls, and a small philodendron languished on the windowsill.

"Sorry, all the interview rooms are full," he said, gesturing for her to take one of the two chairs facing the desk. "Borrowed the office from the chief." He sat in the other chair and twisted to face her. "I'm not recording this. It isn't an official interview. That okay with you?"

Odd. "Sure. I suppose you don't know yet how Carlos died."

He shook his head. He leaned forward, his hands on his knees, his gaze on Cam's face. "What's your mother lying about?"

Cam's eyes widened. "What do you mean?"

"She refuses to say what she was doing in the house. I wondered if you knew."

"I don't." Should she tell him about Deb's reaction to seeing Geneva? This was her mother they were talking about. She didn't want to get her in trouble. She was sure Deb wasn't a killer, but she was definitely lying about something. "Um, I don't know if you know that my mom knew Nicole Kingsbury in Florida for a little while. Maybe she met Geneva down there, too? I've never asked her, though." That was innocent enough, wasn't it?

"No, I did not know she knew Ms. Kingsbury in Florida." He flipped back through a notepad he pulled out of his jacket pocket. "And she said on the phone she'd never met Ms. Flores." He looked up. "What do you think? I could use some help here." He looked frazzled, even more than he had earlier in the day when he'd come to the farm.

"I honestly don't know, Detective. I've hardly seen either of my parents for years, and I never went to visit when they were in Florida. But my mom has been acting a little oddly this week. She would never kill anyone, though. That much I know."

"It's the timing," he murmured. He cleared his throat as if catching himself. "Officer Dodge says the incidence with the car and the parade was at eleven-fifteen. What time would you say your mother headed over to the house?"

"It was probably half an hour later, say eleven forty-five."

"And you went to find her at what time?"

Cam thought. Albert had mentioned it was noon when he'd said he and Marilyn were leaving. "It was a couple of minutes after noon."

Ivan nodded slowly. "Of course it's only Brunelle and Flores's word about when the victim showed up. They had plenty of time to stage a heart attack before your mother arrived."

"But that doesn't work. My mom said he was still alive when she walked in, that the three were arguing and he fell down shortly after."

"Okay. They still could have given him something with a delayed reaction." He stood abruptly. "Thank you, Ms. Flaherty. I appreciate your help." He motioned toward the door. "You think of anything else, please call."

"Are you finished questioning my mother? I know we'd both like to get home."

"Not quite yet."

Cam's stomach let out an audible gurgle.

"Sorry to detain you." Ivan smiled faintly. "We have vending machines in the lobby. It shouldn't be much longer."

He ushered her out. The steel door clicked shut behind him like a death sentence.

"We have company," William declared happily as he pulled the car into the farm driveway. Ivan had released Deb at a few minutes before two, and Cam's father had come promptly to pick them up. Deb hadn't said a word in the car on the way back, despite Cam's questions.

Cam stared at the small black Nissan pickup with a cap on the back that sat in the drive. "Is that Bobby's?"

"Bobby Burr. Sure is. He and someone named Lucinda came over a while ago, said they'd promised to help with the farmwork after the parade."

Cam pressed the heel of her hand to her forehead. "They did, and I totally forgot." She'd promised them a cookout, too. "But you'd never met either of them, had you, Daddy? Did you just turn them loose on the property? I mean, it's fine, but they could have been anybody."

He smiled at her in the rearview mirror. "They sounded like they knew you pretty well. And Bobby showed me the work he did on the barn. I wasn't worried. They're working out back somewhere."

Deb climbed out of the car. She leaned back in. "I'm going to go lie down. Spitting headache."

"Keys, honey." William pulled the key out of the ignition and handed the ring to her. Cam had given them an extra house key when they'd arrived.

Deb took the keys.

"Mom, when you get up we need to talk." Cam leaned forward from the back seat and tried to grab her mom's attention with her eyes. "Will you promise to talk to me?"

"Yes," her mother said slowly. The dark patches under her eyes were new, as was her sagging posture. She made her way to the back door, also slowly.

William turned to look at Cam. "Go easy on her now, honey."

Cam let out an exasperated sound. "I don't understand the first thing about my mother and what she's up to. She needs to come clean about her connection to those two, Geneva and Rudin. Daddy, Nicole's murderer is still out there. And now Carlos is dead. He might have been killed, too."

"I'd say let the police do their job." He rubbed his hands together. "Now, I picked up a few things for a cookout. Hope you don't mind."

"Mind? That was exactly what I meant to do and all this other stuff got in the way. You're a gem."

198

He laughed off the compliment. "Well, I know I'm hungry and you must be starved. Why don't you light the grill and we'll get a late lunch under way. Invite your friends, too." He climbed out of the car and ambled into the house.

Cam uncovered the small gas grill on the brick patio behind the house and lit the fire. She'd lunched on only a bag of corn chips from the vending machine in the station lobby. She could easily put away a burger, or whatever her father had planned for the meal, with a beer or two to wash it down. She hadn't been able to find out if Geneva and Rudin had also been released. Deb had just appeared in the lobby and said she wanted to go home.

The storm had already blown through, and now the sun lit up raindrops like tiny diamonds on every surface. Thanking the rain gods, or Mother Nature, for the much-needed soaking downpour, Cam headed for the fields beyond the barn. Lucinda was such an experienced volunteer that Cam had no worries about her being turned loose to work. Better Lucinda than William, any day. She first came across Bobby turning compost. He set the pitchfork into the ground when he saw her and wiped his sleeve across his forehead.

"Bobby, thanks so much for doing that. I've been meaning to get to the compost. It cooks fast when the weather warms up at this time of year, and it needs the air it gets from being turned."

"I like a good, sweaty job. Has the same effect as lifting weights, but with this"—he gestured to the three bins side by side—"I actually accomplish something."

"Well, I appreciate it, and I'm sorry I wasn't here when you and Lucinda arrived. My mom and I were, um, detained for a bit. Listen, my dad is getting lunch ready. Come and join us."

"Absolutely. Let me just finish this one bin and I'll be there." He resumed forking the half-finished compost from the middle bin into the last one. Part of the assemblage of leaves, grass, vegetable refuse from the kitchen, and weeds had already broken down, but the piles had to be turned every few days to keep them cooking.

"Thanks. I'll go find Lucinda."

"She's picking asparagus, I think," he said.

Cam trudged down the wide mown path between the fields until she saw her friend. Lucinda was, in fact, snapping off asparagus from the long double rows and laying them in a wide basket.

"Thank you so much," Cam said. "I'm really sorry I wasn't around when you guys got here. Did you watch the parade?"

"No, we had a lazy morning." Lucinda straightened, blushing until her cheeks matched the bright pink scarf tying back her black curls. "Not a problem you weren't here. I like your *papai*."

"I like him, too. It's funny, either he's changed or I have. Or both. I don't remember feeling so close to him when I was younger."

"Good thing we're given long lives so we can change, right?"

"You bet."

"He was pretty trusting, though," Lucinda said. "We could've been murderers, for all he knew."

Cam laughed. "Exactly what I told him. Now he's making lunch for all of us. Hungry?"

"Sure. What were you doing in town after the parade, anyway?" Lucinda picked up the basket.

Cam shook her head and blew out a breath. "It's all mixed up with Nicole's death, and her ex-husband, and his girlfriend. And my mom. Remember you said you knew that Brazilian guy?"

"Carlos?"

"Right. He died in Nicole's house today." Cam saw his collapsed body in her mind and felt again the flood of sorrow at a life cut short.

"No!" Lucinda muttered something in Portuguese.

Cam cocked her head. That had sounded a lot like swearing even though she didn't understand the words. "Yes. And my mom, Rudin, and Geneva were in the house together. The police wanted to question them, and me too. So that's where I was. I guess I'm lucky to have arrived home before dark, now that I think of it."

"Was Carlos murdered?" Lucinda whispered.

"I don't know. I'm not sure they know. It might have been a heart attack. Or maybe he was killed in a way to make it look like one."

Lucinda stared at Cam. "This is bad juju, *fazendeira*."

"Don't I know it."

Twenty minutes later the four of them sat at the picnic table under the big maple. William had grilled cheeseburgers and chicken sausages, and he'd picked up containers of potato salad and coleslaw from the Food Mart. A plate of Cam's marinated asparagus rounded out the offering. Now the aroma of grilled meat was driving Cam's taste buds crazy. Good thing it was time to eat, and the shade was welcoming in the warmth of the afternoon.

Cam picked up her bottle of beer. "Here's to the chef."

"To the chef," Bobby said, clinking his bottle with the others.

"Dig in, everybody." William squirted ketchup on the cheese that had melted lusciously on top of his patty. He added the top bun and took a big bite. He'd never looked happier as meat juice and ketchup dribbled down his chin.

Lucinda split open a chicken sausage and laid it on a bun, then layered it with Dijon mustard, lettuce, and a dill pickle slice.

"Your mom isn't joining us?" Bobby asked after he swallowed his first bite of burger.

"She said she had a headache and went to lie down." Cam followed Lucinda's lead and fixed a sausage burger. Preston put his front paws on the bench next to her and mewed his tiny mew of supplication. She smiled at him, tore off the end of the sausage, and laid it on the bench.

"Bobby, Cam found another dead person today, in your cousin's house," Lucinda said. "And her mom was there. That's enough to give anybody a headache."

"You're kidding me." Bobby arrested his burger-laden hand halfway to his mouth and set it down. "In Nickie's house? Who was it?"

"Carlos Griffith." Cam repeated the facts as she'd relayed them to Lucinda. "I called the police, since none of the three had thought to do it. That alone is pretty suspicious." She thought back.

"This sucks." Bobby's nostrils flared. "I can't believe it. So it has to be linked with Nickie's death, doesn't it?"

"I sure think so," Cam said. "First of all, why were Rudin and Geneva in the house at all? Second, what were they arguing with Carlos about? Third, why did my mom go over to see them? Fourth, why didn't they call it in the minute Carlos hit the floor?"

"Wow," Lucinda said, the edges of her eyes turning down. "Lotsa questions. Poor Carlos, nobody taking care of him." She crossed herself.

"Rudin and his girlfriend went over to the house after they were interviewed at the station," Cam said. "When they were walking back, we saw them from across the street. They looked like they were arguing even then. Right, Daddy?"

William followed this exchange as if he was watching a tennis match, but he'd kept quiet up to now, working his way through his burger. "Mmph," he said, nodding his head and chewing.

"At first Rudin was trying to drive into the parade, and he was really steamed he couldn't," Cam went on. "It was a ridiculous stunt to pull. Ruth showed up and made him go back into the parking lot. So he and Geneva must have gone into Nicole's house after that."

"How'd they even get in?" Bobby asked. Preston made his way around to Bobby and begged again. "Okay to give him some meat?" Bobby asked Cam.

"Sure," she said. "Rudin said Nicole had given him a key."

Bobby frowned as he fed a morsel to Preston. "No way. Nickie was all done with her ex. She never would have given him a key to her new house." He shook his head, hard.

"That makes sense." Cam took a bite of her sandwich. Despite having seen a body only a few hours earlier, she couldn't help but savor the slightly salty, juicy meat flavored with roasted garlic and dried tomatoes.

"So where'd Rudin get the key?" William asked.

"He could have lied about that. Maybe he stole it or jimmied a window. Or picked the lock." Cam shook her head. "I wonder if Ivan managed to extract any answers out of them. Rudin seems like the type who would shut up and lawyer up instantly. But maybe Ivan played Rudin and Geneva against each other."

"Like in the shows, where the cop tells one suspect that the other one said something they didn't really say?" Lucinda asked, eyebrows raised.

"Maybe." Cam sipped her beer. A small black and white woodpecker rapped at the trunk of the tree above them, as if reminding her of the other questions. "I guess the obvious thing for Rudin to argue with Carlos about would be his affair with Nicole." She rapped her finger on the table, not to keep time with the bird but to keep her brain working.

"Sir, do you know why your wife went over to Nicole's house?" Bobby asked William.

"Can't say that I do. She tells me what she wants to, but she's always kept a lot close to the chest." Cam's father tapped his own chest.

"She promised me she'd tell me later," Cam murmured, more to herself than to the group.

"And we have the question of why they didn't call nine-one-one," Lucinda said.

"That one is really confusing," Cam agreed. "Did they think they could keep it secret? A guy falls down, you call for help. Not phoning it in is the most suspicious thing of all, as I see it." Her brain ached from the strain of trying to figure out events that didn't seem to have a sensible explanation.

"And now you'll never know what Carlos was doing snooping around last night," William pointed out.

"Carlos was snooping around here?" Lucinda wrinkled her nose. "Why?"

"I don't know. Pete found him, but Carlos only said he wanted to talk with me."

"And didn't just call you or ring the doorbell?" Bobby asked. "That's crazy."

Cam pursed her lips "I'll say." She looked at Lucinda and Bobby across the table. "And I found a rosary on the ground outside the house this morning."

"Carlos must have dropped it," Lucinda said.

"It had to be him," Cam said. "I called the detective, and he came and picked up the beads. Which looked exactly like the ones Nicole had in her hand when I found her."

Lucinda cocked her head. "What were the beads on the rosary like?"

"They looked like little beans or something," Cam said.

"Not plastic?" Lucinda asked.

"I don't think so. The surface was a bit duller. They were red with a black dot at one end. Not quite round."

"Those belonged to Carlos," Lucinda said, nodding in recognition. "I saw him praying with them at Mass. Pretty unusual these days. They're like the ones *Avó* said her Hail Marys with back in Brazil. They're made of real beans or seeds or something. My grandma liked the traditional stuff."

"So maybe Carlos had given Nicole a matching rosary," Bobby said.

"Or she'd given him one," Cam said.

"That makes sense." Bobby sank his forehead into his hands and stared at the table. "Except now they're both dead."

Chapter 28

Cam sprawled in a lawn chair in her backyard at six that evening. Bobby and Lucinda had stayed to work after lunch. William had said he would clean up the food and then needed to rest, claiming a strained muscle in his back. With Bobby and Lucinda's help, Cam had accomplished a lot of needed farmwork in a few hours. The couple had just driven away, a dozen eggs and a bag of asparagus in hand. It would be good to have Ellie as a regular employee on the farm for the summer. Cam couldn't do it all alone.

Now her muscles twitched as she relaxed, still in the work T-shirt and old jeans she'd changed into after lunch. What a day it had been. Working in the morning. A lovely small town parade with all of her favorite people except Pete. Seeing Rudin's anger across the street. Watching in bewilderment as her own mother left to join him and Geneva. And the terrible scene at the house, starting with Deb's strange behavior about calling in the death and ending with Carlos's unseeing eyes. She blew out a noisy breath. Not a single fact of the two murders was clear to her. What she wouldn't give to sit down with Pete and talk it through. And speaking of the police, no officer had come back to do a more thorough search today, as far as she knew, but it probably didn't matter. She'd found the rosary and couldn't imagine what else Carlos could have dropped.

Cam gazed at her phone. She'd promised to call Albert and fill him in, but she didn't have the energy to explain what had happened at Nicole's house. She'd send him an e-mail later.

When she heard the screen door slam behind her, Cam craned her neck to see her mom walking down the steps holding two glasses of white wine. Maybe they were finally going to have that talk.

Deb handed Cam one of the glasses and sank into the chair at a right angle to Cam's. "Thought you could use this," she said.

"You're right, I can. Cheers, Mom." Cam held up her glass.

Deb reached over to tap her glass against Cam's, then she took a hearty sip. "I owe you a story, it appears." She gazed at the big maple tree. Preston stood from where he'd been resting next to the trunk and moseyed over to Deb, rearing up to rub his side against her leg. Deb reached down to stroke him.

Cam sipped her own wine, the cool alcohol soothing her still-scratchy throat. She waited for her mom to speak. Cam had asked enough questions without getting answers. If Deb wanted to talk, she was going to have to take the lead.

Gazing at the barn and not at Cam, Deb took a breath, her shoulders rising and falling with it. "I met Geneva in Florida, during that time I told you about."

"I wondered about that."

"She worked at the rehab facility." Deb looked straight at Cam. "I did something bad. Illegal. And Geneva caught me at it. I'm ashamed and never did it again, but she's been threatening me ever since."

"Do you mean she's blackmailing you?"

The skin around Deb's eyes was strained, and her head

hunched into her shoulders. "Sort of. I also know something about her, so we each agreed not to tell on the other, so to speak. But I hadn't seen her since we left Florida."

"What bad thing did you do, Mom?" Cam kept her voice soft and laid her hand on her mother's. Deb was clearly in pain. Cam had never seen her this way.

"I think I'd like to tell you and your father with your detective present."

"Daddy doesn't know, either?"

"He doesn't. I have to come clean to both of you about what happened. I owe you that. But I also have to tell the police."

It must have been something pretty bad if her mom wanted to confess to the police. But what?

"Will you call and see if Pete can come over?" Deb clasped Cam's hand. "Please?"

Chapter 29

By seven o'clock Pete sat in the living room with Cam and her parents. Cam had fixed tea for them all, but Deb hadn't touched hers. Her lips were pressed together as if she was keeping them from quivering. Pete leaned forward, his forearms on his knees.

"Thank you for inviting me to hear your story, Dr. Flaherty. Just so you know, I'll be obliged to share any account of possible criminal activity with the appropriate authorities. I want to be sure you're aware of that."

Deb nodded from the couch, where she sat holding hands with William. "Yes," she said. "I can't keep this secret any longer."

"Go ahead," Pete said.

He wasn't smiling, but Cam thought his calm, open face would encourage her mom to speak.

"William and I had a sabbatical semester in Miami. What was it, three years ago, Bill?" She glanced at him.

"That's about right."

"As I told Cam, I volunteered in a nursing rehabilitation facility. I told stories about our travels and our research. It was a kind of entertainment for the shut-ins. Nicole had been in a serious accident and was living at the rehab while she regained her strength. We became friendly."

Preston wandered in and jumped up on the back of the couch behind William.

"What was the accident?" Pete asked.

"Nicole fell down the stairs in her house. People talked at the time that her husband might have had a hand in it, but Nicole could never prove it."

"Really?" Pete sat up straight.

"Yes. Anyway, Geneva worked at the rehab. She was the receptionist."

Cam cleared her throat. "Mom told Ivan she'd never met Geneva before. Is that going to be a problem?" she asked Pete.

"Let's let her finish the story. Please go on, Professor."

"You can call me Deb, you know. I had left the rehab at the end of the day. It was my last day visiting with the residents before William and I were to depart on our research trip to the Maldives. I was driving west, and there was terrible solar glare." She swallowed. She squeezed William's hand and let it go, laying her hands flat on her thighs. "I heard a thud. I felt it, too. I couldn't see anything. I panicked and drove away."

Cam's eyes widened. "You hit somebody and you didn't stop?"

Deb shut her eyes for a moment. When she opened them again, they glistened. "Yes, Cameron, I hit someone. I kept on going. I'm a coward, and I've been living with it."

William laid his arm across Deb's shoulders. "You were very eager to watch the news in the airport the next morning, as I recall. You could have told me, honey." The corners of his mouth and eyes dragged down.

"I know. But I didn't. I was terribly ashamed of myself. I'd never been that kind of person."

He squeezed her shoulder. "And you're still not. You made one mistake, that's all."

"Geneva wrote to me after that," Deb went on. "She tracked down my e-mail address, said she'd seen the whole thing, that she knew I was at fault."

"But it wasn't like you were trying to hit this person," Cam said.

Deb gave her a look. "A hit-and-run is a terrible thing, and illegal. Isn't that right, Detective?"

"Yes," Pete said. "The law varies from state to state, however, and I'm not familiar with the Florida statutes. In Massachusetts it could result in a prison sentence."

Her upstanding, disciplined, successful mother in prison? Cam couldn't believe this was happening. From the worried look on her father's face, he couldn't, either.

"Cam said you know something about Geneva, as well. I'm very interested in hearing about that," Pete said. "Did she also commit a crime that you witnessed?"

"She was an addict. Probably still is. She often acted odd. She sometimes had unexplained absences. Once I came upon her trying to break into the pain meds cabinet. She knew I saw her and made up some excuse."

Pete watched Deb. A few days ago he'd wondered to Cam if Deb herself might be an addict. Was he still thinking that?

"Usually nursing homes and rehabs lock up narcotic meds like it's Fort Knox," Pete said. "Could Geneva have stolen any?"

"It wasn't a very well-run place. I heard they went out of business a year later."

"Please go on." Pete rolled his hand.

"Geneva e-mailed me and said she was going to inform my

university about my involvement in the accident unless I paid her quite a large sum of money. I wrote back and suggested I would let the rehab as well as the local police know of her drug use."

Pete opened his mouth to speak, but Deb held a hand up.

"I was about to report her trying to steal the meds when the accident happened. We agreed to form a mutual silence society." Deb squared her shoulders. "And now you know. It's been hanging over my head for years and I've had enough. I don't care what happens to me."

Oh, Mommy. Cam's heart went out to her mother. The burden she'd been carrying. The secret she'd been hiding even from Cam's father. The prospect of going to prison, and the likely end of her academic career, which had been her life up to now.

"I appreciate your including me in this session," Pete said. "I will need to relay these facts to Ivan, and possibly to the Miami police. Depending on how the victim fared and the state laws, they might bring criminal charges."

William frowned, but he kept his arm close around his wife.

"I tried to find news of the accident," Deb said. "I located one article reporting on an older woman who'd stepped off a curb and was hit. But after the first day's report, I wasn't able to find out whether she recovered. Part of the problem, of course, was being in the Maldives with sketchy Internet access while the news was fresh."

"I'm sure we can track back the victim's status. I'll need the name and location of the rehab, and the date of the accident."

"I'll e-mail them to you," Cam's mom said.

"Fine. Cam knows how to reach me." Pete stood and held out his hand to Deb, who also stood and shook hands. "We'll be in touch."

"I'm sure you will, Detective." Deb lifted her chin, her face pale and still.

"Wait," Cam said. "You both have airline tickets for tomorrow, don't you?" She looked at her parents.

"We called and postponed the trip," William said. "What with all this going on."

"A wise choice. Deb, you did the right thing tonight," Pete said. "And you can call me Pete, you know." He pulled a wry grin. "Good-bye," he said to Cam's father.

"Take care, now," William said.

Pete turned to Cam. "Walk me out?"

"One second." She stood and held her arms out to her mom, who stepped into them. Cam didn't speak but just hugged, feeling her mother's strong, slender back under her hands, smelling the herbal scent of her shampoo. She wasn't sure she'd ever hugged her mother like this. Certainly not since she'd grown taller than Deb in middle school. "You're going to be okay, Mommy," she whispered, the first time she'd called her that in twenty years.

Deb squeezed back for a moment. She pushed back, her eyes full of tears. "I suppose I will. Thanks, honey. I feel like a box of bricks has slid off my back and I don't have to pick it up again."

Cam smiled, wiping away the overflow from her own wet eyes. "I'll be back in a minute."

Pete took Cam's hand as they walked down the back steps and stood on the driveway. "You obviously didn't know anything about that experience."

"I totally didn't know about it."

"Are you all right?" he asked, squeezing her hand. "That's a lot to hear, especially considering how distant your mom has been."

"It's hard to think she could do something like that." She gazed at Pete. "My mother is such a straight arrow, Pete. She . . ." Cam shook her head. "And to think she might have to go to jail for a hit-and-run worries me so much."

"I know. But we'll deal with that when the times comes. If it comes. Let's sit down for a minute." He led her to the picnic table, where they sat side by side, backs to the table. A cool breeze blew the impending twilight through the leaves above them. Pete slung his arm across her shoulders, rubbing her arm.

"Do you think Mom will really have to go to prison?" Cam asked. Maybe Deb would be able to make the best of the situation. She could lead an anthropology study group with her fellow prisoners or teach something else. But it wouldn't be easy. Not at all. And being convicted and incarcerated would destroy her academic career. *Poor Mom.*

"I can't say. If the victim was only slightly injured and doesn't want to press charges after so many years, that might affect the sentence. I also don't know about the Florida statute of limitations on an unlawful driveaway."

"I hate to think of her in prison. She's just started to open up to me." Cam fell silent. She'd read awful things about prisoners abusing each other. Did incarcerated women do that, too? How would her intellectual mother survive? Sure, Deb was fit and healthy, but Cam didn't think she had any experience with prison populations.

"Your mom's suspicion about Rudin maybe pushing Nicole down the stairs could be important," Pete said. "And frankly, Geneva's using is the least surprising part of what Deb said."

Cam sighed. She couldn't do anything about the case from the past. But she could try to help her mom right now. "Remember when we talked about Nicole being an addict a few days ago, and you said you can't always tell by looking at someone whether they're using or not? Maybe Rudin is an addict, too," Cam said. "Or maybe he's the supplier. He is a pharmacologist, remember."

"That has come up in our conversations about the case," Pete acknowledged.

"He could have been Nicole's supplier, too. She might have become hooked on narcotics in the rehab. I hear that's pretty common. Right? Wouldn't that explain the tourniquet in the greenhouse?"

"It could."

"Or maybe the tourniquet was Geneva's." She turned to face Pete. "I still don't know Nicole's cause of death. You must by now."

"I haven't had a report from Ivan today. They found heroin in Nicole's system, but it wasn't a case of overdose."

"Could she have been poisoned with something?" Cam asked.

"Certainly. But the lab has to know what to test for. And right now we don't know how to narrow it down."

She stared across the yard to the perennial garden. The white flowers of the snowdrop anemone glowed in the dim light. Too bad their almost eerie appearance couldn't pull some answers out of the ether.

"Earth to Cam?" Pete said. He pulled her in for a sitting embrace. "I miss you, sweetheart."

"Mmm." The feeling was entirely mutual.

He pulled away. "And the sooner we solve this case, the sooner you and I can get back to normal."

"I know. And that means you're leaving."

He smiled ruefully. "You got it." He stood.

"Hey, is Dasha doing okay with you working so much?"

"Heading home right now to take him for a walk before I go back to the station."

"You can bring him over again, you know." Cam stood, too.

"I think maybe I will. Tomorrow morning okay?"

"Of course. Speaking of animals, I need to go put the hens to bed."

After another kiss, Pete headed for his car and Cam trudged out toward the chicken coop. Not in a thousand years would she ever have expected Deb to have acted like she did this week. But if she'd learned one thing in her year of farming, it was that the unexpected will happen when you least expect it. She'd also learned the corollary: She, Cam, was way more resilient and flexible than she'd ever suspected.

The latch on the coop clicked shut, with all the hens safe inside. The day-after-full moon hadn't yet risen, and it was dark out here in the field. Cam felt for her cell in her pocket to use the flashlight app, but of course her phone was in the house. Figured, despite all the times she'd vowed never to come out here again without it. The air was cool too, with the post-sundown earth sending up its rich-smelling moisture.

The breeze had turned into a wind, bringing all kinds of new noises. Leaves rustled here, a branch cracked there. Her scalp prickled when she heard the awful cry of a fisher cat in the woods behind the fields. The weasel-relative's call sounded like a baby being tortured. One more reason, beyond the foxes and coyotes, she always secured the chickens for the night.

She hurried back toward the barn on the path, thinking about her mother's prospects, wanting to talk with her more and continue their newfound closeness. Halfway to the barn her toe caught on a clump of grass, and she ended up sprawled on her elbows and knees.

She swore and pushed back up to standing, dusting off the knees to her pants. She straightened, then froze, hearing a murmur. Was that a voice? Was somebody on her property again? She pictured Carlos's face when Pete hauled him into the barn. But Carlos was dead.

The murmuring didn't continue. It must have been the wind. Cam set out for the house again, this time at a long-legged lope. She didn't stop until she was safely on the back steps to the house. *Whew.*

Inside, though, she read a note on the table from her father saying he and Deb had gone to bed and that they'd see Cam in the morning. Talking with Mom would have to wait until tomorrow. Her poor mother. The thought of her spending time in a Florida jail was chilling.

Now that her nerves had settled after falling and hearing the sound, Cam identified the empty feeling she had as hunger. She foraged in the kitchen, settling on a peanut butter toast with sliced bananas. Red wine oddly seemed like the right accompaniment. She sat at the table to eat her supper, but stood again to grab her phone off the kitchen counter where she'd left it charging. What Lucinda had said about Carlos and Nicole's matching rosaries was bugging her. Cam brought the phone to the table and, as she ate, tried to learn more about those rosary beads. Lucinda had said they were made of something natural, a seed or a bean. And she'd said her grandmother in Brazil prayed with a rosary like Nicole's.

Cam tapped in "natural rosary bead." But that search yielded rosaries with beads made out of wood, stone, or glass. She tried "rosary bead plant." She shook her head at the images of a hanging house plant with little beadlike growths. She typed "rosary bean." She stared at the screen. She set down her wineglass with a jolt, making the deep red liquid slosh up the sides. The third result read, "Rosary Pea: 15 Plants that Could Kill You." It was a link to a Web site called Mother Nature Network. She clicked the link.

"Many jewelry makers have died after pricking a finger while handling a rosary pea," she read. "The poison contained within the seed is abrin—a close relative of ricin and one of the most fatal toxins on Earth." Cam clicked the link for ricin and read about the even more toxic substance found in castor beans. She sat back, eyes wide. What if abrin was what killed Nicole?

A few of the peas had been missing on Nicole's rosary. She hunched back over her phone and searched for abrin. Of course the Wikipedia article came up first, but she clicked the Centers for Disease Control and Prevention link instead. It had to be more accurate. She frowned as she read. The article said it could take a person from a few hours to a couple of days to die from abrin poisoning, depending on the method of ingestion. Had Nicole been that ill when Deb had talked to her? Cam thought back. Deb had said Nicole didn't seem to be feeling well that morning. Cam wondered if Ivan had checked out who'd had contact with Nicole the day before her death.

"Gah," she said out loud. Good thing she hadn't picked up that rosary outside her barn. What if one or more of its beads had been broken? Cam herself could have been the next victim. And maybe Carlos had died from abrin poisoning, too. Except his rosary hadn't been missing any peas.

She checked the time on her phone. Eight-thirty. She really didn't want to be phoning Ivan on his cell this late. And she had too much information to convey in a text message. She scrabbled in her bag until she found his card. Yes, an e-mail address. She moved over to her laptop and typed out a message for him with a subject line of "KINGSBURY POSSIBLE CAUSE OF DEATH." She described the rosary pea, mentioned the highly toxic abrin, and included the plant's Latin name, *Abrus precatorius*. "Have you checked it out yet? CDC

Web site has good details," Cam wrote. She pasted in the link to the CDC article. "Remember beads were missing off Nicole's rosary. Thought you should know." And if the lab had a clue the poison might be abrin, they'd know what to test for, according to Pete.

She signed it and hit Send. *There*. He could handle it from here on out.

Chapter 30

The next day's dawn splashed stunning reds and pinks over the horizon. Cam had learned that the adage "Red sky in the morning, sailors take warning" was a remarkably accurate predictor of rain later in the day. Good. The soil was still so dry, despite yesterday's rain. She sat on the back landing, mug of French roast in one hand and an apple in the other, munching and watching the color dissolve into wispy clouds and blue sky. She hadn't been able to sleep past five, but the compensation was getting to see Mother Nature's watercolor art. The beautiful sky did nothing to cheer Cam, though.

She couldn't shake the heaviness of her mom's news last night. It felt as if a lead cloak were draped over her shoulders. She hoped Mom would be resilient enough to survive whatever was to come. And the murder was still unsolved, too. Preston rubbed his head against her knee. She drained her mug and laced up her work boots, tossing her apple core into the herb garden to decompose.

"We're up so early, might as well get to work, Mr. P." Maybe some good physical labor would lighten her mood.

He glanced up at her, then trotted down the steps as if to go fetch a miniature hoe. She smiled wanly and followed him to the hoophouse, propping the door open after her. As she sprayed a fine mist over her seedlings, Orson Page and his run-down greenhouse came to mind. Had Ivan checked out his alibi? Adding Carlos's death to the investigative mix might have slowed the search for Nicole's killer. Unless it was one murderer, two victims. And what was the period of time for an alibi, anyway? If Nicole had died of abrin poisoning, it could have been administered even the day before. Or maybe her death was an accident, in fact. She might have accidentally crushed one of the rosary peas and the poison seeped in through a cut on her hand.

Cam shook her head. She was missing too much information to make sense of the two deaths. She trudged out to the coop instead. She couldn't help but smile again as the hens spilled out into the fresh air. "Good morning, ladies," she said. "Eat, fertilize, lay eggs. Rinse and repeat. What an easy life you have."

She spent the next two hours having her own version of an easy life. You couldn't beat planting and weeding on a fresh new day to bring a sense of accomplishment. By the time her stomach growled, it was seven-thirty and time for breakfast.

Pete's car pulled in as she approached the house. He climbed out, with Dasha bounding out after him, his leash trailing on the ground.

"Hey, guys," Cam said, extending one arm to Pete and the other hand to pet Dasha. "You're here early."

The skin around Pete's eyes was tight, and his Mediterranean skin had that slightly gray hue it took on when he hadn't had enough sleep. "It's a tough case. Or cases, I should say. Our commander is leaning on both Ivan and me to get these deaths resolved."

"I hear you," Cam said. She squeezed him around the waist

and dropped her arm. "What do you know about abrin?" She cocked her head.

Pete narrowed his eyes like he was thinking. "I've heard of it but can't think where."

"So Ivan hasn't mentioned it? Or whoever does autopsies for the police?"

"No. What is it?"

She explained about ricin's toxic relative and its carrier, the rosary pea. "You need to be sure they test for that in Nicole's blood. And maybe in Carlos's, too. If you don't know about it, Ivan must not, either."

"You're right. I would have heard. This changes a lot. How long does it take to act?"

"The article said it varies depending on the means of ingestion. It can get in through the skin, by swallowing, or by injection."

"Sure. Like any poison. And how did you learn this?"

"Yesterday Lucinda was here and she mentioned that she'd seen Carlos praying in Mass with a rosary like Nicole's, and like the one her grandmother used in Brazil. And she said the beads were from some kind of plant. The ones I saw didn't look plastic or glass or even wood. They looked natural. "

"You could have told me," Pete said, but his voice was more inquisitive than scolding.

"I just found out, and I didn't realize it mattered. Lots of people pray with rosaries, right? Last night I got curious, so Mr. Google and I had a little visit. The information was pretty easy to find. And I e-mailed it all to Ivan."

Preston strolled up to them but froze for a moment when he saw Dasha, who perked up and panted happily. Preston ignored him. He groomed an urgent spot on his back before trotting to the trunk of the big maple. Dasha barked once and trotted right after him. He lay with his head on his paws, gazing at Preston. The cat raised a front paw toward Dasha.

"Uh-oh," Cam whispered. "We might be in for a little pet fight."

Instead Preston lay his paw on Dasha's ear and began to lick the dog's head. Dasha didn't budge.

Pete smiled at Cam. "Looks like acceptance has happened, at long last."

"I guess." Dasha had always accepted Preston, but the Norwegian Forest cat had remained true to his feline roots and had taken his sweet time to return the favor.

Pete took Cam's hand. "How's your mom doing? I hate that you all have to go through this."

"She went to bed early last night and I haven't seen her yet, so I don't know. It gives me the shivers to think of her in prison."

"It might not come to that. We'll see." His phone vibrated on his belt. "I gotta go, darling. I'll be in touch."

One kiss later and he was gone. She waved as he drove off, then squared her shoulders. She still had an empty stomach to fill and a farm to run. She hoped after a good night's sleep Deb would still be accepting her situation as well as Preston was accepting Dasha. Cam frowned. But her mom was unlikely to accept Dasha at all. She picked up his leash.

"Come on, Dash. Let's get you out behind the barn, okay?"

He yipped his agreement and trotted alongside her. She found another rope in the barn and tied one end to the bench and the other to his leash. That side of the barn was in shade for the morning. He could rest here until she came back out to work.

Cam headed back to the house, but inside Deb was nowhere in sight. William once again worked in the kitchen, this time pouring pancake batter and tending sausages in two skillets side by side.

"Hungry, Cam?"

"You bet." She watched as he plopped a few blueberries onto each disk of batter. "Where'd you get those blueberries?"

"Your freezer."

"Really? I had no idea." At this time of year she barely kept up with cooking and wasn't surprised her freezer held forgotten secrets. "Where's Mom?"

"Upstairs. I brought her coffee, but she said she's not hungry."

"She's still pretty upset, I'll bet."

"Wouldn't you be?" he asked.

"Of course." She poured another mug of coffee and added a splash of milk before sitting at the table to watch him cook. "How are you doing, Daddy?"

He glanced over his shoulder at her. "I've been better, sweetheart."

"I hope Mom doesn't end up in prison."

William's shoulders slumped as he let out a breath. "I hope she doesn't, too. But if so, we'll meet it together as we've met every other problem in our marriage."

Cam frowned, glad his back was to her. This wasn't the time to ask about other problems in their marriage, about which she knew zero. "So, what are your plans for today?"

"I thought I might go into town and do some snooping." He twisted and grinned at her.

"Snooping, Daddy? What do you mean?"

"Seems to me we need to get this mystery, or mysteries, solved. You don't need it on your shoulders, and your mother and I should resume our travels to . . ." His voice trailed off along with his grin.

"Now you can't go. Is that what you were thinking?" she asked gently.

"Exactly." He grimaced. "But back to the situation at hand, which needs solving no matter what."

"That's for sure. I have to run the farm. But I also have to figure out what happened with these murders. I think it's key to find out who went in and out of Nicole's house and the greenhouse the morning of her death."

Her father turned back to the stove. "I agree. We need to track the various suspects' whereabouts. Including the late Carlos's."

"Right. Hey, Daddy, maybe you could visit the houses near the greenhouse."

"I like it. Ask questions of the neighbors and all. Isn't that what they do in mystery novels?"

"But . . ." Cam frowned. "Why would they tell you any-thing?"

He flipped the pancakes one by one, then faced her. He held the spatula in the air. "I've got it. I'll be conducting a sur-vey about small-town life, with a clipboard and all. And I'll draw them into conversation. Listen, I'm a cultural anthropologist. I have decades of experience getting people to talk to me."

Cam stared at him. "Of course you do. That's a brilliant idea. I think. You're going to have to ask about the day before, too." She told him what she'd told Pete about the abrin. "Since we don't know how or when she ingested the poison, if that was how she died, the period of an alibi could be more than a day long."

"Not a problem. You leave it to Professor Flaherty."

"Do you want me to come with you?" Cam asked.

"I don't think so. People might recognize you. Nobody knows a skinny, older professor from Indiana."

"Okay." She hoped it would be okay. What if he asked the wrong person the wrong question?

"Now set the table quick, honey. Breakfast is ready."

* * *

Cam saw her father off on his crazy quest. She doubted he'd get any more information than the police had, but you never knew. He'd mocked up an ID from a fake national survey company, printed up questionnaires, and borrowed the clipboard Cam used at the farmers' market to sign up newsletter subscribers. He climbed into the rental car just before nine o'clock wearing clean khakis, a button-down shirt, a blazer, and a big smile.

"I like to feel useful," he said.

"Are you sure that ID is a good idea?" she asked

"It'll be fine."

"All right. Well, good luck. And be careful, okay?" Cam cautioned from where she sat on the steps. "If you run into any of our suspects, just call the police."

He counted them off on his fingers. "Rudin, Geneva, or Orson. Right?"

"Right." She waved as he drove off. She'd said "our suspects." Were they? What if both deaths had been accidents? Once again Cam thanked her lucky stars she'd left that rosary on the ground when she'd seen it outside the barn. Ivan had picked it up with a pencil, since the police never touched any piece of potential evidence directly.

Now what was next on her own agenda? Tomorrow was Volunteer Wednesday, and she had to be sure she was organized for that. The soil had warmed up so early this spring, she could assign a couple of helpers tomorrow to spread mulch on the herb garden and on any freshly weeded beds. Finished compost was the best mulch. It shaded the soil so weed seeds wouldn't sprout. It kept the moisture in and fed the soil beneath it when rainwater trickled through. Too bad she couldn't mulch away the pressing issue of murder as easily.

She made her way to the barn. "Dasha, want to help?" She

unhooked his leash. He followed her first to the faucet and then to the compost area. She dragged her longest hose behind her, a sprayer holding back the flow of water until she squeezed it. While air was a key component of the mix, so was enough water for the bacteria to stay alive. She examined the side-by-side bins. Bobby had turned one whole pile yesterday.

Cam set to work turning the least finished pile into the next bin. It wouldn't be ready to be used as mulch tomorrow, but certainly by the weekend. She remembered her experience finding a bracelet as well as a body part in her compost earlier in the spring and shuddered. She hoped that would never happen again. Dasha rolled back and forth on his back under the nearest tree before settling in on his side. His eyes drifted shut as she forked and watered, forked and watered. The physical work set her mind to working, too.

Surely Nicole's death hadn't been accidental. The question of who killed her seemed to come down to motive. Would Orson really have murdered his new competitor? That still seemed an extreme solution to Cam. And what about Rudin? Maybe the divorce wasn't quite final. He'd said something about Nicole being his almost-ex-wife. If he got away with murder, he would inherit everything he'd had to relinquish to her in the settlement. Or the killer could be Geneva. Maybe Nicole had also seen Geneva trying to steal narcotics as Deb had. Or worse.

And that was only Nicole's death. Carlos's was even more bewildering. One death could have been murder and one an accident. She paused with a forkful of rough compost about ready to toss over the wall into the next bin.

"Can I help?" A low voice spoke behind her.

"Ai!" Cam was so startled she threw the pitchfork into the air as she whirled. Deb stood behind her. "Mom, you scared me."

Dasha woke up and stood in one movement.

Deb held up both hands. "Sorry. I didn't mean to startle you. I just wondered if I could help you with anything." She edged away from Dasha, putting the bins between them.

"Dasha, sit," Cam told him, and he did. As her heart rate sank back to normal, she took a closer look at her mom, who appeared to have aged a year overnight. "Are you okay?" Cam asked.

"Not really, but what can I do?" Deb's shoulders sagged as much as her eyes. "I was stupid and now it's coming back to bite me in the ass, so to speak."

"Maybe it won't be so bad. I mean, Pete said he didn't know what the Florida laws are."

"We'll see." Deb stood up a little taller. "But for now, put me to work. You know, I spent my summers here with Albert and Marie, too."

"Did I know that?" Cam cocked her head.

"I'm sure I told you, but you might have forgotten. It was one of the reasons I wanted you to have that time with them, too. I have only the happiest memories of life here on the farm. Mother—your grandmother Helen—and Aunt Marie had spent their own summers here. When Marie and Albert married they bought the farm from my grandparents."

"I knew that last part. Albert told me one time."

"Both my mom and Marie wanted me to have time on the farm to get out of the city and get out of my head. I was such a bookworm as a kid."

"So was I."

"I know." Deb gazed out to the fields beyond the compost area. "And since Albert and Marie didn't have any children of their own, they got to have me for summers. It was perfect, and I loved being here."

"Your summers were just like mine, then," Cam said. "I wish you'd told me, Mom."

Her mom fixed her gaze on Cam. "I wish I'd done a lot of things different as a mother, honey. But letting you come here to the farm was one of the things I did right. You know my parents died when you were a toddler?"

"The car accident."

"Yes." Her mom continued. "Once you were old enough, Marie invited you to spend summers with her and Albert. She wanted to fill the grandparent gap in your life, and she knew your father and I needed to travel for our research."

"They definitely filled that gap." Cam smiled wistfully. "Both of them." She'd had happy summer months with her great-aunt and great-uncle, year after year. "Thank you for letting me come."

Deb swiped away a tear and cleared her throat. "Don't you have some work for me to do?"

Chapter 31

"Orson? Really?" Cam stared at William. He'd just returned from his trip into town, and now sat with her and Deb at the dining table at a few minutes before one o'clock.

"Indeed. The neighbor on the other side of the greenhouse, a keen-eyed senior citizen, said she saw a character snooping around the greenhouse that morning."

"How do you know it was Orson?" Cam asked.

"Tall guy with long arms and lots of teeth? Had to have been him. Oh, and the truck with the Fresh Page logo on the door was a sure giveaway."

"It would be," Deb said. The morning spent working physically in the fresh air had erased some of the strain from her face. Her cheeks held color again, and she had a smudge of dirt on her forehead. "What did she mean by snooping around?"

"He tried both doors and appeared to want to look in. Tried to lift the plastic at one of the corners, but it wouldn't give. According to this lady, anyway."

"That's pretty interesting." Cam drummed her fingers on the table. "Did she know what time it was?"

"Early. She said her paper had just been delivered and that it always lands on her driveway at seven-fifteen."

"Did you learn anything else?" Cam asked.

"Nothing new. Somebody across the road was complaining about the protesters, though." William smiled at Deb. " 'Organic, schmorganic' were his exact words."

"Did the senior citizen say if the police had been by to question her?" Deb asked.

"She said an officer had stopped by but that he only asked about seeing Nicole and Rudin."

"Maybe that was before I told Ivan about Orson. I need to let him know." Cam felt for her phone in her pocket.

"You do that," William said. "Here's her name and address." He slid the clipboard across the table to her. "We'll make lunch, right, Deb?"

Deb glanced at the wall clock. "It's already one o'clock? My goodness, where did the time go? I was working with Cam all morning and—"

William touched his finger to the dirt on her forehead with a tender smile. "I noticed. And I'm glad." He stood and extended his hand to his wife.

By the end of the morning, during which she'd weeded three long beds of beans and two of squash, Deb had even seemed to be less bothered by Dasha. Good, hard, mindless work had many benefits, Cam reflected. She'd left Dasha back inside the barn when her mom and she had knocked off work. She didn't want to rush the détente, but she hoped when Deb saw what a gentle dog he was, she'd get over her fears, at least with him.

Cam checked the clipboard and texted Ivan the woman's name and address.

She told my dad she saw Orson Page near Nicole's
greenhouse Thurs 7 AM. Just FYI.

She tapped Send and pocketed her phone again. Ivan was
bound to be mad at the thought of William gathering evidence. But hey, if Daddy had filled a gap in the investigation,
a gap that shouldn't have been there, Ivan should be grateful.

William and Deb clattered and murmured in the kitchen.
Cam felt antsy just sitting still, and they clearly didn't need
her help. She stood and made her way to her computer. She always sent out a reminder about Volunteer Wednesday a couple of days early and hadn't done it yet. She drafted an e-mail
to herself, blind copying her subscriber list. At the end she
added, "Don't forget Saturday is our first share pickup. If I
don't see you tomorrow, I'll see you between nine and noon
on June 3! Looking forward to it." She signed the message
and sent it out, then posted to the farm's Facebook page, too.

"Soup's on," William announced from the other room.
"Quite literally."

Cam freshened up in the bathroom and joined her parents.
Bean soup steamed in bowls at each place, and a plate of sandwiches sat in the middle of the table.

"Anybody for a beer?" Cam asked.

Deb raised her hand.

William shook his head. "I want to go for a bicycle ride after
we eat. I saw you have two in the barn."

"I do. One is DJ's, Alexandra's boyfriend. He's off on a meditation retreat and he's storing his bike here. He said it was fine
to use it, though."

"Will you go for a ride with me, Deb?" William asked.

"I think not," Deb said. "I enjoyed working in the field this
morning. I believe I'll work with Cam again this afternoon.
But you go on, dear."

Would wonders never cease? Cam smiled at her mom as she went to get two beers from the fridge. Deb not only wanted to work with Cam, she used an actual endearment with William. It looked like Cam wasn't the only Flaherty capable of change.

Twenty minutes later Cam and Deb stood outside, beer glasses in hand, and watched William ride down the driveway. He stuck up his hand and waved as he turned onto the road.

Cam turned to her mom. "Are you sure you're up for more farmwork?"

Deb drained her glass. "I didn't mean farmwork. Will you help me find Geneva?" She stood straight, expectant, looking at Cam.

"Find Geneva? Why?"

"Now that I've come clean to the authorities, I want to tell her, face-to-face, that she no longer has a hold over me." Deb's hands clenched.

"Wait a sec, Mom. I don't think that's a good idea," Cam said.

"Good or not, it's something I feel like I need to do. You in?" Deb headed for the house.

"How are you going to find her? And what if . . ." *What if what?* What if Geneva had killed Nicole and Carlos? It was possible. Or if Rudin had, and Geneva was with him. "It could be dangerous."

"I don't care. I have to do it. And I have an idea about how to find her. You in or not?"

"I guess." Better not to let her mom go off on a harebrained, risky adventure alone. And hopefully they wouldn't even be able to find out where Geneva and Rudin were staying.

Inside, Deb brought her iPad, a pad of paper, and a pen to the table, and sat. "They said they were in an Airbnb, right? What are likely towns to look in?"

"If they wanted to be near the water, I'd say Salisbury, Newburyport, or Newbury. Plum Island has land in both those last two towns. If they wanted to window-shop and go to restaurants, then just Newburyport. But let me call Sim, see if Rudin ever picked up his car. They might have already left for Florida."

Deb glanced up with a frown. "Do you think the police would let them after yesterday?"

"I don't think the police can make them stay here unless they arrest them, same as with you. But maybe Sim talked to Rudin and learned where he's staying. Or I could ask Pete."

"Please don't do that. He'd want to know why you're asking. I have the feeling he wouldn't exactly approve of my plan."

With good reason. "I have the feeling you're right. Okay, Sim it is." Cam tapped the number for SK Foreign Auto. "Hey," she said when her friend picked up.

"Sup, Cam? Your truck okay?"

"It's fine. Loved seeing you in the parade yesterday, by the way. But I'm calling to see if you ever heard from Rudin about his car. We're trying to figure out where he's staying."

Sim swore. "I've left him three messages. It's all ready, he just needs to come pick it up. But he hasn't replied to a single one."

"I wonder why."

"Same here. I'd like to get it off the lot. It's a luxury model, and I have to keep parking it inside at night. It's a pain in the ass."

"I'll bet. And you didn't ask for his local residence when he left it?"

"I did, but he said he hadn't found a place to stay yet. Sorry, friend."

Cam thanked her and disconnected. She shook her head at

her mom. "No information. Except that Rudin isn't returning Sim's calls about his car."

"Maybe he's in jail," Deb said. "Maybe they had enough to arrest him for Carlos's murder."

Cam narrowed her eyes. "I wonder." She sat at her desk. "I'm going to look for news on him. You keep working on the Airbnbs." She searched for online news.

A couple of minutes later, from behind her Cam heard Deb say, "Yes. I'm looking for my brother, Rudin Brunelle. I'm afraid we've had a death in the family and he's not answering his calls. I wondered if you could tell me if he's staying in your apartment. Only because it's an emergency, of course."

Cam smiled. It was a good ruse.

"No? All right. Thank you very much for your time."

Twisting in her chair, Cam caught her mom's gaze. "Nice."

"It's worth a stab." Deb checked the iPad and tapped another number into her phone.

On the laptop, the only news Cam could find was a brief notice about the death the day before. "An area man was found dead in a Westbury residence Monday," the lede read. "Police have not revealed the cause of death but are questioning a couple visiting from out of town who have ties to the deceased. The identity of the deceased is being withheld pending notification of the family."

That was pretty innocuous. Unless they were still questioning Rudin and Geneva, possibly in separate jail cells. Cam decided to poke around for more information about Rudin. She searched, followed up leads, linking his name and Nicole's, until she hit pay dirt. He'd filed for bankruptcy last month. The article mentioned something about failed real estate deals. That was pretty common in Florida, she thought. Developers bought up land cheap and built cheap houses, and then couldn't sell them. But what was a pharmacologist doing developing real estate? Unless he'd lost his job and needed the money, maybe. She sat back, thinking. Bobby had said Rudin bought out Nicole's share in their Florida home. Rudin could have been expecting to make back that money on his other deals but they'd fallen through.

With her success at learning a bit more about Rudin, Cam dove into digging up more information about Geneva Flores, too. It was a fairly unusual name. She had a Facebook page but didn't seem to spend much time posting or interacting on the social media site. Geneva was tagged in a few pictures that looked like family birthday parties, and it was a big family of people with the same dark hair as Geneva. Cam went back to Google and dug until she saw pictures of Geneva as a ballroom dancer in a stunning red gown cut way up her thigh. She'd apparently won competitions for Latin dancing. One picture of Geneva and her tuxedoed dance partner—definitely not Rudin—was staged in a lush tropical garden.

An idea went *sproing!* in Cam's brain. She could almost hear it. She'd Googled Rudin the other day. He was a pharmacologist. In tropical Florida. Where rosary peas grew. Cam had found the tourniquet. Nicole was a heroin user, and maybe Geneva was, too.

What if Rudin had injected Nicole with abrin the morning she died but she thought it was heroin? And if she regularly injected, the autopsy wouldn't notice one more needle site. If the divorce wasn't yet final, as Nicole's husband Rudin would now own the house and property in West Newbury. He must have planned to sell them and pay off his debts.

Both Ivan and Pete now knew about the abrin. All they needed was something to connect Rudin with the poison, and they might have found it in a search of the house. Like his prints or DNA on drug paraphernalia or something else. So maybe Rudin was in jail and that's why he wasn't returning his calls. That would be a blessing. At least he wouldn't be out in the world poisoning others. And that would mean Orson's activities were innocent. She hoped.

"Only because it's an emergency," Deb was saying.

Cam stood, then paced the length of the living room and back. She plopped back in the desk chair again, drained her beer, and returned to the CDC site on abrin, leaning in to read it. Yes. If the poison was injected the toxic effects would act much faster than if it was ingested or absorbed through the skin. That made sense. Anything that went directly into the bloodstream had to act more quickly.

"Really?" Deb said into her phone. "Thanks so much. I appreciate it. No, please don't tell him. It's the kind of thing I have to do face-to-face. I'll stop by and leave him a note if he's not there." She nodded, listening. "I see. Thank you." She disconnected.

Cam hurried to the table. "You actually found him?"

Deb grinned. "And on only the fifth call." She checked the iPad. "The place is off of Northern Boulevard. On the Basin, the woman said, whatever that means."

"It's a tidal inlet between the two branches of land that form the top of Plum Island. They actually look like lobster claws. People paddle kayaks and canoes in the Basin because there aren't any waves and the water is quiet."

"Sounds nice. The owner said the house is behind a restaurant called Mad Martha's."

"I know exactly where it is." Cam and Ruth had eaten several delicious meals at the tiny restaurant after walking the Plum Island beach.

"I thought Airbnb offered rooms in people's houses," Deb

said, standing. "But Rudin rented an entire house. The owner said she lives somewhere else."

"So it's just like a regular short-term beach rental. Interesting."

"You coming?" Cam's mom took a step toward the door.

"Right now? Geneva might not even be there." Cam wasn't sure the visit was such a good idea. What if Rudin wasn't in jail but was at the house? What if he and Geneva were a team of killers?

"Right now. I want to get this over with."

"I don't think it's a good idea, Mom." In fact, it was a terrible idea. Why had she agreed to help her mom earlier?

"You can come or not come. I'm leaving now."

Cam swore. "It could be dangerous. Like really dangerous."

Deb picked up her purse from the shelf where she'd left it and took the rental car keys off the hook.

"Wait!" Cam touched her mom's arm. "Wait. I'll come with you." She couldn't let her go alone. Cam would send Pete a text to let him know the plan. And at least it was two o'clock and broad daylight. "But Daddy doesn't have a key to the house," Cam said. "I'm not leaving it unlocked. And I'm in my work clothes. As are you." She gestured at her grimy shorts and work boots.

Deb made an exasperated sound. "Run and get changed, then. I will, too. We can leave William a key under the mat and text him about it."

Chapter 32

A light shower had blown in as Cam drove along the cause-way toward the long barrier island. Salt marshes stretched out on either side of the road. She'd insisted on driving. She glanced at her mom in the truck's passenger seat. Deb didn't appear to be taking in the swooping purple martins feeding on bugs or the elegant, long-necked great blue heron slowly stalk-ing its fishy prey in a salt pool.

"Are you nervous?" Cam asked as they passed the oft-painted, oft-photographed pink Foursquare house where it sat alone in the marsh on the right. The road sloped up and over the bridge before heading down toward Plum Island ahead. Cam rolled down her window to inhale the salty, vegetative smell of the marsh. The wipers on low lazily cleared the wind-shield, and the few drops that blew in brought a fresh wel-come to the seaside.

"A little."

Cam's phone let out short beeps indicating it was out of bars. She cursed under her breath. She'd gone to a cheaper cell carrier recently to save money, but the coverage wasn't as good as some of the major networks. And one consequence was either paying roaming charges or having no connection at times like this. Before they left the farm she'd sent Pete a text with the address of the house and their plan, just in case anything blew up. But now she wouldn't be able to tell if he responded, and she doubted he had Deb's cell number. If she'd even brought it.

"Mom, do you have your phone?"

Deb held up her cell without speaking.

A large bird, mostly white from underneath but with black elbows and long, dark feather fingers, soared above them across the road from south to north. A helpless fish wriggled in the iron grip of its enormous talons. "Look, an osprey." Cam pointed. "They're incredible. Five-foot wingspan." The bird flapped its wings with a few powerful strokes. It landed on a nesting platform that rested about fifteen feet above the marsh on a thick pole.

Deb shook her head fast, nostrils flaring. "I saw those in Florida," she whispered. "I don't want to be reminded of that place."

Cam couldn't blame her. Just because they were on this ridiculous caper didn't mean the situation with her mom's hit-and-run had gone away.

Cam drove straight through a quarter mile of small businesses and homes until the road appeared to end at a tiny town parking lot. She could spy the Atlantic just beyond the dunes. She glanced at Deb but decided to postpone pointing out any more scenic views. Turning left, she drove slowly up Northern Boulevard until she reached the small building housing Mad Martha's.

"What's the side street?" Cam asked.

Deb checked the map on her phone. She glanced up and pointed. "This one. Turn left. Now."

Cam yanked the wheel, counting her blessings that nobody

had been tailgating her. The narrow street petered out almost immediately into a driveway paved with broken shells that were half covered with drifted sand. A three-story house in a silvered natural siding loomed on the left. The first floor was primarily pillars supporting a covered but empty parking area, with a small, closed-in area under the base of the house. Outdoor steps led up to a deck walkway that wrapped around to the back of the house. Only one house sat between this one and the quiet Basin beyond. She stopped the truck and pulled up the parking brake as the rain shower eased to nothing.

"No red car," her mom said.

"So either Geneva is in the house alone or nobody's on the premises. Did you bring the note?"

Deb nodded. "It's in my bag. But I don't think I'll leave it if she isn't here. It was true what I told the landlady. This isn't something I want to leave a message about." Her eyes had a tense set to them as she shoved open her door.

Cam turned off the ignition and climbed out, too. The thin cry of a gull sitting on the roof of a neighboring house mixed with the drone of a small plane overhead. The sun squinted through the moving clouds, blinked dim, and shone forth again. The high tide in the Basin sparkled in the midafternoon light from the west.

Deb took in a breath and squared her shoulders. "Let's do it." She climbed the steep steps to the main level and pressed the bell next to the door at the top.

Cam heard a peal inside from where she stood two steps down. No footsteps followed it, though, and no one pulled open the door. Deb knocked four times in quick succession. She gazed at the deck to her right.

"I bet it has a back door and a back deck. Or maybe she's down at that little beach." Deb gestured toward the water beyond the second house, where Cam could just make out a strip of sand.

"If she's on a back deck, don't you think she would have heard the bell? Let's go, Mom. We can find her later." Cam touched her mother's elbow.

Deb whirled to face Cam. "Maybe you don't understand how important this is to me." Her harsh whisper stung. "You can wait here. Or in the truck. I'm going around to the back, and if she's not there I'm going down to the beach." She swallowed. "I need to do this."

"Okay," Cam said, but it was against her better judgment. "I'm right behind you."

Cam followed Deb to where the deck turned the corner. Sure enough, the walkway widened to a porch, a back door, and another steep set of steps leading down. The deck was even higher off the ground here because the ground sloped away from the house toward the Basin. On the porch, four chairs were arrayed around a glass-topped table with a furled green umbrella. Thyme, rosemary, and oregano grew in several large earthenware pots. But no Geneva. Deb exchanged a look with Cam. She put her foot on the first step of the back stairs.

"Well, look who's here." Geneva appeared at the bottom of the stairway. A bright yellow sleeveless top showed off both her tanned arms and her pressed white Capris. Her stormy expression, curled lip and all, wasn't as pleasant as her outfit. "The teller of tales herself. You're ruined, Deb. I assume you know that."

Chapter 33

What? Where had Geneva appeared from? She must have
been out for a walk. Or had she hid when she heard Cam
and Deb arrive?

Geneva started up the steps, moving with a dancer's grace.
"Damn cops had me at the station again this morning, thanks
to you." She kept coming, her jeweled flip-flops slapping
against her heels.

Deb backed up to the deck. Cam took her mom's hand and
squeezed it.

Deb stood tall. "I had to come clean. I'll deal with my past,
and I came here to tell you that. What about you? Still using?"
She linked her arm through Cam's, effectively blocking the
top of the stairs.

"What I do is none of your business. Or your nosy daughter's."
Geneva glared at Cam from two steps down. "In cozy with your
little cop boyfriend? Feeding him stories?" She hitched a flashy
black and white handbag farther up on her left shoulder. "Both
of you have been."

"Whoa," Cam said. "Back off, Geneva. We haven't been feeding Detective Pappas anything." One more white lie. *Oh well.*

"Not what I heard." Geneva tossed her ponytail onto her back. She narrowed her eyes at them.

"Why do you care, anyway?" Cam's mom asked. "If you didn't do anything wrong, you don't have anything to worry about, do you?"

Geneva slid her right hand into her bag. "No, I don't have anything to worry about." She drew out a small gun with pink accents. She pointed it with both hands at Deb's chest.

Deb gasped. Cam swore under her breath. The day went silent except for the thud of her heart in her throat.

"I've had it with both of you," Geneva spat. "With the whole stinking state. All this stupid intrigue. That dumb Brazilian dying on us. Rudin dragging me up here from Florida with his little project." She drew out and emphasized the last word.

"What project was that?" Cam asked, as if she didn't already know the project was to kill Nicole.

"Oh, no, you don't. You're not pulling that trope of getting a bad guy to confess at the end of the book so the heroine can stall for time. I need you to get in the house," Geneva demanded. "Now." She gestured with the gun.

Cam scanned behind Geneva. Despite it being two-thirty on a sunny day, no one was out. The window shades were drawn in the house beyond, and their deck faced the Basin, too. Another short street ran beyond this house to the left, but nobody pushed a stroller or carried a kayak. The nearest yard was empty of playing children, and the rocking chair on a front porch was unoccupied. She and her mom weren't going to get any help from strangers.

"What's it going to solve if you shoot us?" Deb asked. Her voice quavered, but she kept her chin up.

Cam squeezed her mom's arm and disentangled her own. She and Deb were going to need all the mobility they had.

"Who said I'm shooting you?" Geneva used a deadly sweet

tone. "This is just my favorite persuasive device. Now go." She pushed her gun-holding hand toward them.

Cam really, really didn't want to turn her back on the weapon-holding Geneva. She was only a yard away from them. Cam wasn't about to be locked in a deserted beach house, either.

Wheels crunched on the shells in the driveway and a horn tooted. *Let that be Pete.* Cam cast a quick glance down, and her heart sank to its knees. Rudin sat behind the wheel of the open red convertible, staring at them. And blocking Cam's truck. Geneva glanced at him, too.

In one move Cam grabbed the post of the deck with her right hand. With a swipe of her left hand she whacked the gun out of Geneva's hand. It clattered down the steps.

"Hey!" Geneva watched her weapon slide away.

Cam leaned back, keeping her hand gripping the post. She delivered a flat-footed kick to Geneva's chest, pushing as she struck.

Geneva cried out. She crashed onto her back and fell down the wet steps backward. Gravity pulled her sliding and bumping off the balusters. She tried to grab for one but missed. When she hit the ground, her head clunked on the concrete pad. Her body crumpled. She fell silent.

Deb stared at Cam. "Now what?" she whispered.

"Let's go." Cam pointed at the front stairs.

Deb took one step and tripped, falling to her knees. Cam swore, extending her hand to her mom. Deb scrambled to her feet but tripped again.

Rudin yelled a curse at Cam as he jumped out of the car and ran to Geneva. He knelt at her head. "Gennie, darling! Wake up," he urged. He pressed his fingers to her neck. A moment later he looked up at them, horror widening his eyes. "What did you do to her?" He scrambled for the gun. It had fallen on the ground to the side of the steps. He slipped in the sand and fell to his knees before he could grab it.

Cam grabbed a heavy earthenware flowerpot in both hands. She leaned over the railing and heaved it. She aimed at Rudin's head, down where he sprawled on hands and knees. The pot missed its target. Instead it crashed and cracked on his hand as it reached for the gun. He cried out.

"Front stairs," Cam said, pulling Deb along. They clattered down. "Convertible." Cam had bet on Rudin having left the car running because he'd leaped out so quickly. But it was quiet. He must have turned it off. She swore and narrowed her eyes at her truck. She'd never be able to back out around the red car. "Run!"

She and Deb sprinted up the driveway for Northern Boulevard. They'd almost reached Mad Martha's when a crack sounded. Deb took two more staggering steps and fell forward, crashing onto her right shoulder.

"Mom!"

Chapter 34

Deb lay on her right side on the ground, her eyes squeezed shut, her face the color of sand, her skin damp with sweat. Cam squatted. "Mommy," she pleaded in a shrill whisper. "Look at me." Cam's heart was going to explode in a minute.

Another shot zinged by and thudded into the back wall of the restaurant. Deb's eyes flew open, staring at Cam.

"We have to get out of here," Cam's voice rasped, urging. "At least around the corner of the building. Where were you hit?"

"My shoulder." Deb extended her left hand. "Help me up."

Cam glanced behind her. She couldn't see Rudin. "Okay, but stay low." She took a deep breath. She had to be strong for Mom. She leaned back and pulled her mom up to a squatting position, too. "Ready?"

Deb gave a faint nod. Cam kept hold of her hand as they scurried forward a few yards and around the corner of the restaurant to the front. Mad Martha's was open only for breakfast and lunch, but Cam beat on the door, anyway. Maybe someone was inside cleaning up. Nobody answered. Deb sank to sitting, her back against the door. She grabbed her right shoulder with her left hand as she slumped, chin on chest. Cam panted, her throat thick, her mouth dry. She had to get help.

As a siren keened in the distance, a gray car approached from the south. Cam ran to the street and waved her arms.

A silver-haired man opened the door of the house across the street. "Do you need help?"

"Yes!" Cam shouted. "Call nine-one-one. My mom's been shot and there's a guy with a gun back there. And another woman is hurt."

The man pulled a phone out of his pocket and tapped it. The car came closer. A sob escaped Cam's lips when she saw it was Pete's old Saab. With a burst of speed it crossed over and pulled to a screeching stop in front of Cam.

"Cam," Pete called as he jumped out. He hurried toward her. "Are you all right?" His face was drawn with worry.

The siren grew louder. Cam nodded fast. "Mom was shot." She pointed to Deb. "Rudin's behind us somewhere with a gun. I pushed Geneva down the stairs when she threatened us."

His expression turned to frustration tinged with anger. "I can't believe you," he muttered, even as he pulled out his phone, tapped one key, and tersely outlined the situation. "Armed suspect. Two women critically injured. At Mad Martha's on Plum Island. Northern Boulevard." He disconnected and stared at Cam.

"I'm sorry," Cam said. "Mom was determined to go on her own, and I couldn't let her do that. At least I told you where we were going."

"One team is already on the way. More are coming. Help me get your mom into my car. Then both of you are out of here. I mean it."

"Fine by me."

Pete hurried to Deb, Cam at his heels. Pete squatted in front of Deb, whose good hand had fallen into her lap. "Ma'am, I need you to . . ." When she didn't open her eyes, he peered at her, gently patting her cheek. He felt her neck and pushed to standing. "She's unconscious."

"But she's alive, isn't she?"

"Yes. Damn it, Cam, now you're both in danger with a live shooter in the vicinity. We'll have to wait to move her until an ambulance gets here."

A Newbury squad car roared up. Two officers leaped out.

"You stay right here with her," Pete ordered Cam. "Please."

"Okay." Cam sat next to Deb. She took her mom's left hand in hers and stroked it. "You're going to be all right, Mom," she murmured over and over. "Everything's going to be all right." Cam's throat was thick and her hand shook. She felt as if she was about to dissolve into tears, too, but she couldn't let herself. That wouldn't help anything, particularly not her mother.

Pete strode to the officers and conferred with them in voices too low for Cam to hear. Two other cruisers arrived, sirens blaring, lights strobing. Pete hurried back to Cam and squatted in front of her.

"Tell me about the gun. And how this all happened, but as fast as you can."

"Nobody seemed to be home and their car wasn't there. We were on the second-floor deck. Geneva appeared from somewhere and started coming up the steep back steps. She pulled a small gun out of her purse."

"Small like this, or this?" Pete placed his palms about eight inches apart, then six.

"The second. Rudin drove in and blocked my truck. When

Geneva looked at him, I whacked the gun out of her hand and kicked her down the stairs, which were wet and slippery."

"You did?" His eyes flew wide open.

"Yep. Her head hit the ground pretty hard. She didn't move after she landed."

"Does Rudin have a weapon, too?"

"Not that I saw. He rushed over to Geneva. He acted like she might have already been dead. Then he tried to grab her gun. I dropped a heavy flowerpot from the deck onto his hand. Mom and I ran for the street. That's when he shot her."

"Any more shots?"

"One more, into the back of the restaurant. No more after that."

An officer let a German shepherd out of the back of police SUV marked CANINE UNIT. He held the leashed dog close to his side, but Cam was briefly glad her mother was unconscious. Having her fear of dogs rise up again would be too much.

"Too many possibilities." Pete frowned. "Stay right here until the ambulance arrives."

He stood and rejoined the group of officers, which now included Ivan and Ruth. Ruth wore a bulky black vest and a helmet, making her already imposing figure even more so. Ivan was similarly outfitted.

At some sign from Pete, a couple of officers headed for the short street on the other side of Mad Martha's. Ruth and another officer pulled out weapons and moved carefully toward the rental house, sticking close to the restaurant until they vanished around the side. The canine officer followed. Pete pulled a vest and helmet out of his car and secured them. He drew his own gun and followed Ruth. Cam sent him and Ruth a silent message to be careful, to come back alive.

Two officers moved cruisers with their lights flashing to block off the road in either direction. Ivan followed Pete carrying a bullhorn. A moment later his amplified voice announced, "Rudin Brunelle, this is the police. Lay down any weapon and come out with your hands on your head. I repeat, come out now with your hands on your head."

Chapter 35

Cam glanced at her phone one more time. It was six o'clock and still no message from Pete. She'd ridden in the Newbury Fire and Rescue vehicle carrying her mom off the island to the hospital in Newburyport. A very nice nurse had let her sit in the ER bay until they'd wheeled Deb away to surgery. Her mom, in a hospital gown, was hooked up to an IV and various monitors. She'd remained pale. And she hadn't woken up. One nurse had told Cam not to worry, but how could she help it? And where was her father? She'd called him as soon as she reached the hospital. That had been more than an hour ago and he'd said he'd come right over.

Cam paced from one side of the hospital's surgical waiting room to the other. The room was blessedly empty. Rain beat against the second-floor windows, and wind stirred the tops of the trees outside.

As soon as she walked in she'd pressed the Off button on the television mounted on the wall. The last thing she needed was the blare of inane reporters. *Wait*. It was six now. Maybe she could catch the local news. She pressed the On button and waited through a couple of national stories and a few commercials. A well-known Boston reporter appeared on-screen, an older woman with perfectly styled streaked silver hair and a red jacket.

"Breaking news from Plum Island this afternoon," the reporter announced in a dramatic voice. "Police have apprehended a Miami, Florida, couple suspected in a recent North Shore murder. The female, Geneva Flores, is in critical condition from an injury sustained in the event. She is under police watch at the local hospital, and the male, Rudin Brunelle, is in police custody."

The event. The event of Cam kicking Geneva down the stairs. She shuddered, remembering the sound of Geneva's head hitting the pavement at the foot of the steps, Rudin's cry when the heavy pot hit his hand, the shot hitting her mom. Cam's efforts to hurt Geneva and Rudin had been in self-defense, sure, but . . .

Footage of a motionless Geneva bundled on a wheeled stretcher flashed on the screen. It was followed by Ruth protecting a handcuffed Rudin's head as she ushered him into the back seat of a cruiser. The reporter went on. "The Coast Guard assisted with a dramatic capture in the Plum Island Basin, where Brunelle attempted to escape by kayak this afternoon."

Cam's eyes flew wide open. *By kayak.*

"No officers were injured in the apprehension. Westbury farmer Cameron Flaherty is being lauded for bravery in the capture, and her mother, Professor Flaherty, is in serious condition from a gunshot wound. Now for the weather."

Cam punched the television Off button again and let out a long breath, not realizing she'd even been holding it. All the possibilities she'd imagined since leaving the island had been circulating in her thoughts. But Rudin hadn't engaged in a shoot-out at the house. He hadn't holed up inside with a cache of weapons. He hadn't taken his own life. Cam hadn't killed

Geneva. And the best part: No officers were injured. Not Pete, not Ruth, not even the difficult Ivan. But she wished her own name had stayed out of the story. She'd had only one possibility: removing the threat of Geneva and her gun. It wasn't particularly brave to want to save your own mother's life, especially when she and Mom had gotten themselves into the whole mess in the first place. The brave ones were the law enforcement professionals.

Cam whirled when the door opened, hoping to see someone in scrubs telling her Deb had come through surgery with flying colors. Instead, William walked toward her. His wet hair clung to his head, and a raindrop hung from the end of his nose.

"Daddy." She rested her face on his chest and wrapped her arms around his waist. She didn't care that his jacket was wet. He again flapped his hands against her back before they quieted into a hug.

He pushed back and patted her shoulder, peering into her face. "No news about your mom?"

Cam shook her head. "No. Come sit down." She perched on a chair that allowed a view of the soaked leafy courtyard. William sat at a right angle to her, but close.

"Sorry it took me so long," he said. "It started raining in earnest, and I wanted to get the hens in. Thought we might be here for a while."

"Thanks. Good idea."

"And I got lost looking for the hospital."

Cam smiled. Her father had always been hopeless at navigation. "It's okay."

"Brought us some sandwiches, in case you were hungry." He set a paper bag on the table and joined her in the row of chairs facing the door.

Cam loved her father dearly, but emotional displays were

not his thing. His wife had been shot and was in surgery, and what did he do? Get the chickens in and make sandwiches. Or maybe that *was* an emotional display. It was a caretaking one, at any rate.

"How is she?" he asked. "Any word about her status?"

Cam's smile slid away. "Not yet." Outside the interior glass wall an orderly pushed a prone patient on a gurney, almost running, while a woman in scrubs strode alongside steering the foot of the bed.

"So you and your mother ran into some trouble, it seems." He patted her hand.

"Yeah." The whole story poured out of Cam. She couldn't help herself reliving the terror of those few minutes this afternoon. "I'm so sorry, Daddy. I told her it was too dangerous, but she was determined to find Geneva. I thought it was better for her not to go alone. And I'm glad I was there."

"Me too. So Deb was shot in the shoulder. By Brunelle?" William asked.

"Yes. With Geneva's gun. Mom's in surgery now because they had to go in and take out the bullet." She brought her hand to her mouth as she choked up. Hot tears stung her eyes.

"What is it, honey?"

"Mom passed out a little while after she was hit. And she hadn't woken up before they took her into surgery. I'm worried."

"Now, now." He took her hand in his. "It'll be all right. She's a tough cookie. Everything's going to be all right."

Cam stared at him as he repeated what she herself had told her mom two hours before. She sniffed. "I just heard some good news on the TV. No officers were hurt, and the Coast Guard captured Rudin."

"Excellent. Glad to hear it. Had he stolen a power boat?"

"No, a kayak."

"Why do I think the man was a little lacking in wits?" William ventured a smile.

Now a giggle bubbled up where a sob had earlier. "Not exactly a high-speed getaway vehicle, is it?" Cam smiled back at him.

The door swung open again, and this time it was a petite woman in turquoise scrubs. A white surgical mask hung around her neck, and her name tag included the letters MD. "Cameron Flaherty?" she asked after introducing herself as Deb's surgeon.

"Yes." Cam stood in a hurry, as did William. "This is my father, William Flaherty."

"Nice to meet you, sir. I'm happy to report that Debra is out of surgery. She did well. We expect her to make a full recovery after the wound heals. She might need a bit of rotator cuff repair at a later date, but the shoulder joint should be functional."

"We're pleased to hear it," William said. "Aren't we, Cam?"

"Thank you, Doctor." Cam swallowed. "Thank you."

"When can we see her?" Cam's father asked.

"She's in the recovery area. Someone will come and get you when she's been moved to postsurgical care. We'll keep her overnight for observation, but as long as her vitals continue strong, she should be able to go home tomorrow."

William extended his hand, and the doctor shook it. She cocked her head at Cam. "Heard you were pretty brave this afternoon, Ms. Flaherty."

"You did?" Cam asked, cringing. She'd let her mother do a foolhardy thing and had gone along with it. It wasn't exactly courageous to try to rescue them both.

"We have another patient in here under police watch," the doctor said. "Word spreads."

"Actually, it was all the law enforcement officers who put

themselves at risk, including the Coast Guard," Cam said. "They were the brave ones."

"Is Geneva going to survive?" Cam's father asked.

"I believe so. I'm off now to set a few of her broken bones so she can stand trial. Thank you for your courage." She extended hand to Cam.

Cam clasped the surgeon's small hand and marveled at her strong grip. "Believe me, it was desperation more than courage. I wasn't about to let anybody shoot my mother."

William and Cam ate their sandwiches while they waited. They finally got the call to sit with a bandaged and groggy but conscious Deb. She opened her eyes and gave them a ghost of a smile, then closed her eyes again. Nurses came and went, checking on Deb's IV and her responses. She gradually grew more alert, but winced when she moved. When she seemed fully awake, William stood and stroked her hand.

"You made it, hon. And we're right here."

Cam's mom looked from William to Cam and back. She opened her mouth to speak, but William put a finger to his lips.

"You just rest now," he murmured.

Deb nodded but beckoned ever so slightly with one finger to Cam. William stood back so Cam could approach the bedside.

"Thank you, sweetie," Deb whispered. "Thank you."

Cam's throat thickened, but she swallowed it down. "I'm just glad you're alive." She stroked her mom's forehead, smoothing her hair back off the cool, silky skin. The lines in Deb's brow smoothed under Cam's touch.

She and her dad settled Deb into her hospital room at around eight-thirty, and the nurse assured them she wasn't in any danger. After the nurse added that William would be a better help to Deb tomorrow if he went home and got some sleep, William drove Cam back to the farm. She let Dasha into the house and fed both him and Preston. William went up to bed after kissing Cam good night on the forehead.

"Told you everything was going to be all right, now, didn't I?" he'd asked, smiling.

"You sure did. Good night."

Now she sat swirling whiskey in her glass, listening to the rain outside, replaying the day, every one of the last five days. Finding Nicole. The questions about Carlos. Seeing Jake again. The business with her mom, the long-ago dog incident, and what happened in Florida. Geneva and Rudin.

Preston jumped up on the back of the couch and purred like a fluffy, well-oiled motor. So many things Cam still didn't know. How had Carlos died? Had Rudin or Geneva injected Nicole with abrin, or had she been killed with another method? Had Cam's surmising about Rudin's bankruptcy been correct?

An incoming text beeped, interrupting her thoughts. She checked to see Ellie's ID.

Cam u OK? Yr mom? Heard about capture on news. OMG.

Cam texted back. Yes. Fine. My mom's going to be okay, too.

Awsm. Thx. XOXO. Frm Vince 2.

Cam tapped out, Thank him from me. As soon as she sent that, a different text came in even as Cam heard knocking. Pete wrote I'm at the door and followed the letters with a winking smiley face.

She rose to let him in. He gave her a hearty kiss before rubbing an eager Dasha's head. Pete held out his arms to her, smelling of fresh rain. Their silent embrace lasted what seemed like an hour.

"I'm sorry," she mumbled into his shirt.

He pushed back. "What's that?"

Cam shrunk into her shoulders for a second. She straightened. "I said I'm sorry. It was foolish to let my mom go to the island to confront Geneva."

He took her face in both his hands. "You're loyal and caring. And wicked brave. And I love you for it."

"And foolish, right?"

He snorted. "Right."

"Come tell me about the dramatic capture." She took his hand and led him into the living room. "You're off duty, I hope?"

"At last. I'd love some of what you're having." He sank onto the couch, his legs sprawled. Preston stayed put on the back of the couch, a true indication he'd accepted Pete into his life.

Cam brought a glass of bourbon for him, as well as the bottle, which she set on an end table. "So you had to call the Coast Guard?"

"It wasn't actually such a bad move on Rudin Brunelle's part. He could have slid into any number of small beaches around the Basin. Walked off and phoned a cab to take him to the airport before we even got the alarm up. But a woman in a neighboring house noticed him stealing her bright yellow kayak, and she called it in. It didn't take long for the Coast Guard cutter to round him up." Pete clinked his glass with Cam's and took a sip. Dasha padded in and sat at Pete's feet.

"The same doctor who took the bullet out of my mom was going to be setting Geneva's bones next, she told me," Cam said. "I'm really glad I didn't kill Geneva."

"You did what you had to do."

"I guess." She ran her finger along the side of her glass. "Pete, when Rudin reached Geneva at the bottom of the stairs, he said,

'Not again!' Mom talked about Nicole's accident, falling down a flight of stairs. I wonder if that's what he meant. So maybe Nicole's was an accident after all."

"Possible."

"Or . . . remember I told you what Bobby said? That Rudin had contacted him and said he'd tried to talk Nicole out of the divorce. So maybe on Plum Island he thought he'd lost another woman in his life."

Pete laughed, but it didn't hold any humor. "He's lost her from his life now, for sure. They don't let couples stay together in prison."

"So were you and Ivan on Rudin's trail?" Cam asked.

"We were close. The actual evidence was pretty thin, though, and the DNA testing was taking forever. Your tip about the abrin was spot on. Once the lab knew to test for that, they easily found it in Nicole's system. The working hypothesis is that Brunelle injected her with powdered abrin in solution."

"Powdered from grinding up the rosary peas?"

"Yes, unless he brought some from Florida and the missing beads were a coincidence." Pete held up his glass and swirled the alcohol, watching it. "He probably injected it the day before she died, or maybe that morning."

"But you'll need to find the syringe or whatever."

"We will. We found a witness who says he saw Brunelle toss something in the Dumpster behind the Food Mart. Ivan has guys going through it right now under floodlights. Kind of stupid. If Brunelle had discarded it in the ocean, we'd never find it."

"Anybody who commits murder has to be a certain level of stupid, in my view," she said, shaking her head. "Right? From what I've seen, even if they think they have it all worked out, they always slip up somewhere along the line."

"That's certainly the hope of my department," Pete agreed.

"Did you figure out how Carlos died?" Cam asked.

"That one looks like an actual heart attack. The pathologist is going to look closely for drugs, especially tropical ones, but so far it's being called natural causes."

"I wonder what he was doing at the house on the day of the parade," Cam said.

"Once again, it could be as simple as he was upset about Nicole's death and he wanted to confront Brunelle."

"Who probably isn't talking."

"No, he isn't." Pete sipped his drink and set it down. "We'll get the whole story out of him, though. Sooner or later."

"When Geneva was aiming her gun at us, she said something about Rudin dragging her up here for his project. I assume that meant killing Nicole."

"Yes. She's definitely an accessory to the murder. I imagine we'll be able to persuade her to give us some details about Brunelle in exchange for a reduced sentence."

"I tried to get her to tell me, but she refused." Cam savored her whiskey. "I read online Rudin had filed for bankruptcy. And Bobby said he thought the divorce might not have been final. Is that why Rudin killed Nicole, to get his divorce settlement back?"

"Probably. Some version of that." Pete twisted to look at her. "So where'd you get your moves, disarming her in more ways than one?"

"It just popped into my head. I didn't exactly have time to plan my moves. I had the height advantage. The stairs were slippery from the rain. And she looked away from us when Rudin drove in." Cam swallowed. "It seemed like the only thing I could do was knock the gun out of her hand and get her away from us. It worked a little better than I thought it would." She yawned, covering her mouth. "Excuse me."

"I know I'm not very interesting." Pete laughed. "How about I fix that by offering you something not quite so boring?" He drained his whiskey and stood, holding out his hand to her.

She took it and rose, as her heart rate rose, too. "I thought you'd never ask."

Chapter 36

By nine-thirty the next morning, Volunteer Wednesday was going strong. The rain had again blown through overnight, and now the soil was a happy and thirst-slaked deep brown.

After a very satisfying night of intimacy and hours of spooned sleep, Pete had said he was taking a personal day. He'd gone off with Dasha for a long walk but said he'd be back to help with whatever farm chore Cam wanted to assign him.

William had gathered eggs and communed with the hens earlier before heading out for the hospital. He carried a map Cam drew for him of the route because she wasn't sure he could manage the GPS on a phone. Her dad's smarts lay in other areas than finding his way around.

Now Felicity was watering in the hoophouse. Lucinda had showed up, saying she'd taken the morning off work so she could help. Cam assigned her to harvest more asparagus along with Sue Biellik. Cam was in the barn when two people on bicycles appeared backlit in the wide-open doorway.

"Look who I found!" Alexandra called. The two dropped their bikes and walked toward Cam hand in hand.

"DJ!" Cam exclaimed. "How great to see you."

Dasha ran up and barked in a friendly way.

DJ rubbed Dasha's head. The young man's formerly shoulder-length hair was now a light brown half-inch long all over his head. "You too, Cam," he said, leaning in for a hug. "Heard you had some excitement. But it's all good now?"

"It is. And how was the retreat?"

"Most excellent."

"Doesn't he just seem so calm?" Alexandra asked, her eyes shining.

"He always seemed calm to me," Cam said.

"So what can we do?" DJ asked.

"Weed the cornfield? But really carefully so we don't disturb their baby roots."

"How about mindfully?" DJ raised one eyebrow and grinned. He sauntered off with Alexandra, again holding hands.

Sim's truck pulled into the drive. She climbed out holding a large, flat box. "Donuts for the farmer?" She grinned.

"Why not?" Cam waved Sim toward her. She startled as Ellie and Vince jumped out of the back of the truck. "Don't you guys have school?" she called.

"Teacher in-service day," Vince said. "Thought we'd do our own in-service here at the farm."

"Sim stopped at the bottom of the hill and offered us a ride, so we threw our bikes in the back." Ellie smiled and took Vince's hand.

"The more, the merrier," Cam said. "Come on back."

"What do you want us to do?" Ellie asked.

"Hang on a second." Cam stared at the driveway.

A large white van with MORAN MANOR written on the side pulled in behind Sim's truck. *It doesn't rain but it pours.* The driver climbed out and extracted both Marilyn's walker and Albert's wheelchair from the back. He slid open the side door and helped them to their metal steeds. Cam hurried toward them as the van reversed with a series of beeps before driving off.

"What a lovely surprise," Cam said. "I didn't know you were coming, Albert and Marilyn." She hugged each of them. "And Sim, you too. I feel like I hit the jackpot."

"I wanted to show Marilyn the farm, don't you know," Albert said as he maneuvered himself into his chair. "Plus hear a bit about your adventure yesterday, if you have time. The van was out taking folks to appointments and whatnot. They agreed to drop us and come back in an hour or two."

"This is a bucolic setting you have here, Cam," Marilyn said. "It's just lovely."

"Come on back and I'll show you as much of it as I can. The path is paved to the barn, at least."

"I'll bring up the rear with the snacks," Sim said. Vince and Ellie followed her.

They were halfway on a slow route to the barn, with Albert pointing out various plantings he'd established decades earlier, when Cam heard, "Yo, Flaherty," from behind her. She turned to see Bobby strolling toward them from his truck, which took up the next-to-last spot on the long driveway.

"What is this, a party?" Cam asked.

Bobby shook Albert's hand and then Marie's, and fist-bumped with Sim. He greeted the teens, too.

"Luce said she was going to be here, and after I heard the news, I had to stop by, too." Bobby's expression was a somber one. "Thanks for getting that monster, Cam. Both of them."

"I didn't really get them. Well, I sort of got Geneva. The Coast Guard ended up capturing Rudin."

"That's what we heard," Marilyn said, her eyes again bright. "It must have been so terribly exciting for you. Or terrifying, like."

Cam let out a breath. "Definitely the second."

After touring the barn, they ended up in the sunshine on the other side of it. Cam grabbed a few of the plastic milk crates from the barn and set the donuts on one. Marilyn sat on the bench next to Albert's wheelchair, and Sim perched on another upturned crate. Vince slung his arm over Ellie's shoulder as they leaned against the barn wall.

"You certainly did a fine job rebuilding the barn, Bobby," Albert said.

"Thank you, sir. It was a pleasure."

"And it's pleasing to look at, as well as functional," Marilyn added. "The best of both worlds."

A tousled-hair Pete strolled up with Dasha and unclipped his leash. Dasha padded into the barn, and Cam could hear him slurping his water even from outside.

"Good walk?" she asked Pete.

He nodded, smiling, and wiped perspiration from his forehead. He greeted everybody. "What's this, breakfast?" He gestured to the donuts.

"Help yourself," Sim said.

"I'm going to go find Luce," Bobby said.

"She's picking asparagus again. Find a volunteer named Sue, too," Cam called after him. "And Alexandra and DJ."

Pete beckoned to Cam and drew her away from the group. "Did some digging. Your mom is in the clear for that thing in Florida."

"She is?" Cam whispered in astonishment.

He nodded. "She didn't hit a person. Somebody had put a roll of carpet out for the trash, and the wind had pushed it into the street."

"Geneva was lying!"

"Apparently, and not for the first time. No wonder your mother couldn't find anything in the news about the accident."

"Incredible." Cam shook her head. "Just incredible. I can't wait to tell Mom."

Cam and Pete rejoined the group. She'd have to wait to tell her mother, but smiled at the image of her mom's surprise and relief at Pete's news. Her parents would be able to get to their summer research as soon as Deb had healed. More important, her mom wasn't a criminal. Cam felt as light as if she'd been hauling a heavy cart piled full of compost that had just tipped out onto the ground.

Felicity appeared from the vicinity of the hoophouse. "Wow. Is this the Westbury organic farming subgroup?" She smiled and greeted them one by one.

"Something like that." Cam gestured at the box. "Have a donut, courtesy of Sim." Cam selected one of the chocolate rings. "Except not this one. Farmer's prerogative." She'd just bit into it when her parents appeared from around the corner of the barn, followed by Ruth in civilian clothes. A little color had returned to Deb's face, and a blue sling held her right arm across the front of her body. William grasped her other arm.

"They let you loose," Cam said, hurrying toward them.

"I gave her the unofficial official police escort," Ruth said, laughing. "Your dad asked for my help so he wouldn't get lost."

"Thanks, Ruthie." Cam kissed her mom's cheek and looked into her eyes. "You all right?" she whispered.

"You told me I would be," Deb whispered back. "I heard you."

Cam's eyes welled. She blinked away the happy tears.

Clapping commenced as William led Deb through the group. Marilyn patted the bench beside her, where Deb sank down to sitting, relief evident on her face. Bobby, Lucinda, and Sue walked up from the direction of the fields, Sue carrying a full basket of asparagus spears. DJ and Alexandra followed, with Preston moseying behind. He ambled over and jumped onto Albert's lap.

"Let's hear it for survivors," Albert said. He held up a piece of donut. "It's not champagne, but it'll have to do."

"To Cam's mama," Sim echoed, holding up her own sprinkles-covered sweet.

"And to Cam," Felicity added, brandishing a piece of asparagus. Dasha trotted over and barked. He sat alert at Cam's feet, gazing up at her.

Cam looked around the circle. All the family she had in the world. All these friends holding a piece of pastry or a spear of asparagus in the air as a toast. All this support. She'd never envisioned such a scene a year ago. And could only hope her relationship with each of them would strengthen and deepen in the next year. Quite the leap for an introvert.

Cam raised her donut. "Here's to all of you."

Recipes

Roasted Garlic Spread

Cam's father William whips this up for their lunch sandwiches. You can use it as a spread, or as a dip with crack-
ers or raw vegetables.

Ingredients
2 small garlic bulbs
¼ cup sour cream
¼ cup soft cream cheese
1 teaspoon minced fresh oregano
1 teaspoon minced parsley
Dash of habanero hot sauce

Directions
Preheat oven to 350°F.

Slice the tips off the garlic bulbs. Place on a piece of
aluminum foil and drizzle olive oil over the bulbs. Wrap
the foil around the garlic and roast in the oven (a toaster
oven works well for such a small quantity) for 30 minutes.
Remove the packet and open the foil to let cool.

Mix the sour cream, cream cheese, and herbs in a small
bowl. When the garlic is cool enough to touch, squeeze
the soft garlic out of the bulb and into the bowl. Mix well,
mashing the garlic with a fork. Add a few drops of hot
sauce to taste.

Edith Maxwell

Kale and Couscous Salad

Cam ordered this delicious and easy salad for her dinner at Throwback Brewery. Brewery co-owner Nicole Carrier was kind enough to share a version of the recipe for this book, which I have modified slightly.

Ingredients
1 cup pearl couscous
1 teaspoon salt
4 cups washed and chopped kale leaves, stemmed
½ cup chopped walnuts
¼ cup dried cranberries
¼ cup grated Parmesan cheese
1 tablespoon cumin
2 tablespoons good olive oil
1 tablespoon rice wine vinegar
Freshly ground black pepper

Directions
Cook the couscous until al dente and drain well. Sprinkle the salt over the kale and rub the kale with your hands for a few minutes, until it wilts. Add the cooled couscous, walnuts, cranberries, Parmesan cheese, and cumin, and mix. Stir in the olive oil and rice wine vinegar. Adjust oil and vinegar to taste, and grind black pepper over the salad.

Brown Rice Vegetable Risotto

Cam's mom orders this fresh, chewy dish at Jake's restaurant, The Market.

Ingredients
4 ounces asparagus, cut into 1-inch pieces
6 cups chicken stock
2½ teaspoons kosher salt
½ cup butter
½ teaspoon freshly ground black pepper, plus additional
    for taste
1 red sweet pepper, diced
2 stalks diced spring garlic (or scallions)
1½ cups brown rice
½ cup dry vermouth
2 tablespoons finely chopped fresh oregano (or herb of
    choice)
2 tablespoons finely chopped parsley (or herb of choice)
½ cup grated Parmesan cheese
1 cup frozen peas, thawed
2 tablespoons freshly squeezed lime juice

Directions
  Cut asparagus just below the tips, then on an angle at
1-inch intervals. Set aside.

  Bring stock to a simmer. Keep on a low simmer.

  Heat 2 tablespoons of butter in a large skillet over
medium-high heat and add asparagus. Cook, stirring occasionally, until the color turns bright green. Season with
½ teaspoon salt and pepper, to taste, and set aside.

In a large saucepan, add 2 tablespoons of butter over medium-high heat. Add the spring garlic and cook until translucent, about 2 minutes. Add the pepper and rice and stir so that they are coated with the butter and glossy, about 1 minute. Add the vermouth and cook, stirring constantly with a wooden spoon, until it is absorbed by the rice. Ladle in ½ cup of the simmering stock and stir constantly, until the rice again absorbs the liquid, adjusting the heat to maintain a gentle simmer. Continue ladling in about ½ cup of stock a time, stirring between additions and letting the rice absorb the liquid before adding more. Continue stirring and adding stock until rice is tender but slightly al dente.

Stir in asparagus and herbs. Vigorously beat in the remaining butter and the Parmesan cheese. Add peas and lime juice, and stir just until heated through. Remove from heat. Cover and let risotto rest for five minutes before serving.

Divide among four warm bowls, grind a generous amount of pepper over each, and serve.

Swedish Cheesecake—Ostkaka

Jake's special dessert, which he offers Cam and her parents at his restaurant.

Ingredients
4 large eggs
½ cup sugar
¼ cup unbleached white flour
24 ounces strained cottage cheese
½ cup almond meal
3 to 4 ground almonds
1 tablespoon Frangelico liqueur

Directions
Preheat oven to 425°F.

Whip the eggs until fluffy. Stir in sugar, flour, and cottage cheese. Fold in the almond meal, almonds, and liqueur.

Butter a 9" x 13" casserole. Pour the mixture into the pan. Bake for 30 minutes. If cheesecake starts to get too brown, cover with foil.

Best served warm with strawberries and sour cream or crème fraîche.